UNNATURAL PRACTICES

JON THURLEY

Unnatural Practices

HAMISH HAMILTON · LONDON

HAMISH HAMILTON LTD

Published by the Penguin Group
Penguin Books Ltd, 27 Wrights Lane, London W8 5TZ, England
Penguin Books USA Inc., 375 Hudson Street, New York, New York 10014, USA
Penguin Books Australia Ltd, Ringwood, Victoria, Australia
Penguin Books Canada Ltd, 10 Alcorn Avenue, Toronto, Ontario, Canada M4V 3B2
Penguin Books (NZ) Ltd, 182–190 Wairau Road, Auckland 10, New Zealand

Penguin Books Ltd, Registered Offices: Harmondsworth, Middlesex, England

First published 1992
1 3 5 7 9 10 8 6 4 2

Filmset in $11\frac{1}{2}$/13 pt Monophoto Palatino
Printed in England by Clays Ltd, St Ives, plc

A CIP catalogue record for this book is available from the British Library

ISBN 0-241-12907-9

Under the Surface of an English Society abroad what rife Greed abounds, what concupiscence, what private abandonment to Vice under the Guise of Christian Virtues . . . The world here is like Bedlam, save that there are no Warders and the Inmates may do whatsoever they please without fear of consequence. The Indian is too gentle for us: we take his home, his women, his living – and he still trusts us . . .

Clive's Diary: Reminiscences of India, 1774

Vice is a monster of so frightful mien,
As to be hated needs but to be seen;
Yet seen too oft, familiar with her face,
We first endure, then pity, then embrace.

Alexander Pope, *An Essay on Man,* ii, 217

Chapter One

The house was in sunlight as I drove between the rows of cypresses. From the distant wrought-iron gates its Palladian, ivy-covered façade, framed by the uprights of the dark avenue, seemed perfectly preserved. Nearer, parking by the south wing, I could see the last winter had peeled and ravaged the stucco still further: the distant view of beauty was transformed into an old tart with loosened stays. It was a habit Father had assumed with the acceptance of his knighthood — 'for services to the Asian community' (whatever that meant) — this careless yet deliberate embracing of decay and neglect. 'One cannot get the craftsmen. They're much happier repairing the red-brick semis of *hoi polloi* in these egalitarian days.' That was one of the ways in which his arrogance showed. Over the portico the legend ran 'Odi profanum vulgus et arceo.' I hate and shun the vulgar crowd.

The engine coughed and died. As I sat in the car for a moment, my heart beat apprehensively fast. My hands were damp with perspiration. I had thought that tragedy had firmed my long held resolve for once to deal with truth rather than enter again the conspiracy of lies we had all created. Yet again, faced here with the quotidian reality of my parents' lives, fear and compassion remade me as the dutiful son: fear most of all, for the truth is too hard to bear for most people, and the bringing of it lies in that hinterland bordered at the one edge by cruelty and hubris, and carries also the responsibility for dealing with the consequences of revelation. Which is why most of us accept the lies by which we all live, aware, even as we speak or accept them, of their dubious provenance. (Such sophistries permit my profession to avoid the simple judgement of cowardice.)

1

I could see my mother sat at the far edge of the lawn under the great cypress, dressed in flowered print, a glass in her hand and a carafe of iced water on the rustic table before her. Two little blonde girls in pink dresses ran across the lawn towards me. Lydia's children, who, as my father sometimes remarked, could have been their grandchildren. The implied coda being if only I had done my filial duty. Rosemary kissed me, soft skinned, smelling of buttermilk. 'Uncle David's here,' they chorused together and Mother waved. Hand in hand we three walked towards her.

She had the fragile show of serenity which grew more marked in times of trouble. Despite her white hair and the Indian summers which had sallowed her skin, she had retained her rounded prettiness. She said nothing, holding me tighter than she usually did for a long moment. 'Your father is down at the vineyard. Dr Bell came round this morning, but there isn't a great deal he can do.' Some instinct guided her. I nodded my acquiescence, looking into her eyes, and her face cleared.

Father stood with one fist on his hip, leaning on his stick. It was always as if I had never been away the very instant I returned. New acquisitions, events in their lives or those of mutual friends, dropped casually into the conversation as though, of course, I was aware of them, had been party to their revelation. Silently he raised his stick to indicate the ordered rows of vines. Under the shadow of his hat his mouth smiled, but I could not see his eyes.

We walked slowly down between the vines, the grapes clustering dense and green under their canopies of leaves. My father wore a broad-brimmed white hat, old cotton trousers, a shortsleeved white shirt. I could see in the distance, half hidden in the copse, the long building which housed all the vats and instruments of his new obsession. Once, pausing in the midst of describing the nurturing of his vineyard, he said wonderingly, almost to himself, 'I thought they'd give Thomas a knighthood at least. After all he's done for the party . . .' But, even as he shook his head, I could see his pleasure. We walked slowly in Indian file to the white table and slatted wooden chairs under the chestnut by the lake.

2

My father's face was dark in the green shade of the tree. It would be a fine vintage this year. Here, taste, he'd said, and held the olive-wood bowl out to me. The grapes were firm, dusted with a pale film, sweet. The viniculturist says that in three years we'll produce better quality than any other English vineyard, he told me, his voice thick with satisfaction. The lawn was emerald green in the sunshine. By the house my mother, hands on hips, was talking to the gardener. Looking at my father, I was suddenly aware of his frailty, the hovering presence of his imminent death. His glaucous blue eyes gazed unseeingly over the vines, bathed in sunlight. The skin on the back of the trembling hand of which he made a fist to rest his chin was marked with liver spots. My mother had gone into the house, re-emerging with a tray which she carried with careful precision, walking towards us.

Father's voice was querulous with self-pity. 'One makes something of one's life, one does one's best for one's children – and then this . . . ! ' He spread his arms wide, as though to indicate the extent of his misfortune.

After the tragedy I had spoken to my mother. These were the first words I had heard from my father. Even if I had not entered the silent contract with my mother, I could not have spoken, for we had no language in common. I knew that what he wanted was the usual panaceas: it wasn't your fault, these things happen, you did your best. The threadbare consolations which his generation would expect for salve and comfort, to enable them to move forward and forget. To give him that – as I had done in the past – would be to diminish myself, to carry the self-engaged, destructive process within myself, perhaps for ever.

'Well, do you think it *is* our fault?'

Mother's hair blew in the wind. She came on steadily, her smile fixed and serene. She coped with tragedy as she coped with everything, by ignoring it. As a child I had felt secure in her resolute sameness: now, versed in such matters, I knew that the walls which had kept everything out over seventy years had trapped her behind them. The price she had paid for her apparent serenity had been to feel nothing at all, for feelings might be dangerous. She had learned the outward show, true enough, but nothing had touched her heart, or ever would now. The ice tinkled in the glasses. 'Cooee,' she called. Behind her the house shimmered in the heat haze.

'What I think isn't important.'

'A lovely cold drink. You'd better come in and clear up before lunch. Remember, we've got visitors . . .'

As I took his arm to assist him to his feet, I could feel his anger.

Back in London, I reinstate my cancelled appointment with Beckenbauer. Nominally we are co-editors of the *Psychoanalytical Journal*, though in practice Fritz does most of the work. There is in him a sardonic Mittel-European disconnectedness from the surrounding Anglo-Saxon conformity which I sometimes find comforting. His roots run further into the deep, dark soil, and he is less preoccupied with cricket scores, transient scandal and the machinations of the government than most of my acquaintances. He does not, of course, believe my half-proffered suggestion that I was passing and thought I would offer some thoughts on the journal over a drink.

He is late forties – fifty perhaps – with grizzled grey hair, a neat beard. He dresses impeccably; is between wives at the moment, though his elegant Mayfair penthouse usually sports a languid, suntanned blonde. A hint of German in his accent still. A long way back a polyglot ancestry of Christian Maronite and Sephardic Jew. A reputation as a polymath (though I think he works at it), wealthy enough to indulge his passion for Bacon, Max Ernst and, incongruously enough by contrast, Cotman and Palmer. His book on the dialectical theory of the treatment of neurosis was an unexpected bestseller, probably on account of the quotable aphorisms he levels at our profession. He operates discretionary portfolios with three stockbrokers. 'There is always the fear that you might leave for one of the others if they don't perform.' He is rarely serious.

'A surprise, David.' His hand on my shoulder, drawing me in. It isn't, of course. Helping him on the journal these last months, I will have betrayed distress, despite my care. Even we cannot control the silence that extends for a moment too long, a fumbled word out of context which betrays. He has studiously avoided asking me for my late contribution on Irma's dream for the journal.

There is a blonde girl. She brings us drinks — a whisky for me, vodka tonic for him. A hint of the acolyte in her manner. She bends over Fritz, taking the curtain of hair back from her face with one hand, her grave profile against the light for an instant as Fritz takes his drink from the tray. He glances at me, smiles. When she has left, closing the door behind her, he says, 'What the hell. It took the first thirty years to escape the provincial mores of my parents. I promise nothing beyond the pleasure of the moment — nothing beyond what I am willing and able to perform. They are young enough to survive, to derive something from the experience and pass on.' He laughs gently at himself, getting up to refill our glasses. A police siren wails in the distance. 'Does that sound defensive? Curious how we return in time to right and wrong — those shackles we threw off with such dispatch when we first entered the discipline.'

He phones a local restaurant to bring us dinner. Stephanie — I catch her name in their barely audible exchange — *en chemise*, puts it into the heated trolley. She stands absolutely still for a moment, framed against the window as he kisses her forehead, then leaves in silence. Tonight something has started in Fritz. He has discarded his customary cynical jokiness. Over dinner he talks about the abrogation of responsibility. A Latinist (again, so the reputation goes), he has been reading Cicero's *De natura deorum* — On the nature of the gods. 'The idea of man as the plaything of the gods runs through literature. The harmonic of the old alchemists — as it is above, so below — so that the haphazardness and irrationality of our lives are a reflection of the unknowable. For who may know the nature of the gods or the causes of their anger? Sometimes I wonder if the way the ancient world considered such matters makes more sense than our existential insistence on the primacy of the individual in determining their own fate.'

5

After dinner he lights a Havana and we drink Janneau. 'Curious,' he says, 'we get it no more right than others when it comes to our own lives. Look at me. I had that age-old double standard at my heart. The women I loved, I married, knowing that they did not love me in the terms I use the word – that in time I would no longer be able to make love to them or sustain a true intimacy with them. The slow accretion of half-truths drives us apart. Yet I can confess my basest desires, my worst fears, to these uncomprehending transients whose ten-ancy will soon be over. You never married, of course ...' It is a statement, the nearest Fritz ever comes to a question.

'It was close, years ago. But it was too complicated.'

He laughs, looking away. I know he does not want the burden of intimacy: nor do I wish to offer it. Once, when I first knew him, we talked of the ideal upbringing, children held in common to a large community of generations living together, where each child might see the processes of growth at work and could make their own associations based upon need, instinct. When he spoke of his own family, I felt an immediate sympathy. He observed, as I had, that their genera-tion could not discuss things openly, that they held the busi-ness of living to be concerned with the trappings of success, recognition, important acquaintances, saving face – that all the criteria of the good life were held between these matters alone. We think too much, that is the problem. Perhaps the answer is to live blindly without bringing everything into the light.

He hugs me at the door. So close, his eyes have a goatlike impersonality. The air on the landing is cool, clear. He hesitates before speaking, looking down the long corridor. 'Mothers are different. Women are closer to the earth, to the rhythms of change. There is only the possibility of confronta-tion with fathers. When one has the strength, then compassion and guilt bear away the resolve. That is my experience.'

As I walk to the car, I feel warmed by gratitude.

I am angry. It is not the anger which flares up at some particular grievance and is then extinguished. I am angry

6

because Thomas has ruined my life – the only one I have. I am angry, too, that he is dying, and I cannot vent my fury upon him.

I have seen him twice in the past week. He has the apologetic air of a dog which has misbehaved and cringes whilst begging forgiveness. 'My fault, old man. Probably the reason I never got as far as my talents deserved. I've always reached my conclusions before working through the facts to support them.' An epitaph for a social criminologist, which is how he describes himself. And again, sitting in the stifling front room of his Kensington house, while the bright sunshine threw trapeziums through the window on to the silk Kelim – 'You were right, after all. The book was all about revenge. The rest was bullshit.' The nearest he has ever come to apologizing for what he has done.

This is a country for old men. Septimus came round unexpectedly to visit me yesterday. Huddled into winter coats, our breath smoking in the bitter air, we walked through the woods by Esher Green. The birches were bare, their bark leprous with sores, and the skeined earth underfoot, thawing slightly now, had the tilthy bounce of rotting vegetation. He still likes a challenge: I followed him down the steep bank to the river, slipping and sliding down the worn red earth. We forded the stream and climbed over the token fence. The great field had been ploughed, and frost still lay in the declivities as yet untouched by the weak sun, the perspective of the white lines converging towards the row of pastel houses at the far edge, framed by a tracery of trees and a slate-dark sky. The smell of reeking woodsmoke caught in my throat.

As we walked along the path by the side of the furrows, we came across a few bobs of grey hair where a rabbit had been caught in the blades of a plough. 'They gas the burrows and those that survive come out into the open to die.' This delivered with the Luddite anger of one who was dispassionate about the events in the Gulf until he saw the pictures of sea birds maimed by the oil spillage – who has fundamentally never left the priesthood with its unrealistic cavillings about the wickedness of men. One of Septimus's passions is the preservation of wild life: along with other causes like the reduction of CFC emissions, the halting of seal culling, the end of all weapon production, it gives him a safe, impersonal vent for such emotions as he has.

I knew that in his oblique, elliptical way he had come to offer me the comforts of companionship — on his own terms. His is the mute support which will never address the issues directly, for to do so might expose him to the muddiness and irrationality of human feelings. After all, I speculated, as we stood hands on hips, he is of the same generation as my father and Thomas: men whose very existence — bolstered by such words as honour and truth and duty — depends upon their denial of what they have done.

I suspect Septimus to be motivated by the need certain people have to witness disasters, to gain that curious affirmation derived from seeing and participating at second hand in some awful happening which they themselves have survived unhurt. He proceeds by similes, by metaphors, by skirting the issues narrowly, taking the care of an archaeologist to ensure that his scratching does not damage or disturb whatever may lie beneath. And — as one does — I modify my responses to what I feel he can accept. He has a passionate desire to know how things fit together because, for all his intelligence, the mysteries of contiguity, of precedence and consequence, of the springs of love and hate, remain impenetrable to him. Father Gregorio, who raised him, was undoubtedly a saint upon earth, but was not much qualified in the ways of men. And I know from my profession the coldness that can lie within the human heart which has not been immersed in the visceral, animal closeness of the family from the beginning. Septimus reacts to atmospheres — but cannot understand people. Such instincts as he once had have atrophied.

'I'm a bit cold. Shall we get back?' He hunched his shoulders so that the collar covered his ears.

'A cup of tea'll revive us. Come on — at the double.' Septimus lengthened his pace, giving me a wry smile.

Such is the bond between us. It is not cynicism to say that

it is as good as most, given my daily exposure to such matters. His presence gives me something – a period of avoidance of the doubts which return when I am alone. 'It is not insuperable. You will survive.' His voice as I prepared tea and crumpets carried the vague certainty of a social worker's *obiter dicta*. 'These things happen to all of us. They are merely part of life.' How like Sep to have all the pieces in his hands, and not to see how they fit together. His naïvety inspired a sudden rush of affection and I suggested he stay to dinner. He too is lonely and, unlike mine, his loneliness shall have no surcease because it is founded upon incomprehension.

He has the fussy efficiency of a man who has always looked after himself. Peering dubiously at the vegetable drawer, some steak from the freezer, his tone was unconvinced. 'Perhaps I can make a casserole. I don't suppose you have a bouquet garni?' I laid the table and then, at his insistence, covered the hibiscus on the patio with a black plastic bin-liner. I would have let it fend for itself but he was primly determined. 'You'll appreciate why when you see it flowering. It would only die if you neglected it.'

Once during the evening he reminded me of my anger. 'I saw Thomas last week.' Turning, I saw he was preoccupied in slicing onions on the chopping board. 'Ah hah,' I said, noncommittally.

'Perhaps you are too hard on him. I know the whole thing began out of revenge, but he regrets what he did. He visited the graves, you know. Eleanor and Dora . . .'

'The point is, Septimus . . .' I was surprised to find myself almost incoherent. 'Thomas has spent his life making mistakes at others' expense – and being rewarded for them. Please don't give me an *apologia pro vita sua*. The only good that has come from this is that at last he is face to face with what he's done.'

'He's an old man. What pleasure can his discomfort give you?'

'Not tonight. Let's leave it.' He shrugged and resumed his preparations while I went into the sitting-room to light the fire. I cannot attack Septimus, simply because he belongs to the same generation as Thomas and my father, whose ethic has been to imprison and control people. Like them, he fears the liberating thrust of my profession — for where will such liberation lead?

By some strange reversal Septimus — almost seventy now — seems to have remained the same while I have aged, and I find myself granting him the indulgences I allow to children — the freedom to test their new-found strengths against me. Physically he has changed little: one or two grey hairs, a suspicion of arthritis in the knuckle joints, but few other evidences of ageing. Like my father, like Thomas to a great extent, he has escaped the *Angst*, the guilt of my generation. He has a rumpled boyishness, an aura of enthusiasm, as though he wakes each morning to a brilliant new world open to discovery, full of opportunities, thronged with people who — *au fond* — are decent, moral, sympathetic. The limp from the old accident adds to his charm. He still has the looks and manner which endear him to certain kinds of women: they think — wrongly — that he is malleable; they wish to smother him with affection, to civilize him towards some ideal in their minds. It may be because he has never been threatening in any sexual sense: he is *curious* about women in the same way that he is curious about everything, but I have never found in him any evidence of strong physical passions. Again, I suspect, it is the sense of connectedness in such activities which eludes him. Such instincts wither early if never used, and I know, from what he has said in unguarded moments, that he has felt the lack, though without precisely being able to articulate his sense of loss.

Last night (one is always learning) I first noticed an endearing vanity in him. He has always been neat, his hair cut *en brosse* and his fingernails shaped and clean. I caught him angling his head to look at his face in the hall mirror. 'Thought I had something in my eye,' he said disarmingly, pulling a handkerchief out of his pocket and dabbing at the corner of his eyelid. Much of his behaviour is collusion — the acting of a part which he feels meets with my approval.

Recently, talking to me, he has developed the good-natured

banter which old-style physicians would sometimes employ with their patients to cover the embarrassment of their own rude health. A slight bluff heartiness, a hint of stoicism, of implying that we are all in this fearful business of living together, all subject to the same mortifications of the flesh and spirit: that we must all smile in the face of adversity and battle, head down, against the encroaching storm. He often quotes Henley – rolling the words round his mouth with theatrical relish: 'Under the bludgeonings of chance/My head is bloody, but unbowed.'

Behind me Septimus said, 'Just getting a glass of wine. Fancy one? Told you it was going to freeze, didn't I?' His momentary self-satisfaction was palpable.

I said, 'I've got some Napa Valley. I'll bring it in a moment.' Septimus is devoid of real malice, but I know he feels that my depression might reveal a flaw in what he calls 'your damned assumption of the rightness of your opinions'. He does not realize that I had simply sought to make a reasonable pass at the time remaining to me: scarcely laudable – a modest enough ambition. It is that which has gone beyond my grasp.

He cannot negotiate disclosures with me, for he has none to offer. His own feelings have somehow remained fixed – the secret, I suppose, of his optimistic boyishness. He is trapped in youth, as an insect is preserved in amber. 'Life isn't a game played by known rules. You mustn't dwell on the past. You must just accept that such things are beyond repair.' He delivers such threadbare philosophizing as though it is the product of profound thought.

'This is very good.' The casserole was excellent, and my compliment deflected him from further probing. Only once, years ago, I attacked him, telling him that he produced panaceas and aphorisms like a child, without any true understanding of their import: that he cannot appreciate the significance of the facts he holds in his possession. (If that sounds smug, I offer the certainty that possession of the entire picture is no prophylactic.) He was so hurt, behind his frozen façade of dignity, that I knew I must never confront him again.

11

After, I loaded the dishwasher, and we moved to the sitting-room. Everywhere there are the reminders of my sister's eclectic taste. Angela always brought something back from her travels. She had the enviable ability to buy widely discrete artefacts with absolute confidence. In the end I could buy nothing unless she had approved it. Everything reeks of her; sometimes it seems as if she is next door and will walk in and things will be as they were.

Septimus sprawled before the fire, his long legs encased in buff corduroy stretched out over the Isfahan, his hand clasping a glass of Napa Valley: his eyes gave the game away – never still, pausing momentarily upon my face to query some response of mine. The occlusive rictus of his lips indicated some insight gained, stored against some probable future use.

He proceeds by points, as in a debating society. The old sore still rankles – as it has always done with my father and Thomas. 'The problem with you psychoanalysts is that you assume everything to be explicable, soluble, ultimately controllable.' I poked the fire, unwilling to be drawn. My apparent certainties about people's behaviour anger Sep, though they are not certainties at all, merely models with some provenance of precedence behind them. It is his personal crusade to dispossess me of them – because he wishes to bring me to his own level, wherever that might be.

'Nice drop of wine. Oaky.' He held the near-empty glass to the light and I took the hint. Without his Calvinist streak Sep could become a boozy old lush. His social work in Southwark calls for 'community services' – most often carried out away from his home patch in a journalists' pub once named 'The Stab in the Back' and rechristened 'The Stab in the Front' a couple of years past. Thatcher's Britain has, paradoxically, given Septimus a *raison d'être*: he possesses inexhaustibly benign feelings towards the generality of people and particularly towards the halt, the sick and the lame.

It was sacrilege to play *Turandot* as a background to his late night philosophizing. If I held a finger up to suspend his monologue while I listened to a phrase, he might pause dutifully, but his incomprehension would be total. His mind was engaged in quite different matters. Little moves him beyond some pure, abstract reasoning which he now pursued. God! He's driving. I felt a momentary pang of concern.

There is still comfort in this companionship. The room glowed with the colours and the textures of the East. The pain is momentarily dulled: I have survived and shall, so far as I can see, survive next week. Septimus was preparing himself to deliver some polemic.

'For the last few decades we have been convinced that we are close to controlling our lives and our environment. True, we haven't solved the riddles of thermodynamics − that progress requires the production and use of energy which in turn promotes entropy. I've recently' − here he fidgeted self-consciously for a moment and rubbed his forefinger against the side of his nose − 'been studying the latest developments in chaos theory science which Edward Lorenz began to formulate about meteorology in the 1960s. Scientists had been unable to explain the discrepancies between computer forecasting and actuality. The chap with the piece of seaweed in Margate was doing as well as the whole shooting match in Bracknell. What became evident was that not enough information was being fed in to provide an accurate picture. There is now' − he peered over his steepled fingers to ensure he had my full attention, his open mouth a startling black void in the firelight − 'a school of forecasters who believe that the movement of a butterfly's wing, amplified millions of times, may spark climatic upheavals on the other side of the world. Physiologists at Oxford are applying the same principles to attempt to find how tiny effects in the heart can trigger an ultimate heart attack. Like the butterfly's wing, such minute alterations generate a rhythm into a kind of chaos we call fibrillation. Some go further in proposing that literally every event, every consequence, is caused by tiny and discrete happenings whose resonance will ultimately affect the outcome of matters far removed, like the ripples caused by a pebble spreading outward.'

'So life is just chaos, without the possibility of imposed order?'

'I didn't say that. According to these theorists, where we

have fallen short is in constructing sufficiently detailed basic models from which to make our predictions.'

'You're the one who believes we are progressing towards perfection, Sep – not me. I've always recognized the random messiness of life.'

I felt suddenly weary of Septimus's abstract passions. I know that he is one of those who – having lost God – must yet attempt to impose some order and hierarchy upon the random irrationality of life. It is the good father he seeks in another form: some principle, however incomprehensible it may be in its totality, which has meaning at its core, and within whose mechanism each individual has some place and function. The trick of his endurance is both in this belief in a system and in his dissociation from people, from the possibilities of loss and betrayal. If there is ultimate redemption, there is no tragedy. The potential for pain comes only from the abandonment of structure and the acceptance of the ultimate nature of human relationships. In the silence I thought of Angela, ashamed to feel the sudden prickle of tears behind my eyelids.

There is an unexpected occasional gentleness in Septimus, as though, momentarily, even he is moved from his obsessive quest by human considerations. 'There is no help anyone can give you until the pain passes. But pain often comes as a consequence of the belief that things might have been different – that there was a moment when you might have controlled the sequence of events. When you abandon that fallacy, the pain will be dulled.'

The house creaked, settling for the night. I looked at my watch. Past midnight. The wind must have changed to the east: the windows began to rattle and vibrate as a plane slowly flew past on the new flight path. 'Good Lord,' Septimus said, 'Is that the time . . . ?' He drained his wine glass and uncurled his long body, following me out to the hall. Septimus must be one of the last people in the world still wearing a duffel coat. He struggled into it with absent-minded gawkiness.

By the door he hesitated, half turning towards me so that the light angled across the bottom part of his face. He surprised

14

me then, holding my forearm in an uncharacteristically fierce grip for a moment. 'I know you are distressed. I won't presume to say I know how you feel – but remember you have friends who are concerned about you.'

It was that, more than anything, which finally underlined the permanence of what has happened. The one act, in the whole time I have known him, even as a child, in which I sensed Sep reaching beyond the Jesuitical control he imagines he has escaped to offer me a gesture of warmth. And the irony is that he does not know the real situation. I wondered if he would reject me in horror if he knew the truth. As I watched the brake lights flicker and the car move into the road, I felt the wearisome burden of the knowledge I shall never lose again and, at last, the start of my resumption in the real world. And, knowing from my profession the value of being thus brought to face such things, I was grateful.

'. . . ich für Schmerzen jetzt habe in Hals, Magen und Leib . . .' Irma's dream as related by Freud, upon which I have been preparing a paper. It could apply to me. I had no stomach to finish the thesis now. Perhaps in a few months, when the time of iron has passed again.

The buds of the magnolia are there, small still, but tight, fecund. A promise of renewal.

Once drawn, where does a circle begin? This last year has brought back my past, robbed of the cosiness with which Angela and I invested it. It was not always summer and picnics. The adults were not nice: they were human. What has happened is a process which should have happened years ago for me. Transmuting the conscious memories into the bone and sinew and muscle which lay beneath. Setting aside those selective fictions called memory which mutate with repetition into a polished, finished form bearing little resemblance to the first untidy sprawl of their birth, before they were indexed, annotated, filed. My work with my patients is to represent their experiences in that first form without the mind breaking, taking refuge in fugue and darkness. And now I ask myself the same questions. Was it really that lunch with Thomas which led to the place where I am now, or did the butterfly's wing begin to beat years ago, in Iskanderabad?

Chapter Two

So long ago, it seems. Thomas had just finished at the MoD and had accepted the mastership of his old Cambridge college. I'd seen him once or twice over dinner during the last months of his tenure of office. He'd received the CBE some years before, but, behind his façade of effortless superiority, I detected some hint of chagrin, as though matters had not turned out quite as he expected. One of the heavy Sundays had called him 'the conscience of the party' in the early eighties and that had probably been enough to slow his progress in Thatcherite Britain. At the Home Office he had presided efficiently enough over messy and overdue reforms, but the quantum leap beyond had eluded him. He'd moved sideways, briefly, to the MoD, to preside over what he described as the dismantling of the props of Empire. Once, uncharacteristically, he had sneered at his position as 'a sort of door-to-door arms salesman'. If he'd taken that job with the intention of easing his way back into hardline favour, it hadn't worked. The mastership spelled the end of his ambitions, and he was too shrewd to harbour thoughts of a return. 'I have done the State some service,' he would say, in tones which clearly implied that the State had been less than properly grateful. The bitterness surfaced most when he mentioned my father, who had received a knighthood two years before. Talking of Father, Thomas's face would become veiled, sly: 'they sometimes get things badly wrong, you know'. I assumed it to be the good-natured rivalry of old friends, mildly spiked with malice and envy but no more than that. There was nothing overt at first.

Thomas probably knew of the proposed honour even before the arrival of the tentative official letter asking if I would accept it were it offered to me. I was certain of one thing at least — that he had not proposed me: in common with Septimus and my father, he had a Victorian repugnance for what I did. In foreknowledge of matters such as this, though — and, I suspect, many others — he had always been ahead of me with a smug, twinkling jollity which I bore without pleasure. He was part of the politicians' grapevine, that great web of gossip and bitchiness and preoccupation with trivialities which was as easily stimulated into life by salacious incident as the graver concerns of State. I remembered the stories as far back as Eden's accession, when Thomas had told us that Churchill, favouring Butler, had mistakenly left it to the Queen to nominate his successor. And of course there had then been stories of Ayub Khan and Prince Philip and 'two common little tarts' (for Thomas was a snob) well before the drama burst out in the press.

Evidently the club, once joined, was for life, for Thomas had blotted his copybook once or twice, yet, according to him, was still party to their privy councils. Perhaps to distance himself from his role as moral arbiter of the party, or because he saw his way ahead held little more, Thomas had eschewed the writing of his dull, worthy books on penal reform, and had written two positively *louche* novels pseudonymously. It was *Private Eye* who had revealed their authorship, wittily juxtaposing a choice of purple passages from the novels side by side with excerpts from his speeches on penal reform over the years. There was a hint of a libel action, settled out of court, which boosted his sales, and it was rumoured that Thomas's political friends tended for a time to avoid his invitations. None of which had any permanent effect, and he had once again demonstrated his inside knowledge by telephoning to invite me to lunch at the Garrick just prior to the official announcement, while I was still feeling bound by my naïve observance of the convention of absolute secrecy.

Thomas had been part of my childhood. As a young man he had come out to our north Indian colonial community in Iskanderabad as a criminologist on brief secondment to the Indian Civil Service to help, in some capacity, salve the conscience of the Raj, then moving with slow, portentous steps to exile, whilst in the other direction passed the generations emerging from the shadow of their protectors – from the fabulously wealthy nizams and maharajas who felt betrayed by the British, to poor harijans walking upon lamed and wearied feet towards the uncertainty of the future – towards Nehru's proud boast of India's tryst with destiny and their shrugging off of their imperial shackles. 'I came,' Thomas Henne used to say later, with the *gravitas* appropriate to a senior Tory, 'to give them their first experience of a forensic approach to solving crime based upon firm evidence, rather than the infinitely corruptible anecdotal and circumstantial models they had hitherto employed. To permit access to justice equally for the poorest sweeper to the proudest maharaja.' Such phrases were expressive of Thomas's self-image – the purveyor of Truth at all costs.

He had proved an indifferent godfather in that youth. He had no facility with children, treating them with uncertain avuncularity, patting them on the head as though they were some species of pet. Later, it seemed that this gave way to a grudging affection, which did not embrace my choice of profession. He once told me that he believed psychoanalysis to perpetuate an endless preoccupation with self, which was the condition requiring treatment in the first place. Long runs, cold showers and pure thoughts were the answer! My equanimity in the face of his jokes at the expense of my profession infuriated him: his gibes were wide of the mark and, anyway, the understanding of such resistance is built into our views of the human condition.

I had an idea, as I stood in my dripping Burberry browsing in a nearby bookshop until the time came to present myself a respectable five minutes early for our one o'clock appointment, that there was more to this lunch than mere congratulation. It was hard to imagine what I might have to offer him, but Thomas did nothing for its own sake and without good reason.

In the dark lobby, musty with old smells, he looked the same as ever, plump, red cheeked, grey haired, twinkling, benign. I had to suppress my invariable urge to hug him, instantly aware again that he was of that older generation for whom anything beyond a firm handshake between men might hint at some perverse intimacy. (My profession would categorize this as Thomas's unconscious fear of his own latent homosexual impulses, but I see this as a catch-all judgement, too wide to cover the case. Thomas, I suspect, has never been able to bear the onus of intimacy. He operates best under the compulsion of a three-line whip.)

I ordered potted shrimps followed by poached salmon, and Thomas, showing the new indifference of age to his food, said, 'And the same for me, George,' and ordered a bottle of Pouilly-Fumé. The dining-room, too, had the indefinable smell of comfortable old age, overlaid with roast meats, boiled cabbage.

Resumption had always been difficult with Thomas, as though he must first relocate his page in a half-read book. To set the stage again, we had the idle, half-heard exchanges of long acquaintance. The progress of Julia's chemotherapy. Their son Julian's recent advancement to first secretary in Tokyo. By the time the salmon arrived, Thomas had advanced to *sotto voce* opinions on the present state of the party ('never really been the same since Macleod and Macmillan') and to offering defamatory comments on two of the Cabinet ('giving a speech for our candidate in the by-election with his wife on one hand and his mistress on the other. As for M——. Still soliciting in Underground lavatories despite that cosmetic marriage.') All of which, mildly intriguing as it was, was merely Thomas walking crabwise towards the real substance of the lunch.

'I'm thinking' – he leaned forward conspiratorially, warming his brandy bubble in his plump, cushioned hands – 'of writing a novel which deals with the decline of British adventurism and the departure of the Raj from India.'

I felt a momentary unplaceable unease. Angela and I always reminisced of childhood as a time of sunlight: but there were shadows. 'Isn't that rather *passé*? It's been well picked over and, besides, it's almost half a century ago. I would have thought people would be far more interested in recent developments in Eastern Europe, or home politics.' I was genuinely surprised. Out of curiosity I had read his last novel, a narrative of petty crime and sexual antics under a lurid paperback cover. Its most serious suggestion being that over half the House of Commons regularly played away from home to the accompaniment of swishing whips and ladies dressed in gymslips and suspenders.

Confronted, Thomas took refuge in portentousness. 'There are more parallels between the fall of regimes than may be readily apparent. Under the guise of paternalism we exploited the Indian as we had exploited the Malay and all the others we colonized. Much of what is wrong in those nations today has roots in our tutelage. Besides' — he took a sip of his brandy, avoiding my gaze — 'I feel I should be attempting something with a bit of weight. The others were just a bit of fun, really.'

Julia, I remembered, had not been amused by the *Private Eye* exposure. Julian, an egregious, humourless man without his father's charm, had joined her in castigating Thomas. 'You might have thought of me, Father. These things do count at the FO, you know . . .' I'd felt a little sorry for Thomas being thus set upon at his launch party at the Ivy. Now he was looking vaguely into the corner of the dining-room, preoccupied with some private thought, his old mouth working.

'Sounds very laudable. Have you started?'

He wriggled suddenly, reminding me of an overweight schoolboy pinned by his master's accusing glance. The casual ramble was over: we were coming to the heart of the matter.

'Well, as a matter of fact, I have sketched out the first draft . . .' He gestured vaguely with his free hand. 'I've got a few months' work to do . . . some more research and rewriting. A bit of polishing . . .' He gave me his insincere politician's smile, the one his heart and mind never accompanied. Watching his eyes suddenly avoid mine and his fingers start to play with the cruet, I knew that he was calculating some approach to me. He cleared his throat. 'It never occurred to me . . .' (such phrases arouse my professional instincts: if never, why now, whatever is to be said?) 'that your family could . . . might . . .

21

think that I had based some of the characters upon . . . um . . . all of you.' He pinched his jowl and looked up as though examining something of interest on the ceiling.

Hindsight, that fallible modifying agent. It seems to me now that I saw the shape of things in that instant; saw that Thomas was trying to set his conscience at rest for what he was about to do; saw that there was nothing so inexorable as revenge taken by one old man upon another, with no regard for what else might speed the plough.

'And have you?' I asked, knowing Thomas to be too much of a politician to answer a direct question.

'Every writer bases his creations upon personal experiences. Of course there isn't any direct correlation between life and a completely fictional work. But fiction must derive from life to be valid, and it is strange how often people completely erroneously identify themselves . . .'

'I suppose the laws of libel offer some protection. Anyway, if you're so concerned, why not put it aside – do something else?' An idle question. I had seen the hunger in his face. This lunch was part of some exorcism so that he might go ahead with what he had already made up his mind to do.

There was occasionally a strange, childlike sincerity in Thomas, restoring him to me momentarily as a person who, under the facile sophistries behind which he hid, might merit the all-embracing affection parents can at best give their children – where disapproval of what the child does is quite a separate matter from the unaffected continuing love for the child. In such brief glimpses I thought I saw someone who, though flawed, held the eternal verities at his centre, and had merely used the platitudes of politics to protect some soft underbelly of worth. It was not that I thought Thomas was right; more often than not I felt that he had made the wrong decisions, in the sense that he had said and done things which had denied him the advancement he craved. I think, though, that he almost invariably knew what was right, even though he often chose to ignore it. This time he did not avoid my eyes.

'I believe I've written something quite extraordinary. I think when Julia's . . . cancer . . . came along I suddenly realized two things: that my own death approaches and that I wanted to leave something . . . more . . .' He waved his hand generally in the direction of the other diners, as though consigning them to some realm of no importance.

'Here lies one whose words were writ in water? Remember, there's no fool like an old fool.' (God, I thought, I'm beginning to sound like Septimus.) The words were harsher than I had intended, so I followed them with as warm a smile as I could muster.

He gave me a reproachful glance, but the shaft had gone wide. 'I suppose being constantly confronted with the sick makes you cynical. I know that it may be an illusion, but I feel that this gives a pattern and shape to my own life . . .'

'But life is chaos and there is no shape in that. All the patterns and meanings are only the artificial ones that we create. And there is rarely little truth or worth in the specious memoirs of a politician. So you will appear in the book too?'

The waiter appeared with some more coffee. Thomas gave a short, exasperated sigh, biting his lower lip in thought for a moment. 'None of us appear in a representational sense. The book isn't meant to be a record of gossip or actual events — rather it is intended to provide a context for certain things that happened . . .'

'You mean the exploitation of India by the Raj?'

He glanced at me covertly, licking his full bottom lip. 'I think that the historical overview has been covered time and again. The problem with histories is their distance. They deal with wars and treaties, dynastic ambitions, the statistics of battles. I am dealing with a community at an interior level, where, if it works as I hope it does, the characters will show in their day-to-day lives what the relationship is between ruler and ruled . . .'

'Not Edwina Mountbatten and Nehru again?'

He reddened slightly and coughed behind his hand. 'Well, not quite at that level, but it is certainly about people rather than social history.'

It was then I might have found the key. Might have stopped

the whole sequence of cause and effect. Might have left the past undisturbed. Or was that falling into the trap that Septimus spoke of, the fallacy of presuming I ever had any control over what might happen? Something in Thomas (when I suspected him of being devious — which was much of the time) prompted harsh responses from me, which were later followed by guilt. I already felt badly about my comments. He was an old man now and for that, if for no other reason, merited my compassionate protection, if not my unqualified love. So far as he was concerned, it seemed the time had come to suspend the laws under which I expected people to earn my affection. I knew he had reached that age when he felt it permissible to make summary judgements: when time grows short one cannot maintain the debate for ever; and (he would argue) there was an obligation to pass on one's wisdom without the restraints of polite social usage.

Still troubled, but unwilling to carry on the attack, I said, 'Why not give what you've written to Father to read, if you're so worried about it? Surely nothing can be important enough to risk hurting your friends . . . ?'

With seeming irrelevance Thomas said, 'I was consulted and supported your nomination, you know? I'm sure that surprises you . . .' and then, signing the bill and giving the waiter his politician's smile, 'Perhaps at Christmas when we're all together in the country. Eh?'

Chapter Three

After my last patient had left, I walked down Harley Street to collect the car from the underground car park in Cavendish Square. I felt uneasy, but it was not focused yet beyond the vague knowledge that Thomas had stirred something in me.

Stuck in the traffic on the Cromwell Road outside the Natural History Museum, I began to think reluctantly along lines that had become more and more familiar of late. I remembered, when I first began to practise, the pleasure of intellectual discovery, the feeling of well-being that I was – in a small way – helping to order a world driven mad by excess. One of my first patients was Ronald – in his early thirties, his big body cowering in the chair as I explained the processes of analysis and therapy, his eyes averted as he nodded in apparent agreement to everything I said. With the assumptions of inexperience I formed an opinion after a few weeks: he at first showed the resistance towards the necessary collusion of analysis which is characteristic of the abnormally insecure. In small asides – barely noticeable in his artificially bright anecdotes about his work as a banker, his visits to rugby matches, his reading – I caught the flavour of an ever present wife whose each appearance demonstrated her dominance in their relationship. I forbore to introduce any concrete proposal until I had amassed more evidence, discovering, as we progressed, that there was a symbiotic base to the relationship which could not easily be set aside – that his present predicament (a sense of deep, pervasive depression, a fear of some unspecified infection, very low self-esteem, an inability to make love to his wife, a sense, as he put it, 'that each day seems the same, and yet each day seems severed from the one before, as though there is no continuity in my life') was a repetition of some previous relationship. He compartmentalized his emotions: he would express himself with sudden, extreme, uncharacteristic violence towards his wife or a member of his family ('I could take a meat cleaver to him . . .' and so on) and then, confronted with his own words later, profess disbelief that he had expressed such feelings.

In time, when he had ceased to try to produce interesting material, or to treat me like some deity who could guide and protect him from the world, he suddenly told me that his father's chauffeur had once tried to rape him as a child – instantly qualifying the admission by suggesting it may have been a dream. It took some weeks for him to return to the theme with reluctance. It was a hot afternoon. His parents were out and he had been left in the charge of the chauffeur. The man had suggested that they tidy the bedroom together, sitting in the chair and directing the boy. He knew instinctively of the man's arousal, the claustrophobic, sudden intimacy between them. He had known what was happening – trapped into stillness by an uneasy sense of excitement. Watching him, the man had begun to remove his clothing, while the boy, fascinated, afraid, had continued to tidy the books into the shelves, barely aware of what he was doing. He knew that now he held the power – that one word to his parents when they returned would result in the chauffeur's dismissal. He was curious too. There was a moment, as the man, naked himself, tried to undress him, when he had at last felt a revulsion in himself. At that instant the doorbell had rung and the man had ejaculated instantly – 'like millions of white worms all over the bed'. He had been unable to say anything, conscious of a tremor of guilt at his own collusion, but later was furious with his mother for not knowing what had happened without being told.

It never happened again. Shortly after he was infested with threadworm. The family Labrador was put down when the doctor suggested it might have been the cause – much to his distress – and Ronald began to develop an irrational dread of infection and of being touched. 'I felt that worms would invade my body – crawl into my brain and make me mad.'

26

As we progressed he professed to comprehend – amongst other things – the close relationship between fear and desire, that often our feeling of repulsion towards something is merely the other aspect of our desire for it. From his own experience he volunteered his views upon the interchangeability of symbols, by which we preserve ourselves from true self-knowledge. Quite casually he said of a recurrent dream in which he made love to a faceless woman who then castrated him, 'It was my mother, of course. The forbidden relationship.' I was cautious, for there is a class of patients who learn to produce material they think will interest the analyst. At about this stage he mentioned in passing that a young man – 'who reminds me of my fag at school' – had come to work for him. In the next few weeks he surprised me with his insights: the salient point of his memory of the chauffeur (he said) was the simultaneous revulsion and excitement of the encounter; the worms that were going to invade his body were the sperm that he had seen at the moment of trauma; he could see that desire and apparent revulsion might be closely related. His references to his wife and family became less violent – often affectionate, sometimes pitying, occasionally valedictory. Eighteen months after he first came he told me he had accepted his homosexuality: he and Howard had decided to move in together. (Strange that I felt a faint pang of revulsion – as though I had not controlled events towards a conventional ending.)

A little later he stopped coming. I was by this time partly working for the Health Service and partly in private practice in the unfashionable end of West Hampstead. Angela's taste permeated the four rooms, so that it had a comforting sense of home. I'd had a number of papers taken by the Institute, and a gratifying list of referrals from senior practitioners unable to take on new patients. I'd been there six months, and had plans on taking consulting rooms in the West End. The name Jennifer Harmby on my list of prospective new patients meant nothing.

She was petite, with the sort of elfin good looks which age might later mock. Wide-spaced grey eyes, a short nose, a wide mouth accustomed to either smiling or being used a lot. Briskly she told me I wouldn't need my notebook: she was Ronald's wife. Ronald had been knifed to death in his flat, apparently by Howard. 'A sordid poofs' quarrel . . .' she said, the anger suddenly showing through her detached brusqueness. 'Do you really feel that you did the right thing? If he had never come to you, none of this would have happened . . .' I was forced to resort to being at my most silent and psychoanalytical, but she was not intimidated. 'If you call this creating happiness, contentment, well-being – whatever your jargon for it may be – I feel sorry for you.' Looking through the window, I could see her anger in the way she walked down the road. The canker, the growing awareness that we cannot know the grand design, that we, too, stumble in the complex dark, began there.

I hadn't thought of my own childhood for years. Many people are drawn again and again towards the things they most fear, in order to conquer them. I had done the opposite, caching the pain of childhood in some dim recess in my mind, where it might have lain undiscovered for ever. I was dimly aware of things: that there had been accommodations I had made, things I had done, which I could forgive and whose provenances I understood, though others would probably not. Again, shadowy as parents' lives often are to their children, there were events I had never fully acknowledged which threatened to break into conscious memory. I cursed Thomas for this, and also because I had begun to realize that it might fall to me to defend the family.

The cars moved forward a few yards and then stopped. (The Cromwell Road seems constantly under siege from excavators.) When the official letter mentioning the CBE had arrived, I remembered the first two thoughts which followed hard upon the pleasure: the first, that I might, at last, enjoy the acceptance of my father. I was surprised to find that I still needed his approval and love. I began to realize that I did what I had done as a child: I sanitized him, ennobled him, discarded those perceptions which would not fit because I knew that to see him whole would make it impossible to continue that love, and would by association diminish me. The second thought had been for the blindness of the world

Thomas inhabits, concerned only with the outer show. Far deeper even than the *obiter dicta* of my profession, with its emphases upon self-knowledge and self-acceptance, ran the true root and branch of the feelings from childhood: already I could feel the shape and texture of the things I had done, and with them, the bully's fear of challenge, the forger's fear of discovery. I wondered, as the traffic began to move forward again, if my father had experienced such doubts about himself, or had ever really considered the consequences of his actions upon Angela and myself.

Time runs short. This is all we have, or shall have. I knew that, and found in myself the desire to make a reckoning upon my own account so that for once, before we too went into the dark and were lost, we might see each other and the past without veils, without evasions. For without that what had it all meant?

That evening I rang Angela. (Again, I have often wondered if *there* I made the first mistake.) Standing by the polished rose-wood table, I waited, looking down the dark hall through the conservatory, past the patio and the pool, to where the far bank of the river caught the last dusky rays of the sun. Nico, Angela's son, was staying with a friend, and Angela had just returned from a few days' holiday in Rhodes with 'someone'. She persisted in using such euphemisms, though we both knew what they meant, and I always knew how such liaisons would end. (Yet, even there I was wrong.) Knowing, it made no difference: the profoundest truth had been expressed in her involuntary cry years before: 'I can never escape. Why do I try?' And, though I knew the answer, or as much as one person may know of another, I had remained silent until the moment of despair had passed.

I sensed some anger in her. Perhaps she saw my not telling her of the proposed honour as some betrayal. Her returns were always awkward, and it was almost with relief that I noticed her growing preoccupation when I told her of the lunch.

'What does he know?' We always go to our own secrets first. Her voice, though anxious, had an edge of asperity.

'I've no idea. I'm afraid Julia's cancer seems to have acted like a *memento mori.*' I mimicked Thomas's phrasing: 'He wants to leave something behind.'

'He's your godfather. He's known us since we were children. He wouldn't want to write anything which could . . . hurt us?'

I felt a sudden affection at the naïvety. 'The length of time means nothing. It might as easily have promoted envy or dislike as the converse. We could always avoid Christmas and let them get on with it. Besides, it's months away. Anything might happen.'

'It's unlike you to take refuge in optimism. Besides, we must go. It may be the last Christmas we all have together.' She paused for a moment. 'Are you coming over?' I could read nothing into her tone.

'Tomorrow, perhaps. I've got some case notes to write up.'

I swam thirty lengths of the pool. The midges carried out their complicated dance above the water, and the evening wind began to stir the ringlets of the laburnum at the far end. Left to my own devices, I would have found some reason to avoid Christmas. My *métier* is avoidance, not confrontation. When one has secrets, any alteration to one's normal pattern of life creates the fear of discovery. I had managed to seal over that past life and now I dreaded the tines of memory scraping the decent covering of tilth and leaves from the past. But I needed to remember, to find some way of dealing with whatever Thomas might be preparing for us.

Ancestral voices prophesying war.

Chapter Four

Now I can say that re-examining the past is a complex business. There is the past as it happened to me as a child – that imperfect mixture of recollections of individual events, of smells, sights, feelings: accompanying which was always the awareness of never quite seeing the whole picture, never really comprehending the glances covertly exchanged, the fragmentary asides, the whole subtext of the adult world. Then there is the past as now revealed to me by Septimus and Thomas and others – so different that I am only just able to piece together what happened. As for truth, well, that is an idea which may only flourish in fairy tales: it has no substance in the real world.

There are some concrete things. In the escritoire in my study, under the picture of Angela and me as children, sepia, smiling at the camera, our arms round each other, there is a pink folder containing a number of things from childhood, including a history of the family which my father wrote for the April 1951 issue of the *Iskanderabad Gazette*. As a child I believed it all implicitly. Now I am less sure.

A LITTLE LOCAL HISTORY

by

Amyas Lawrence

Delving into one's past is fraught with dangers. If one is not equipped by nature with the fortitude to accept the possibilities of bars sinister, felons, practitioners of the black arts, miscegenation, even murder in the history of one's forebears, it would be wise to leave such matters to those of stouter spirit. I decided to go back because I believe that we and our children might benefit from

31

knowing our own history and credentials. It is these things, after all, which give us our substance, our place in the world. And, readers, you too might find this story interesting.

When Clive of India arrived in Calcutta in 1757 with 900 European troops and 1,500 Indian troops in five transports with five men-o'-war, he was secretly resolved not to reconquer and hand back the city to its previous rulers, but to serve his own interests and those of the East India Company by emulating de Bussy's success in sponsoring the Hyderabad state in the French interests. On his successful completion of the campaign, Clive ('Sabat Jung' − the tried in battle) was awarded official entitlements of over £$\frac{1}{4}$ million and land grants worth £30,000 a year. The financial bleeding of Bengal had begun, and a pattern which was to persist for centuries was established. Once the Company's forces had subdued the Nawab the entire country was at their disposal. Any merchant who could muster a few followers could intimidate the Nawabi officers and the peasants as they never could have done when the redoubtable tribesmen were led by their local chiefs in the Deccan. In the new state of Bengal − nominally administered by the Nawab − the military power was in the hands of the Company, who used it to plunder the revenues at will.

My own ancestor, Henry Lawrence, was very close to Clive and privy to his troubled conscience. A contemporary sketch of Henry shows a regular-featured, slightly feminine face under a high brow, with an aquiline nose and rather weak mouth. Some of the notes to him from Clive (preserved in our family bible) − most notably two written in the last months before Clive was finally successful in taking his own life − suggest that Clive was burdened with guilt at the consequences of his own success. 'Can it be right thus to plunder the wealth of this most gentle and hospitable of people?' he asks, and then, 'I fear that I may not be properly shriven, nor shall I be successful in my suit for Pardon before my Maker.'

Henry seems to have possessed a more pragmatic nature. Between 1760, when Clive went back to England, and his return to India in 1765, Henry had moved northwards to establish a base in Iskandera-bad with a plundered fortune in land and cash grants. It is pure speculation on my part, but I believe that his journey north was partly prompted by the fear that Clive, recanting, might attempt to stop such profiteering − as indeed turned out to be the case. However, to appease his own Christian conscience and, probably more importantly, to conciliate his wife, Matilda, Henry commissioned the building of our church, designing the great granite tower himself, and ordering a great bell to be cast at the foundry in Hyderabad and transported overland here by oxen cart.

Henry's private diary records a note in 1765 – the year the church was finished. 'Persuaded that Jesuitical Bishop [indecipherable] to consecreate the Church in consideration of £300 in gold given personally to him, the whiche he tells me is for The Southern Missions, whiche I beg leave to Doute, despite his High Calling.' The cornerstone of the church still carries the barely legible dedication: 'To God and hys Humble Servantes of the East India Coy. whose Christian Fellowship shall bring lighte to thys darke land as Englishmen have done for centuries past throughout the Globe.' Two years later Henry founded our school, ostensibly for the sons of officers of the East India Company. For a time after that it seems that his troubled conscience and new-found piety troubled him less, for he conscripted an army of irregulars and added to his wealth by extracting tithes from neighbouring villages. His wife, Matilda, records stoically in her diary on 10 April 1790: 'We have our own French Revolution here. There was affix'd to the Church door with a kukri a marvellous ill-spell'd Notice to say that My Deare Husbande and his issue in Perpetuity shall be curs'd for the hardships he has lain upon the people.' Nursing him through his last illness with their grown son and daughter in attendance, she notes: 'He is sore afraid of the Judgement to come, knowing that the Building of The Church shall not buy him a place in Paradise. Further, he tells me that the tower, which, being set upon a Hill, is visible for miles, has become a Symbolle of the Rape of India by the British.' Henry duly died and was interred in the graveyard, only for his mausoleum to be broken into one night and his body stolen, to be discovered days later upon the khudside gnawed clean by *feowls* and jackals.

The *Iskanderabad Gazette* for May 1827 carried an article by Amelia Fearnshaw on the church, in which she observes in passing that local legend has it that the English will rule India whilst the tower stands. Almost one hundred years after it had been built, in 1858, the year after the Mutiny had been quelled, a relative of Mangal Pande (the sepoys' hero, who was strapped to a cannon mouth and blown to pieces over his disarmed comrades by the British) gathered together a band of his supporters to stack bales of hay soaked in ghee against the church tower and set light to them. An unexpected storm arose, extinguishing the flames, and the *goondas* were captured and crucified upside down by the British as an example to deter those who would dare oppose their presence in India.

Many of us will remember being roused in the early hours of one Sunday morning in March 1947 by the tolling of the great bell. Who was able to ring the bell while the tower was engulfed in flames remains a mystery. Miraculously the bell itself fell intact upon the rubble from the tower, but by morning the wind blew across blackened masonry, and the gravel was littered with shards of glass from the stained windows depicting the Twelve Stations of the Cross. The subsequent Inquiry presided over by Colonel Whitworth (with ministry sanction) could not reach any firm conclusion regarding culpability, merely concluding that 'the fire was started by a person or persons unknown . . .'

As some of you in the community already know, I have taken upon myself the task of restoring the church. I belong to that school of thought which believes that the unextinguished obligations of each generation pass to its successors. I have proposed the setting up of a fund for this purpose. Colonel Whitworth and Mrs Dora Wheeler have kindly agreed to sit with me on the committee, and work is scheduled to begin as soon as we amass sufficient finance in the fund to purchase the necessary materials and to employ two good workmen for a year. I hope you will all wish to contribute to this worthwhile venture. Though we have no desire to rule India again, this restoration will be a symbol that our beliefs have stood the test of time.

Almost two years before my lunch with Thomas, Mother had called to give me the news. I could tell from the tone of her voice that something exciting had happened, though she teased me as she had when Angela and I were children. 'You'll never guess. Get your copy of *The Times* and I'll tell you where to look.' And there it was. A picture of Father's best three-quarter face and his name in the list of knighthoods under 'Services to the Commonwealth'. Well, to those whose rules were laid down in 'Vitaï Lampada' and 'If' this must be some sort of *summum vitae*, and I managed to say, 'Marvellous, marvellous,' in a hearty tone, glad that my mother could not sense the hollowness of my congratulations. Of course I'd tell Angela. Yes, I'd certainly come down for the celebration at the weekend, and I expected she'd join me. How easily I was trapped into filial obligation!

Angela said, 'Oh, shit! Do we have to go?'

'It means a lot to them. I'll be going, anyway.'

A long silence and then she said, 'I suppose so . . .' without much conviction.

Braced for the worst, the party was even harder to take than I had anticipated. Television cameras, the press, numerous local dignitaries and George Rydell, the local constituency MP, bucolic, over-loud, and eyeing Angela in a black dress as though he intended to exercise some droit de seigneur. Passing me early on, she lowered her voice. 'Mother's trying to get me off with that awful man. If I get stuck with him, you will save me, won't you?'

I talked to Lydia Folkcroft. Years ago she had been one of Mother's plans for me. We had enjoyed each other's company for six months in a totally asexual way, and she had then told me she was marrying Peter Folkcroft, a local farmer. She'd laughed at my incredulity, her brilliant smile making her thin brown face almost beautiful for a moment. 'I know. He's stupid, boring — and rich. He dotes on me, we'll have two or three kids, a good life, and I don't think he'll look at anyone else. That's all I want.'

She still glowed, clever girl. It had turned out exactly as she had foreseen. Two beautiful daughters, a lovely home, a devoted husband. She was one of the lucky ones who had chosen what lay beneath her hand, and was satisfied. 'God, Amyas loves all this. He must have done someone a big favour.' A girl in chinos with her hair in a pony-tail was flicking a paintbrush over his face while the camera lined up.

'That's cynical,' I said.

'When you spend half your life surrounded by the smell of manure helping lambs to give birth or feeding pigs, you discard the inessentials. Still single?'

'You know me. Professional bachelor.'

'I think that phrase carries the wrong connotations these days. But yes,' she said, her eyes flicking towards Angela, who was trying to avoid Rydell's tactile hands, 'I know you.'

Angela came over. 'Can I take refuge for a few moments? He doesn't take no for an answer.'

'Of course,' Lydia said. She smiled at Angela and then at me.

Later, it was the same as it had always been. As though we were children again. Father relaxed by the fire with a whisky soda. The old pictures, furniture, rugs from Iskanderabad all round us.

'Did you like him?' Mother asked Angela.

'The MP? He was awful. A real groper.'

Father said, 'We want you to settle down, Angela. We've forgiven and forgotten that old business now. But you didn't marry Nico's father, whoever he was, and the boy does need a man's hand.'

The past in the present. The belief that we — Angela more than I — owed my parents a debt for being born and nurtured which they had every right to call in. I could see Angela's body tense, and the lines of strain in her face. She brushed her hair from her face with her hand, throwing her head back in a familiar gesture. I said, knowing from long experience that the confrontation couldn't be avoided, 'It's Angela's life. She has the right to make her own decisions.'

I could see the red flush rise in Father's face. 'You know I can't bear that *laissez-faire* attitude. You'll never convince me that we don't have obligations to others. If Angela doesn't think of Nico, she should think of her mother and me.'

'I'm sure she does,' I said. Angela shot me a grateful glance.

Towards the end of the evening Father said, 'It was the Bishop of Lahore who proposed me,' and then, with seeming irrelevance, 'Did you talk to Gobind, by the way? Gobind Dass?'

Something fell into place. I could picture the small, ever smiling Indian holding his champagne glass. He'd struck me as vaguely familiar, but I hadn't been able to place him. He and my father had fallen out very badly, years before. Presumably that had all been made up now. I nodded, moving on. 'I thought you would have invited Thomas and Septimus.'

Father smiled his patrician's smile, the one which I always thought was accompanied by some sense of superiority.

'Septimus sent his regrets and congratulations. I got the most grudging four-line letter you could ever imagine from Thomas, pleading a prior engagement.'

Mother moved her foot suddenly and her glass shattered against the brass fender. 'Oh dear,' she said, stooping to pick up the shards from the carpet. 'The best crystal.'

Chapter Five

Looking back, it seems strange that I didn't even think about the possible consequences of the lunch with Thomas for some time after my immediate anxieties had quietened. I suppose I thought it would pass, that he would recognize the difficulties in pursuing the course he had planned and set it aside. And the possible effects on others just didn't occur to me: on Angela and Nico, and the whole family. For a while things went on as usual. Thomas sent his excuses that Christmas. Julia was too ill. We got through the festivities, Angela and I.

'I can't seem to help myself. And I always hate the man afterwards.'

And before, did you but know it. I sat behind the head of the couch, silent in the approved manner, my hands folded over the notepad on my knees. Miriam Cohen's hennaed head on the pillow began to shake. She started to sob like a child, gulping in huge draughts of air. Schooled to neutrality, I waited. Beyond the window the leaves of the chestnut flapped in the wind. In theory I must be impartial, non-judgemental. In practice (though I have not so admitted to my own analyst — for this is how my profession operates, in a wide, far-flung circle — nor to my colleagues, nor in my recent psychoanalytical papers on impasse and interpretation) I have begun to toy again with the absolutes of childhood: to find myself assigning varying degrees of importance to distress by reference to some objective standard. Thus, say the loss of Simeon Joseph's father and mother in Dachau gave a score of ten, Miriam Cohen's fear of ageing could not rate more than three.

There was a frivolity in this game (which I used to counter

the boredom of being the auditor of numerous neurotic repetitions), for distress is what is felt by the analysand and may not be further quantified. The pad slipped and I scuffed my shoe on the carpet as I caught it.

'In each relationship you are seeking the father you have lost. When each man fails to treat you as though he were the good father, you hate him. These are the inappropriate feelings of childhood.'

'I hated my father.'

'When he died you wept for a week.' I consulted the pad on my knee. 'Three weeks ago you put flowers on his grave.'

A sudden memory of the time of iron. In the morning the lawn glittering white, and the great black lesions in the bark of the silver birches, like open sores. The time, those few days, when it seems that winter will never end. The acrid smell of woodsmoke from Nico's bonfire, before which he stands, scarfed and mittened, his cheeks red, as Angela and I watch him through the leaded windows.

'Every man I sleep with turns out to be a bastard.' Again the circularity, the repetition. The same premises which inevitably lead to the same conclusions. This is no country to inhabit beyond one's thirties.

'We have to leave it now until Thursday.'

Angela and I climbed the dark stairs. Such places were not her *métier* at all, and I could sense her fastidious unease. The stair carpet was orange, cheap and frayed, and the dirty emulsioned walls carried graffiti in black pentel: 'Dyslexia lures − KO.' 'Anyone for Denis? Maggie.' A thin coloured boy in a faded T-shirt stood against the balustrade to let us pass, pursing his lips in a silent whistle as he looked at Angela. On the landing a naked light-bulb illuminated an old tallboy and a door with peeling paint carrying a handwritten card stuck with yellowing sellotape which proclaimed the legend 'Mr Septimus Brown'. Septimus had never cared much for appearances.

Septimus opened the door to my knock. He kissed Angela, enfolding her in a sudden, fierce hug, then shook my hand. He was wearing a suit that night, in honour of our taking him to dinner.

There was a ridge of dust on the shoulder where it had hung on the hanger, and the material had the shine of age. Angela had only seen him twice in the last few years. 'You see,' I said, 'he's just the same,' and she laughed, more at ease now in this neat room with its rows of bookshelves and potted plants.

I felt some reserve in him about my honour, though he produced all the stock phrases about how proud we must be. Later, I thought perhaps I had imagined it. He had brought some old photographs. Chez Victor was almost empty when the waiter brought our coffees and an Otard for Septimus. There was one of Angela and myself as children standing on either side of Latif in front of the Mughal Reservoirs. Some memory stirred. (Septimus was amused to see me don my half-glasses to look at them.) There was the tower in sepia, part built, with Septimus standing in mock-heroic pose, pointing at it. The man by the side of him had moved so that his face was a blur. 'Johann Neidermayer' – Septimus pointed – 'd'you remember him?'

Angela said, 'The man who never spoke. Who helped you with the building?'

Septimus nodded. 'I've seen him a few times over the years. You know how we ex-colonials seek each other out. He came round about three weeks ago. Seems to have done well for himself. But . . .' I could tell he was going to ask a favour. 'I wonder if you'd see him professionally?'

'What's the problem?'

'Never thought I'd hear those words from you. I don't know, of course. Something he wants to get off his chest. He's rich enough to indulge himself. I'll get him to call.'

There was a picture of Thomas and Julia at the White House in Iskanderabad with our parents. How cruel time is! The cricket match against the Nawab's team, both sides sat formally outside the marquee with the Nawab himself seated in the middle with a huge turban, holding a bat. The band. A group of people with a very pretty girl standing by the side of a lean man with piercing eyes and a moustache in a shikar suit. 'Vivienne James. You were very keen on her. That was a tragic story.'

Walking back to the car in the fine drizzle, Septimus said, 'I gather Thomas is writing a book about Iskanderabad.'

Surprised, I said, 'How did you know about that?'

Septimus smiled wryly. 'I knew something was up when he attended the last Iskanderabad reunion. He's always considered that sort of thing rather infra dig — nothing in it for him. He was questing round like a truffle hound, treating people he wouldn't normally offer the time of day to liberal doses of charm. He said something ponderous to me about reflecting the history of the Raj through a novel rooted in experience. And Gobind Dass, who was with us, gave that filthy laugh of his and said, "Another dirty book, but this time with real people." Thomas was most offended.'

'Did he question you at all?'

Septimus laughed, touching my shoulder lightly. 'I gave nothing away.'

'What is there to give away?' Without turning I could sense the sudden tension in Angela.

Septimus opened the rear door of the car for Angela and went round to let himself into the passenger's seat. I nosed out into Shaftesbury Avenue. The crowds were beginning to spill over the pavement from the theatres. As Septimus talked, I could see Angela's eyes in the mirror fixed on the reflection of my face.

'I have never been judgemental. I am aware that the exposure of many of the things I do know, which I accept to be part of humanity's usual foibles, might be awkward for some of the people I know. It would not occur to me to say anything about them. But Thomas — well, there's another question.'

I drove down Charing Cross Road towards the Embankment. Septimus said, 'You will see Neidermayer, won't you?' and I nodded.

Angela slept. Driving along the rain-slicked streets, I felt a flicker of fear. There was something inexorable in Thomas which I had seen before in the old: a decay of compassion in favour of expediency as time grew short; a desire to pay off old scores. And I knew, too, that things had taken place which had not all lost their importance with the passage of time, but still worked under the surface like worms in the dark earth.

Chapter Six

It was after that dinner that the memories began to return, as though from some common compulsion. Sometimes just a few words, a recollection of the look on someone's face, sometimes like a film I was compelled to watch.

I was about twelve. We were going on a picnic to the clearing by the Mughal Reservoirs.

Angela and I were the only two children. A hot day with a piercing sun. There were about twenty of us and the servants ambling down the rutted red-earth path threading through the *maquis* and scrub which sprouted over the great clavicle of the hill along whose ridge the new hospital was being built. There were smells: of woodsmoke, pine resin, the pungent reek of decaying shrubs. Mother and Father were accompanying Thomas and Julia Henne, who had just arrived from England. Brother Septimus from the monastery, Dora Wheeler, Colonel Tom and Mrs Whitworth.

I watched Vivienne James from the corner of my eye, hoping that Angela wouldn't notice and start to tease me. She looked like the beggar maid in the picture by Burne-Jones in my father's study: a sad, beautiful oval face framed by brown hair which hung down her back. She seemed not to notice the young lecturers from the Iskanderabad college who followed at her heels, exchanging jokes for her benefit, jostling and nudging each other in the ribs. There was Mr Weaver ('Not one of us,' my father used to say) and his wife, Eleanor, very tall, ugly, with narrow shoulders and big hips. Dora Wheeler had once told me that every group had their scapegoats, and Mr and Mrs Weaver were ours. I smiled vacantly, not knowing what she meant. Mr Latif walked alone, suited in grey, with a malacca walking-stick. The day was oppressively hot, full of the sounds of humming bees.

I accompanied Dora Wheeler. She walked fast, with purpose. She was about sixty, though she looked younger, and she talked to me as though I were an adult. She still had an arresting beauty, high cheekboned and autocratic, and a skin which was pink and white, protected from the sallowing suns.

'To what do I owe this honour? Why aren't you gathering pearls of wisdom from your father? Or making moon eyes at that girl, like all the other young men?' Her eyes in the shadow from the wide brim of her hat were clear, unwavering, but I could see a hint of a smile at the corners of her mouth.

'It's more interesting with you. Besides, you walk faster.'

She laughed. Leading the party, I could see the big lizards of northern India scatter and run to disappear into crevices in the rocks.

'Keep away from that young woman, David. There is something destructive in her, despite her beauty.' I was never certain with Dora, confronted by the thin, clever face, the comments which seemed to partake of some different order of reality from that of most grown-ups.

I hadn't been quite honest (even then). I had joined Dora from an instinct for her loneliness. Angela and I heard much that was not intended for our ears. As children, unable to influence matters one way or the other, or even to pass on gossip, the grown-ups rarely bothered to modify their conversations in front of us. 'It won't hurt them. It'll go over their heads,' Father once said. So I knew that Dora was worried about her son, Charles, who drank too much and was unable to hold down any job for more than a few weeks. Father had laughed, saying something about 'loose women, too' to Mother, whatever that meant. I liked Charles: until a couple of years before he had played with us and joined us down at the house quite often, until Mother had come to feel he was unsuitable company for Angela. Not like Dora's other son, Henry. He always seemed heavy, dour, as if life were a succession of great disappointments.

'I don't suppose your father's said anything to you about

the progress of the Church Restoration Fund?' Behind us Eleanor Weaver gave her loud, affected laugh in response to something my father had said, and a slight, ironic smile twisted Dora's lip for a moment and then was gone.

I reviewed the adult conversations I had heard over the past few weeks, and shook my head. Almost to herself, Dora said, 'All that Tom Whitworth said when I asked him was, "These things take time, my dear," as though speaking to a child.' She caught the Colonel's dry, patronizing tone exactly. 'Nothing to laugh about,' she said, in apparent reproof, but I knew she wasn't angry.

Dora was one of the two people from whom I learned as a child. Not book learning, for what she showed me was not taught in books but came from her astute insights, her ability to eschew the literal and, seeking behind it, to juxtapose things in a new focus, a perspective which gave them a deeper meaning. And she shared these with me as with an equal. If it had not been for the fact that her dead husband, Theodore, had proved such an ally to my father and Tom Whitworth during the dark days leading up to Partition and after, I suspect my parents would have tried to keep us away from her. As it was they tried to render her impotent by ridicule. 'She's quite batty. Harmless, of course. And look at the way those boys have turned out.' But already, under my acceptance of my parents' wisdom, I knew that this apparent contempt was motivated by fear. Dora Wheeler was — well — if not overtly subversive, not quite normal.

Now she said, speaking to herself, 'It is the last year. Probably.'

'What do you mean, Mrs Wheeler?'

But instead of answering me, she turned her grave regard upon me for a moment, smiling, and we went on.

Father walked with Mother. (Seeing him again last week was to see the ruin of what he once was.) Tall, lean, with regular classical features. At forty, as he was then, a proud, imperious face, with only a dusting of grey hairs amongst the thick gold. ('A young Apollo, golden-haired,/Stands dreaming on the verge of strife,/Magnificently unprepared/For the long

44

littleness of life.' So Dora had characterized him. How seriously I never knew, as with so many of her pronouncements.) Mother was small, dark, reserved. I knew she didn't like Eleanor Weaver, who was walking with them, partly because it was an open secret that Eleanor considered herself in love with Father. A few weeks before, my parents had invited the Whitworths and the Hennes for lunch. The servants had brought *burra* pegs of whisky water to Thomas and my father, *chota* pegs of gin and tonic for Julia and my mother. Julia had a sharp, angular beauty, and a composed stillness. She watched Father's face as he talked. Father had just received his latest copy of the *Iskanderabad Gazette* (of which he was the literary editor) and, caricaturing Eleanor Weaver's voice and delivery (chin jutting, mouth pursed over the vowels, short-sighted eyes squinnying at the manuscript down her nose), he read a part of a story she had written for the magazine: the beautiful young heroine (undoubtedly Eleanor) was on the verge of violation by the cruel, dark, demonic mill-owner to whom she had decided to sacrifice herself to save her ageing parents from financial ruin, but was saved by the intervention of a blond, handsome stranger. Torn between her instant love for him and her duty to her parents, all was resolved when he turned out to be the wealthy landowning heir of the Duke of Midlothian.

Spurred by Thomas's laughter, Father dropped his voice, imparting a confidence. 'Poor Eleanor. She once told me that she stopped looking in the mirror when she was fifteen after convincing herself that beautiful thoughts and a life lived for others would render her beautiful.'

'She has some lovely things.' Julia Henne's voice was low, musical.

'And not all her own,' Father said. He had the expression I feared as a child: the look which accompanied the sarcastic witticisms with which he sometimes punished Angela and me. 'We went round for sherry after church a couple of weeks ago. I spotted a Chinese vase we thought we'd lost on the sideboard.' Mother nodded in confirmation, and Thomas made tsk-tsk noises. 'She's been doing that for years. But, as you'll find, we're a tolerant community.'

High above our party on the path traversing the shoulder of hill upon which the hospital perched, I saw Neville James come into sight, standing for a moment with his hands on his hips and his legs apart, like some victor surveying the spoils of war. Above him two shite-hawks veered and wound slowly in their gyres against the painful blue-white of the sky. Neville shouted, his voice carrying faintly, and began the descent with long, confident strides. Suddenly Vivienne James held both her arms wide in greeting, her customary sullenness dispelled by a wide smile. Her thin cry of pleasure reached us and Dora looked down at me and said, 'You will find out what I meant, by and by.' (Such are the fragments which return.)

The party behind had begun to catch up. Far ahead the sun glinted on the water of the Mughal Reservoirs through a gap in the trees. 'Visitors,' Eleanor was saying in the tone of an excited child, reaching to touch Father on the shoulder. 'Mr Henne and his wife and now the new curate. Father Carey, isn't it? We were wondering if he is . . . well . . . normal?'

The duplicity of grown-ups worried me. It seemed strange to me that my father could talk perfectly amicably to Eleanor Weaver after what he had said about her over lunch. Now again, hearing him say noncommittally, 'Seems nice enough. His sermons are a bit more interesting than Prichy's were in recent years – God rest his soul,' I was aware of a whole subtext overhead at home which ran counter to the remark. Father coming into the house after Akbar the barber had cut his hair, saying, 'Told you, my dear. Akbar confirms the young man is queer as a three pound note.' And, with the perception of children, I knew that Father Carey would be a prize in the community, to be invited from house to house and exhibited until the novelty wore thin and he became the butt of cheap gibes ridiculing his accent and humble origins.

Mr Latif, walking on his own, talked to himself and nobody listened. He would be talking of his son, killed in the Burma Campaign ages before, his death only confirmed three years after the end of hostilities.

The picnic ground was soft and springy from its covering of innumerable pine needles. It was in a clearing bracketed by trees and dense ambuscades of thorny brambles. At its southern edge an inadequate barbed-wire fence snagged with tufts of goat hair afforded bare service in protecting the two thirty-foot-deep Mughal Reservoirs from unwary intruders. It had the desolate fascination of legend. Standing by the fence, I looked across the slime-covered water, glistening with opalescent streaks of oil. A jarring colour caught the corner of my eye: a dead hoopoe lay half concealed in the reedy sedge near my feet. Years before it was here that Akbar the barber's brother, Sharif Ali, was found drowned after escaping from Iskanderabad jail, where he awaited sentence on the charge of murdering his wife. I remember asking Angela, 'Do we really drink that?' and feeling the warmth of her hand on my shoulder through my thin shirt as she told me how it was pumped up through the *galis*, filtered first through successive beds of pebbles, gravel, sand before it reached us. I saw her serious grey eyes in the oval brown face with its straight nose and full bottom lip, her later beauty already foreshadowed in the features which were beginning to assume the sharper definition of maturity. I wanted to believe her passionately, because she was my bulwark in an uncertain world, my mentor who could sometimes explain the behaviour of adults, but I thought, too, of the detritus I found floating in my bath. Did it come from the cold water tanks in the *galis*, or did it fall into the water while the *bhisti* was heating it in ghee tins over an open fire? The impurity of the water was only one of the many things which had begun to trouble me lately.

Mr Latif walked slowly up to the fence to join Angela and me. These days his face was heavy, saturnine, and he showed none of the old warmth, as though he was forever preoccupied with something private, absent. He waved his cane towards the water. 'These were built in Shah Jehan's reign to work the fountains in the grounds of one of his palaces in the plains. They were so constructed that the water could also be diverted to neighbouring farms in the event of drought.' He nodded to himself, and I smiled back uncertainly. Here was another hard pass: the defection of Mr Latif from his role as friend to some passive, brooding place since the death of his son.

Septimus. This is where the pure recollection of memory becomes complex, for Septimus remembers that day clearly for his own reasons. He was, he told me, at a spiritual crossroads. He had reached a point where he felt he was drifting, without volition, down a stream, borne by the current. He'd been brought up by Father Gregorio, and had never before considered the possibility of any other life than entering the order. He told me that he saw himself as if he were a character in a play or a book, as though this first pass in life were some rehearsal in which he could try out the postures, characters, costumes for the real thing which would come later. It was his means for getting by — the shaping of his own life as a fiction in which the drama of his renunciation of the world, the flesh and the devil held both the qualities of vicariousness and a novelettish completeness — a sense of romance. But, at thirty, his thoughts were now sometimes visited by heresies: by occasional, sudden fears that this life might after all be no mere rehearsal for some more polished future performance but all there is. 'Perhaps small beer to you — but a revelation to me,' he'd said, defensively. Without the vistas of a bifurcated life ahead, alternating between abandonment to fleshly desires and pursuits for a period on one hand, and redemptive episodes of self-flagellation and penance on the other, it had begun to seem that a life governed by the twin strands of humility and chastity might, perhaps, be a waste. He was barely present, at the very edge of consciousness: the clink of china and glasses as the servants set out the picnic, the sound of Ernest Lough singing 'Hark! Hark! The Lark' on the wind-up gramophone, the endless stridulation of the cicadas. And he'd confessed to savouring his own memory of walking down the path behind Vivienne James, as oblivious as she to the laughter and chatter of the young lecturers. At the back of her head a coil of brown hair had escaped to lie across the milky-brown skin of her bare shoulder. Father Gregorio had questioned Brother Septimus about his state of spiritual readiness for his final vows: chastity, poverty, obedience. 'All I could recollect was St Paul's prayer, "Make me chaste, Lord, but not yet!"'

But I remembered him lying in the sun. My mother, supine,

resting on her forearm by Father in the resin-scented, dappled shade, called across to Angela, 'Not too close to the pit. Lunch in a few minutes.' I felt Angela squeeze my elbow in complicit defiance even as she nodded. I followed her down the path through the whipping brambles, almost immediately lost to sight of the adults in the green shade. In front of us four small goats broke from the thicket and scattered towards the raised plateau bordering the lime pit, standing to watch us with their yellow, slit-pupilled eyes. My legs stung where the thorns had raked white lines, and my ankle smarted where a nettle had brushed it. I knelt to tear off a dock leaf and wipe the juice against the sting. The ramp surrounding the lime pit reared before me, deckled with flaking Roman brickwork, and the pungent smell of lime caught in my throat so that I gagged, stifling a cough behind my fist.

'Look!'

Angela pointed downwards, standing on the crumbling rim, her calves quivering as she struggled to maintain her precarious balance. The air above the pit shimmered in the heat, distorting the goats behind so that they seemed wraith-like, insubstantial. Angela's eyes were wide with excitement, and her voice was urgent. I took her hand and struggled up beside her, sinking to my knees to follow her forefinger, which pointed at the surface of the lime, four feet below us. A kid had fallen into the lime, which hissed and smoked around it. Half buried, it struggled hopelessly to escape, its thin bleating barely audible above the sound of the wind through the pine tassels. This is what happens when you disobey grown-ups, I thought. It seemed another phenomenon of the adult world: the visitation of unexpected punishment which left a sense of injustice. Aloud I said, 'They'll know we've been here,' already beginning to scramble down the bank. Behind me Angela said, 'It'll die anyway. There's no need to say anything.' But the secret was too big for me to keep. Father would know what to do.

After Partition and the ensuing anti-British feelings Father's Waziri-made bundook had always been taken on picnics, discreetly cached in the bottom of a hamper basket wrapped in an old linen sheet. Saeed Mohammed reverently unwrapped it and gave it to Father. Father said, 'There will be nothing we can do for it. I think the ladies should stay behind. This isn't the sort of thing they should see.' Holding the rifle, he pointed it in the air and inserted a bullet in the breech. Eleanor Weaver put her hand over her mouth, her eyes shining as she watched Father. I was standing near Dora Wheeler, who sat on a cushion next to Vivienne James and her father, who were seated back to back, resting against each other. Drily, quietly, she remarked to no one in particular, 'Trust Amyas to find a bit of theatre.' Colonel Whitworth rose stiffly to his feet and limped after Father and Brother Septimus, closely followed by Mr Latif and three of the young lecturers. My mouth was dry, and I could feel my heart thumping painfully. I started to follow them, but my mother said, 'David. No!' sharply, shaking her head.

The shot sounded disconcertingly loud. Nobody spoke. Father arrived in the gap at the end of the clearing, his face flushed and angry, followed by Mr Latif, who was laughing. 'It was already dead, Mr Lawrence. Why did you waste the bullet?' Colonel Whitworth was already giving his wife an *aide-mémoire*, to remind him that the pit must be securely walled and roofed, and must have a door with a padlock.

In his deep, soft voice Neville James said, 'Bravo, Amyas. So you killed the scapegoat, eh?' His voice was mocking, combative. Vivienne, lying on her back, watched her father's face shadowed under the brim of his fedora.

'At least I did something out in the open, Neville. Where everybody could see . . .'

The silence was embarrassed now and the others averted their eyes from Neville and Father. Neville's face was flushed, dark: I wondered if he was going to get up to strike my father. Vivienne laid her tapering white fingers on his forearm for a moment and he relaxed, giving her a half-smile. Father was busying himself with instructing Saeed on the repacking of the gun. Only Dora seemed unaffected — looking first at Vivienne and her father with her ironic, detached gaze, before turning her eyes towards Father.

After lunch Septimus was a little drunk. (That he confirmed

50

to me, too, with the apologia that the sun was very hot, he was unused to beer and that I should be the first person to recognize — all these years later — that he was going through a crisis.) The sun had passed its height, the savage heat of noon, but the Europeans still lay on blankets in the stippled shade from the trees, while the servants squatted on their haunches a respectful distance away, talking in quiet voices and smoking their *bidis*. There was an air of apathy, almost of melancholy, as though the energy which had fuelled our walk, the laughter and the conversation had been dissipated by the heat. I could not forget the struggling kid: I sat with my chin on my knee, tracing whorls in the dust with my forefinger. It was not only the tragedy, but some dim apprehension of currents I could not understand which oppressed me: Dora's comments, Mr Latif's laughter, the exchange between Father and Neville.

Septimus stood in the middle of the clearing with his hands clasped in front of his chest. Eleanor said, 'Give us one of the old ones, Sep. "Allan Water" or "The Harp that Once — "' but Septimus had already begun to sing 'The Ash Grove' in a clear tenor, stumbling a little over the phrasing when he came to the phrase, 'ah, then never thought I how soon we should part'. Slowly a replete bathos seemed to steal over the party. When Septimus stood erect, forsaking his customary stoop-shouldered posture, he was surprisingly tall. His thick, rufous hair sprayed from his head, and the triangular, discoloured birthmark under his right eye shaded his thin face with a sinister aspect. After, he fell asleep against the bole of a tree.

At dusk we returned up the hill. Behind us the sunset was glorious, blood red, reeking across the horizon of my known world. 'Silly,' Angela whispered, pinching me. She was still angry that I had told the adults about the kid. 'You don't know anything about grown-ups.'

Chapter Seven

'Good afternoon, Dr Lawrence.' Neidermayer's voice is guttural with a hint of a German accent. He has a high, domed forehead, a few wisps of grey hair combed carefully over a nearly bald head, a thin grey face with liverish pouches. He doesn't look at me, and his handshake is damp, perfunctory.

I ask him the routine questions and he answers in a flat monotone. He is seventy-three, a retired importer–exporter, lives in Islington, was widowed four years before. He has repetitive, troubling dreams: sudden irrational fears of imminent death. I explain the process to him and he looks past my left shoulder and nods from time to time.

My memories of him working on the tower in Iskanderabad do not chime with this figure, but we will come to that, by and by. I should not really have taken him as a patient, having known him, even if ever so slightly. (Once he smiles and says, 'You were so high,' exaggerating, his hand two feet above the floor.) We should not see people we have known, for that association in the greater world might distort the passages of our dialogue in the narrow room where everything is permissible. But I have my own curiosity about the past, too. I know I shall have the strength to put his interests before mine if it comes to that. When I have taken the notes, I ask him what he expects and hopes for from seeing me. 'I have learned to expect nothing but I hope for peace,' he replies, with a strange dignity. It is odd to see him thus, as a confessor.

He begins by offering platitudes, small fragments of our common memories, to which I make no response. He is disoriented by my silence and because he cannot move his head far enough to see me where I sit behind him. In the last ten minutes he furtively looks at his watch three times, eager to be gone. I gather hints that he is still weighed down by the hidden incidents of nearly half a century ago. It is here that I acknowledge something to myself: that Neidermayer might help me in my own search for the past. He is another probable repository of some of the secrets from my childhood. I must wait in silence, knowing it to be the one condition which people in pain and distress cannot long bear. He shall tell me all, though whether or not I can help him is another matter. 'Friday. Ja. That is all right.' He annotates the time in his diary.

At first, conscious of my unprofessional interest, I try to apply the rules stringently. No forced congruences, no unfounded suggestions, no preconceptions. Solely the attempt to understand his disordered psyche and then – and only then – to help him find his own stability in the time left to him in the turning world. It is difficult in the circumstances – perhaps impossible – which is why the rules are there. In my own analysis I have voiced my difficulties to the silent figure sitting behind the head of the couch upon which I lie in my turn, but have received the response I most fear: silence. The problem with silence is that we fill it with our own interpretations.

Initially he is surprisingly intractable. Not in the vocal, aggressive way which characterizes some patients, whom one has to remind gently that they made the approach, not I. No, his is a capacity for silence which does not perceive it as oppressive. Within a few weeks he has begun to be late: the traffic has been bad, he has been held up in a meeting, his watch has stopped. Or, in our infrequent exchanges, he suddenly says, 'I can't see the point of this. You cannot expect me to believe your explanation.' He had paid twice, with reluctance. Though he has not articulated anything, I suspect he feels that I should provide this service for love, or in expiation of what he sees as the sins of 'my' community against him. Money means different things to people – possessions, love, warmth, security: one of the first tasks is to explain its meaning in the psychoanalytical process. The payment of fees, for example. (I am convinced we deserve the criticism of smugness: for truly we seem to arrange matters in the way which suits us best.)

53

On the twelfth session I notice that he is wearing old clothes. The suit is shiny with wear and the trousers have long since lost their shape. 'There was much traffic,' he says defensively, waving his hand in the direction of Cavendish Square. He lies down carefully, exhaling with a long sigh when his head touches the pillow. He is at the stage where things might go either way: he will dismiss me as an incompetent fool, or he might manufacture symbols, dreams, pieces of material to please me — the wise teacher, the good father. Or we may begin.

'Last night I dreamed of the tower . . .'

He assumes our common memory. After a pause, I prompt him. 'And . . . ?'

'It was the tower and not the tower, if you follow my meaning. I was on a battlefield surrounded by the dead, lying where they had fallen: a grey army, rotting already. I was walking in a daze and I stumbled over a body. It was the body of your father, shot in the back. He wore the camp uniform of the Vopos. There was no sound — only the smoke and the smell of cordite and blood. I was weak — barely able to stand. Through the smoke I saw the tower. There was a man attacking the tower with a pickaxe . . .'

I see his eyes close and tears begin to slide down his cheeks. Outside the window the wind tinkles in the elms, just audible above the low hum of the traffic. In the building the lift is creaking arthritically as it descends.

'I know that I must rebuild it . . . to achieve something . . .'

I wait until I know he will say no more. 'What are your associations to the dream?'

'Septimus and I talked about the tower the other night. The war I always remember. Last night I watched a documentary about the survivors of the camps . . .' He cries easily now, his shoulders shaken by the sobs.

'What did you think you would achieve in the dream by rebuilding the tower?'

'I don't know. It might take my grief away. It might change something . . .'

'Who was the man destroying the tower?'

54

He says nothing. The minutes pass. As the session is almost at an end he laughs suddenly. 'Arbeit macht frei. That wasn't true. We were enslaved by working on that tower. Bloody Septimus. He thought his sacrifices would make him a saint. He thought he was better than us.'

'I'm afraid that is all we have time for today.'

'But I am ready to talk. I have things to tell you that you would never have known because you were too young to understand.'

Temptation comes in many guises. Somehow he must have sensed that I was curious – under pressure. Perhaps Septimus has said something to him. Suppressing a sudden, unprofessional urge to let him stay, I get up and open the door.

He stands in the doorway for a moment, so close that I take a backward step. Despite his money, he has not looked after himself. His sallow skin is creased, puffy, pocked with black indentations. One of his eyes wanders so that I feel a momentary confusion over which one I should look at.

'You may find some of the things I have to tell you very difficult . . .'

I write up his notes in the late afternoon. There is little tangible to go on so far beyond his symptoms: acute and irrational fear of death or punishment, palpitations, attacks of sweating, of dizziness, inability to get to sleep for hours, early waking. Occasional physical vomiting, possibly of a nervous origin. Omnipotent fantasies.

Fortuitously, I go to our annual party at the Institute of Psychoanalysis that evening. The house is superb, lofty ceilings decorated with oval frescos from classical mythology, a winding central staircase under a glass cupola. The fashion this year is buff: Harris tweed jackets in dun and buff check, worn beige cords and Hush Puppies. In deference to the recession there is Chablis instead of champagne, and the canapés are decidedly home-made. Fritz Beckenbauer stands out from the rest; not only is he wearing a rather *outré* suit, but he is smoking. He has moved on from what he calls his dilettante period of researching arcana to begin a study of the decay of the hold of social observances in the aged. 'People who don't bother to put their teeth in, or are unaware of their incontinence. The old are the most dangerous for they have least to lose,' he told me once.

He gestures humorously towards the bulk of the party crowded in the middle of the room. (Our work together on the journal has fostered in us a complicity against the old guard.) 'What would our patients make of this, eh?' he asks conspiratorially. 'All of them watching each other for evidence of primal jealousy or anal fixations. It often seems that in our attempts to analyse the human condition we have become less than human ourselves. We've become obsessed with methodology. We can't accept that a large range of verbal and semiotic responses has no real subtext. We cannot reduce them further and they have no frame of reference beyond themselves. Much of what we do is meaningless – but it helps to pass the time.'

'How's the research going?'

Beckenbauer holds out his glass to be refilled by the waitress. 'You know how children quite literally wish to annihilate their rivals? It comes both from a sense of great frustration and also from an inability to temper aggressive impulses by reference to a long-term view. They don't really want to kill their parents or their siblings . . .' He sticks his little finger delicately into his glass and removes a piece of cork. 'What I have found in one geriatric patient I am dealing with is a regression to infantilism when faced with daily frustrations, allied to an inability to take the long-term view because, for him, there is no long term. I suspect I'll find that people become more authoritarian as they grow older because they feel there isn't time to solve problems any other way . . .'

'I'm sure you're right,' I say. A picture of Thomas has come into my mind.

'How's the work on Irma's dream going?' he asks. The piece was due for inclusion six months ago. I sidestep neatly, telling him it has involved me in retranslating the work to see if Strachey's version has missed any nuances which may offer some insights.

He nods, chewing a canapé, only half listening, his eyes

never still. 'What, off so soon? I can't think how you can leave such a glittering assembly so early.' His ironic eye lingers on me for a moment. It may be there is compassion beyond those defences.

In the cold drizzle I walk to the car. The rain has been heavy and there is a faint smell of sewage. It is one of those moments when I am suddenly visited by a sense of being the last man alive treading upon the thin crust of a dying earth. Almost, I have to prevent myself from going up to the stolid burgher in his blue raincoat holding a gamp over his head as he steers past me with an incurious glance and proceeds on his way to Langham Place. To say what? To plead, perhaps, for some brief warm acknowledgement of our common humanity.

It comes from childhood: from that time when Angela and I first crept together to offer each other such comfort as we might against the unwitting cruelty of the adult world. In the car I am assaulted by the imagery of childhood. After the fear this is often the case. The picnics, the tower — growing slowly under the patient hands of Septimus and the silent stranger, until I am finally brought to the place where memory ceases, and I am again confronted by the enigma of myself as a child, standing by the barely open door while tears run down my face and I gaze upon some unseen vision of terrifying incomprehensibility, towards something which could not be understood and was put away.

There is a police car by the gate. I turn into the drive and park, seeing in the mirror a policeman walking slowly towards the house adjusting his hat. He is polite, but firm. They would like me to accompany them to the station to answer a few questions.

Chapter Eight

Angela's birthday. Tradition runs strongly in our family.

I groaned inwardly as I parked by the side of Robert Southern's green BMW. Robert, I suspected, had been one of the mysterious companions of Angela's past. He had a flashy, overblown charm, which apparently stood him in good stead for selling houses, and affected twill trousers and loud brown-check jackets. Angela chooses people to whom she feels superior. It saves her from true intimacy. Perhaps – on both counts. The front door was open and I could hear the faint sounds of laughter from the garden beyond.

'Hello, David.' Nico had grown again in the months since I had last seen him. He was on a break from his VSO – or whatever they call it these days: next year he was going to Peterhouse to read natural sciences. I shook his hand and jerked my head towards the back garden, raising my eyebrows in query.

'Oh, just some of Mum's friends. Robert,' – he made a face – 'three of the journalists from the paper. Thomas and Julia couldn't come. Apparently they've had a burglary. Quite shaken up.'

'I know,' I said. 'I had to spend some time with the police persuading them that I'd been at a business party at the time.'

'I don't understand. Why?' He was almost shocked into laughter.

'Who knows?'

'They've had to put off their holiday in India.'

I felt my stomach lurch, registering the fact automatically. Thomas did nothing for pleasure alone. Undoubtedly this trip would be connected with some research for the book. Nico was fingering my present to Angela with expert fingers. 'One of those things you put plants in for a conservatory?'

'A jardinière. Yes.'

It was still light, unseasonally warm enough to be comfortable in shirtsleeves. Septimus was tending the barbecue. I recognized the farmer from down the lane with his wife and daughter. Robert and two women, one of whom I vaguely knew, were talking to Angela. Watching her in the moment before she turned towards me, I knew I was right about Robert and her. He was the only one I had identified: a surprise, in that he was coarse and obvious. But then, no different from Judith in my own past.

I was still shaken by the visit to the police station. Thomas had rung two days later, plainly ill at ease, to give me the unconvincing story that he had been so upset that he hadn't known what he was saying: he'd been terribly embarrassed when the police told him that they had interviewed me. I wondered if he protested a shade too much, but gave him the benefit of the doubt. The policeman who interviewed me had been taciturn to the point of rudeness, only revealing why I was being questioned with great reluctance after I had established my bona fides beyond argument. No, there was nothing missing so far as he could ascertain, except a few papers and a couple of Julia's rings which were only of sentimental value. Again, I sensed the slight hesitation which suggested I was not being told everything.

By this time I had begun to appreciate that there might be more to Thomas's research than malicious gossip. When he was home secretary, one of the serious papers had labelled him the scourge of the Tory party: profiles had suggested that his passion for truth, his known sympathy for the conspiracy theory of both politics and history, his support of awkward lines of questioning on such topics as the conduct of the Falklands War, Westland, the Kincora Homes investigation, would hold him back from the highest office. And in his heart I believe that Thomas accepted these valuations – perhaps because they gave him an excuse for failure – and assumed the persona given him by the media. A few days after Father's knighthood I'd run across Thomas at a party. '"Truth lies within a little and certain compass, but error is immense." Bolingbroke's "Reflections Upon Exile". D'you know it?' He'd been a little drunk, a shade aggressive. When he'd asked me to give his sincerest good wishes to Father for the well-deserved honour, I saw where the wound lay.

Then I'd dismissed it as the rivalry of old men, flaring up for a while and soon to be forgotten. I thought little further of it, as I had thought little further of my childhood. Stay below the parapet and you won't get shot. That had been one of Father's adages from my childhood. I saw no point in seeking trouble until it found me. Now I was certain that there was more in this than a few weeks of jealousy on Thomas's part.

Angela smiled at me and put her cheek up to be kissed.

'Happy birthday. Your present's in the hall. Nico's guessed what it is already.'

'You know Thomas and Julia cried off. Apparently they've had a burglary.'

With an attempt at lightness I said, 'And the police evidently suspected me. I had to spend a couple of hours at the station giving them my alibi.'

'I take it,' said Robert, 'You are talking about our distinguished ex home secretary?' His face was flushed and his voice slurred, a little over loud. The smaller of the two women, the one with the elfin features whom I knew, said, 'I read his last book.' Quite an imagination. Is he any relation, Angela?'

I had to stifle an impulse of anger at Robert's assumption of intimacy. 'He knew your family in Iskanderabad. And' — flicking his eyes towards me — 'he's your godfather, isn't he? I've heard he was quite a lad in his day.' His laugh was common, knowing, as he held out his glass for Nico to fill it.

I excused myself and walked across the lawn to Septimus, now taking tiger prawns from their marinade in a perspex dish and laying them out on the grill. 'Who's the loud gentleman in the check jacket and twills?' he asked and I said, 'Oh, just one of Angela's friends. I've only met him a couple of times,' with deliberate vagueness, avoiding his direct gaze. He made no comment while I told him the story of the burglary, carefully lifting the prawns one by one and basting them with the marinade using a small brush. A dish of chicken breasts was propped precariously on the edge of the barbecue.

'Shouldn't you have done those first? Prawns take no time at all.'

Septimus laughed, taking a long mouthful from his Frascati, and then put the glass down carefully. He seemed, as always, at odds with the company, as though he had left his truest self behind when he had finally left the monastery. There was a sudden burst of laughter from the group at the other side of the lawn, and Robert's voice repeating the denouement of his joke: 'It's fried rice, not flied lice, you Gleek plick.' Septimus said casually, 'Is he the one she's thinking of marrying?'

I felt cold. Angela had been reserved after her last holiday. We had barely seen each other since then, but I had relied upon the gradual resumption of our usual intimacy. Over the years we had lived apart I had become aware of imperceptible changes in her, of the fact that I no longer knew instinctively what she thought or might do. I tried to keep my voice light. 'First I've heard of it.'

Septimus shrugged, starting to remove the prawns from the hottest part of the barbecue to the periphery. 'There's probably nothing in it. She was very angry with your parents for suggesting she should marry for Nico's sake. After all, he's almost a man. But I have the impression she's lonely. Does she ever see his real father?'

A trap in my mind closed. I could see Robert's proprietorial arm around Angela's shoulder. 'I don't know,' I said. Next to silence, the fewer words the better.

It was still warm at ten o'clock. The distant orange glow of Guildford's lights shone in the distance. Bats skittered over the lawn. Septimus said, ''N came to stay for a couple of days. I wonder if it's wise for him to remember the past. He had a terrible nightmare the other night. And he looks so unwell, as if he is brooding.'

We used the name by which we had known him all those years ago. ''N used inappropriate devices to avoid dealing with the past and to avoid pain. We all do, to some extent. For some of us the struggle is too much and we repeat ourselves, remain stunted, caught in unreal situations which are distorted representations of those past events. It is only by confronting the truth that we can move on.'

'I'm too old to understand such things.' It was Septimus's way of closing the subject, of disapproving, which had so much in common with my father and with Thomas. The old school. We talked about Romania. One of Septimus's colleagues had visited a children's home outside Bucharest, and was endeavouring to arrange adoptions. 'If the local authorities in their wisdom permit it,' Septimus said.

When the guests had all left, I sat out on the patio under the stars. The grass of the lawn seemed silver under the moonlight. Somewhere in the distance a dog barked. Nico had gone to bed an hour before and Angela came out, shimmering palely in her white dress, to sit by me. The light from the kitchen window lay along her cheekbone. 'God,' she said, throwing her head back, 'that's over for another year. Next year I'll just let it pass unnoticed.'

I told her about the burglary and the police questioning me. The surprise had faded and I felt distanced enough to make a story of it. The solemn sergeant, the Kafkaesque setting. But she was shocked, listening with her hand over her mouth. 'Is he still planning to write this memoir?' she said, and her voice trembled on the verge of tears.

Later, when she was recovered, we drank a glass of wine together. I could think of no way of asking her obliquely what was in my mind. 'Septimus gave me a fright tonight. He said he thought you may be thinking of getting married. Is it Robert?'

She was silent, looking towards the end of the garden. After a while she said, 'Would that be so awful? For appearances' sake. When Father and Mother brought it all up again, I thought how ridiculous they were being. Nico's grown beyond the need of a father in permanent attendance, now. It's just that, with Thomas in pursuit, that might deflect him in some way.'

I felt angry with Thomas, hearing the tone of resignation in her voice. 'Your marrying Robert now would draw Thomas's attention rather than deflect it. Do you really think Nico could take to Robert? What do you think Mother and Father would make of him?'

I'd gone too far. Her voice was defensive. 'I know he comes across as brash. I've grown quite fond of him. It's not passion – but – he's always there.'

'I wish you'd stay,' she said, later, walking with me to the car. 'It would be quite like old times.'

Everything passes: everything dies. The roads were empty as I drove home under a full moon. Old times never return.

Chapter Nine

In the beginning was the monastery.

Forty years later, Septimus still rises at six to pray for half an hour. The fine framework of committed belief has become indistinct over the years, the prayers themselves a comforting habit.

The act of prayer induces a sense of contemplation. He is aware that his memories of Iskanderabad forty years before are still clear, brilliantly defined, whilst he finds it difficult to remember what he did three days ago. Time, too, seems to have telescoped.

The photographs he took to dinner with David and Angela (here I go again, he thinks) last week, last month, are still on the sideboard. It is Sunday. He takes the photographs to the table and spreads them out, looking at them while he drinks his coffee.

People are inclined to underestimate Septimus. Because his conversation is often hedged by moral considerations, by reference to a scale of values, many feel uneasy in his presence and disinclined to take him seriously. Their mockery is predicated upon the fact that Septimus is an anomaly in Thatcher's Britain: he has no interest in money or possessions. No aspirations which require lip-service to others, no unfulfilled ambitions which demand he temper his own nature.

With most their mockery is compounded with − not fear, exactly, but respect; for they have recognized without articulating it that there is some dangerous quality in him. For Septimus has a vision of truth, justice and the good life.

He hears the newspapers being delivered through the letter-box and goes down in his dressing-gown to pick up his

Sunday Times. In the kitchen he fills the kettle and takes the egg timer and a saucepan out of the cupboard, places two slices of brown wholemeal in the toaster. Working methodically, he is suddenly aware of his anger towards David Lawrence, acknowledging at the same time that he is hardly being fair. He'd had lunch with Johann Neidermayer the day before Angela's birthday party. He'd been struck by Neidermayer's appearance. Accustomed (at least in these recent years) to seeing Johann smartly dressed, and to his usual manner, which was staccato, brisk, punctuated by sudden laughter and sharp comments, he was momentarily shocked into silence. Neidermayer looked his age and more; his suit was old and shiny and his sparse grey hair straggled untidily over his domed head. There were stains on his shirt and his breath smelt carious, bitter. The change was so marked that Septimus had for once forsaken his normal obliqueness. 'You look terrible, Johann. Are you all right?' At first Johann had stoically affirmed how well he was, his tone almost suggesting a sense of affront, but over lunch he had said, 'It may be these dreams. I feel as if something terrible is going to happen . . .' Yes, he admitted, the dreams had only recommenced since he had been seeing Dr Lawrence, but the psychoanalyst had assured him that they would stop once they had dealt with the root cause, whatever that might be. Picking his teeth, he said, 'There are many bad things I just put away and tried to forget. Perhaps it is time to bring them out and throw them away.' Septimus was angry with himself. Some time ago Johann had wished to unburden himself to him, an old friend with whom he had shared so much, and it was then that Septimus, panicking that he might become the repository of God knows what secrets, had suggested Johann should see David Lawrence.

He pours himself another cup of coffee. Looking at the photographs, thinking of Johann, he begins to drift into reminiscence: remembers the way in which he left the monastery. It is strange how events that change one's life may have such small beginnings. If he had not walked down to the picnic behind Vivienne James, feeling that sense of desire as he watched the back of her neck, her bare legs, her naked feet in flimsy sandals, his life might have assumed a different course.

The memory had teased at him for several days. A week after the picnic he was summoned by Brother Nicholas to see Father Gregorio. It was eight-thirty in the morning. Father Gregorio would have been at prayer from five to seven-thirty. The tray on the table by the door carried the remains of his frugal breakfast of dhal and roti. The room – a little like Father Gregorio himself – was dark, sparely furnished. There was a rush mat on the flaking flagstones by the door, a deal desk behind which he sat on a rush-seated chair, another rush-seated chair for interviewees on the near side of the desk. On the whitewashed wall Brother Ambrose's copy of a Simone Martini triptych representing the crucifixion. Septimus was struck by Father Gregorio's frailty, the wrinkled hand covered in liver spots with ridged, cyanosed nails which picked irresolutely through the papers on the desk. As he walked to the chair, he could see Brother Ambrose, who wore his distant, perpetual smile, a pace behind Balaam, the monastery mule, loaded with produce from Gobind Dass's depot near the market. Sitting, he noticed that it was the accounts prepared by Brother Nicholas which lay on the desk. He smiled to himself. Father Gregorio had once confessed that figures meant little to him, and accounting terms even less: 'receivables' put him in mind of the promise of divine justice and 'double entry' conjured up speculation about the dualistic nature of the human soul.

Septimus sensed Father Gregorio's uneasiness that morning. He knew that his mentor had moved so far along his own path towards some hidden prospect that communion with others had become more difficult. When Father Gregorio had started by asking him if he knew Romans 8:6 – 'to be carnally minded in death' – the exchange he had heard between two lay brothers the afternoon before came into his mind. He took a deep breath and looked at the sunlit vista outside the study window. It was here that the vexed question of his own motive in what he had done arose, whenever he recollected the scene.

Father Gregorio's goodness was uncomfortable. Upright in

the chair, Septimus was aware that by the other man's standards he had fallen into Error, and possibly into both Venial and Mortal Sin. His *chupplees* still rubbed uncomfortably at the heels, reminding him of the walk to the Mughal Reservoirs, and the impurity of his thoughts. He folded his large hands in his lap, wondering a little at his own fear and irresolution confronted only with the familiar, tired face.

'My son,' Father Gregorio began softly, turning his head to clear his throat nervously behind his hand, 'is there anything you wish to confess to me?'

Septimus always remembered the precision that dealing with Father Gregorio induced in his thoughts. How he had pondered the precise meaning of the words before answering (perhaps seeking some means of escape?). He had concluded that though there were many things he might confess to Father Gregorio, there really was nothing that he wished to confess. He shook his head mutely, looking down at his clasped hands. He had felt a strange breathlessness, a sense of some great change about to take place which he both wished for and feared.

Father Gregorio sighed, taking a letter written on blue notepaper from a buff folder on the desk. Septimus could see Father Gregorio's reluctance. He knew that the old man had chided himself for the paternal affection he felt for Septimus, which was against the rule. He knew also that the rule was stronger, and the rule would prevail.

'I've had a letter from the Mother Superior at St Theresa's Convent. Possibly best if I read it to you.' He took his rimless half-glasses from a battered tin case and adjusted them on the pinched bridge of his thin nose. His voice echoed in the quiet room.

'Dear Father Gregorio, Our Brother in Christ. Occasion has arisen for me to write to you on a matter of grave concern, and my heart is heavy that this will cause sorrow to you and the members of your order. One of our sixth form girls, Grace Chaudhury, has recently complained of feeling ill and, despite the careful and frugal diet we provide our scholars, has been observed to be putting on weight.

'Yesterday I was called to the sick bay by Sister Mary, and

this child was asked to tell me the story she had just related to Sister Mary. She told of how she was sketching on the hill above the convent after games one afternoon three months past, when a young monk walking by came to sit by her. She was unconcerned, knowing him to be a man of God, and permitted him to sit and talk with her. She says, then, that this monk took her by the hand and offered to show her an object which had stood in the forest unseen for centuries. The object, she says, hidden beneath a bush which the monk parted carefully so that she could see, was a crude stone figure, grossly disproportioned. I cannot express even to you, Dear Brother in Christ, the words Grace used to describe the figure, but suffice it to say it was undoubtedly male and that the distortion affected the nether regions. Upon showing her this, she says that the monk began to breathe very heavily and she suddenly felt faint. She remembers the priest catching her before she fell and the next thing she remembers was waking up to find him by her side. He then escorted her to the upper gates of the grounds.

'Sister Mary tells me that the girl is with child. Grace is insistent that this cannot be so, unless something has taken place without her knowledge. I have prayed for guidance, even to the verge of wishing this to be some miracle, but I am forced to conclude that events during that afternoon must have been responsible for her state.

'She tells me that the monk was tall, with red hair and a thin face bearing a brown mark.

'I beg you, please give me your thought upon what may be done.

'Your Sister in Christ.'

Listening to the letter, Septimus had remembered Grace Chaudhury. A pretty girl, precocious, made up. He'd met her with Charles Wheeler in a café in Iskanderabad. 'My English fiancé,' she'd joked, linking her arm with Charles's. He'd known, even before Father Gregorio had finished reading the letter, that Grace would lack the courage to confess the truth, whatever that may be. He could imagine her, trapped by the nun, confronted with the prospect of eternal damnation. Perhaps she had come to believe her own story. He knew that he would not say anything about Charles, his first thought. Dora was an old friend. She and Theodore had known his own long dead parents. And, as he recalled his own doubts, the feelings Vivienne had stirred up in him, he thought to himself, perhaps this is the way God works.

In the silence that followed Father Gregorio put the letter aside, resting his chin on his steepled fingers. Septimus could almost sense his indecision, the slow loss of his earlier certainties with his daily awareness that the silence of his cell would soon become the profounder silence of the grave. He knew that Father Gregorio was too set in his ways, too unworldly, to follow the dictates of his feelings and deny the order the gratification of their moral outrage. And how could he? Brother Septimus knew that such charity did not exist within the monastery.

'What will happen to the girl?'

Father Gregorio sighed. 'There are precedents. The order will bring up the child and look after the girl. She will probably work for them in some capacity.'

Septimus looked down at his hands in his lap. With surprise he realized that the moment was upon him, and that he need take no thought for the words he was going to say, because they were awaiting delivery. He felt a certainty he had never felt before, mixed with sadness. He cleared his throat. 'I have only recently understood, Father, that your path is not for me. I cannot repudiate human warmth. I cannot prevent myself from bearing the human feelings of a son towards you. I cannot comprehend why our Lord would find such sentiments unacceptable.' He paused. Even having made his decision, he was unable to accept the blame unequivocally. 'As for the girl – well – things did not happen in the way the Mother Superior describes, but I shall say no more. It seems I must now leave this place where I have been happy these last years.'

He thought Father Gregorio had looked at him with something approaching gratitude. With age he knew that Gregorio had lost much of his Jesuitical sophistry. Sometimes, studying some text together, he had the sense that old instincts of the animal stretched and stirred within the older man as though, too late, he had found that the love of God alone had become too cold and abstract for him.

Almost pleadingly Father Gregorio had told him of the fund to rebuild Iskanderabad Church. 'I might have some influence in the matter . . .' Not all men were suited for the monastic life, but this, too, would be a service to God. And, as he spoke, Septimus had felt moved, excited, already imagining the tower beginning to take shape again under his hands. It was the first time, he thought later, that he had been able to grasp the shape of some ambition.

Father Gregorio loaned him Balaam to help transport his meagre belongings down the hill to Iskanderabad. He had arranged that Septimus would stay in a godown owned by one of the contractors to the monastery, Gobind Dass, until such time as he was more settled. He had also surprised Septimus by giving him a generous sum from the contingency fund. 'Are you sure, Father?' Septimus had asked, touched by the gesture but aware that Brother Nicholas would almost certainly disapprove. Brother Ambrose would accompany them to bring Balaam back to the monastery.

In the Gothic doorway Septimus felt of the unspoken censure of the brothers as he embraced Father Gregorio. Brother Stephen's thin lips curled slightly and his eyes flicked towards Brother Nicholas, who nodded almost imperceptibly. Father Gregorio gave the blessing in his old, reedy voice, and Brother Septimus bowed his head before the old man. 'Go with God, my son.' The brilliant sunlight cast the porch into deep shadow and, for a moment, it seemed to Septimus that Father Gregorio had disappeared. By his side Brother Ambrose hummed tunelessly as they walked down the long drive towards the excluding iron gates.

The sound of shouting in the street returns him abruptly to the present. Throwing up the casement, he looks out. A boy with blood running down his face and his shirt torn stands surrounded by bigger boys. 'Give us the money, then,' a tall, crew-cropped youth says, hitting the boy so that he falls against the wall. 'Come on.' Septimus's heart beats faster, propelled by anger and fear. 'Leave him alone,' he calls, conscious that his voice sounds quavering and old. One of the youths looks up and gives him a V-sign. 'Fuck off, grandpa. Mind your own business.' The others move towards the boy, who is sitting on the ground with his back against the wall. When Septimus arrives to help the boy, who is bleeding from a cut above his eye, the boy pushes him away. 'You heard what he said. Fuck off.'

Chapter Ten

Miriam Cohen had missed two appointments. My receptionist had got her answering machine on several occasions, and then a lady who had eventually suggested calling the London Clinic. Even after I had identified her as a patient and they had called me back as some sort of verification, they were very professional, very guarded. There had been a slight accident. Miss Cohen would be free to leave in a few days. Was there any message?

When she came in two weeks later, she was very pale. At the wrists of her long silk blouse I could see bandages, and when she lay on the couch I saw grey roots showing in the parting of her hair. I felt a mild sense of shame at having questioned her despair, even in my own mind. I waited. The tapes on the voice-activated recorder on the table were still.

'I couldn't bear it any more. I lay in the bath and took some pills with whisky and cut my wrists. The bath overflowed and the downstairs tenant called the fire brigade when she couldn't get any response . . .'

A safe bet. A cry for help. But the neighbour might have been out. After a silence I said, 'What was the "it" you couldn't bear?'

'My life. I'd been reading some letters from a man I loved. He was – is – much older than me. Just retired from a very senior post in the government. Everything seemed all right until his wife became very ill. Then he was burgled a few weeks ago . . . and for some reason he seemed angry with me . . .'

We will come to the matter by and by, I thought, feeling a *frisson* of excitement in the pit of my stomach.

'Love letters?'

'They were about everything. He was . . . is . . . a writer.'

I felt both a sense of triumph and a momentary guilt.

'He abandoned you. Like your father.'

It was still all in the balance then. I mean my self-respect, the preservation of the ethics of my profession. There were approved ways of continuing. I could have found an excuse to refer Miriam to another therapist; I could have set my mind against deriving a personal advantage from her disclosures; I could, in other words, have ensured that I followed the correct principle – that of putting the patient's well-being first. It is hard to explain without sounding pi. Asked to isolate the most important property of my working life, I would always have said moral probity, the Aesculapian ideal, the pure, altruistic desire to do the best in one's power for another human being. Without that, all the theory becomes a manipulative bag of tricks, a *trompe-l'œil* painting without a vestige of reality upon close examination.

Miriam began to cry, like a child, putting her fist up to her mouth.

'And now,' I prompted, 'you feel angry. You wish to attack him for what he has done.'

'He had no right . . . It isn't fair.'

'It is best to forget categories such as right and wrong, and fair and unfair. We must make the most of what there is, not waste our time in being frustrated because life is not ideal.'

Despite what Septimus says, that was the moment when I could have made some other decision. But we go to protect our own secrets first. If I had to protect us against Thomas, I needed weapons.

Later I called Angela. There was an uneasy peace between us. We hadn't talked any further about Robert, but the omission itself was obtrusive. I'd got the tickets she wanted for Gluck's *Orpheus and Eurydice*. I'd rather have booked for *Alceste*, but Angela had a passion for the theme. Eurydice condemned to the Underworld because Orpheus could not help himself looking back. She was always more moved than I by the literary and narrative qualities, I more than she by the music. Afterwards we ate at Poons. I did not tell her about the letters. I had at least preserved the confidence of the consulting room. I was noncommittal about Thomas. 'Do you know anything about libel?' she asked, and I replied that I thought Thomas far too worldly-wise to chance his arm thus. What I didn't tell her was my own fear: that if Thomas did proceed to cannibalize us for his story, any action we might take would only serve to identify us.

It is strange how one's views alter. When we were children, I remember Father talking about 'our obligation to extend hospitality to visitors'. This meant Thomas and Julia Henne, Father Carey and others passing through on a brief excursion from England. It was much later that I saw there were other things involved: ennui, a temporary fascination with new people, new liaisons and experiences, anything which momentarily might bring some wider perspective.

What always remained was the core of old blood. In years – for it took years – those who stayed on might be ingested, absorbed, accepted by the resident community when the newcomers' horizons had narrowed sufficiently for bigotry and patronage to become the ruling indices of their lives. Primacy was given to the years a family had stayed in Iskanderabad, then to the family connections and profession of the breadwinner. There were those whose progress was for ever barred by reason of their schooling or their work.

Father used to go out riding with Julia Henne. 'She's so patronizing, Amyas. I don't know how you can put up with her,' Mother used to say, and Father would laugh and say that it was company and they didn't really talk that much. Thomas, meanwhile, spent his time with Gobind Dass and Inspector Malik. We saw the Hennes at parties and picnics, and pretty soon they became part of the Iskanderabad set as if they had always been there.

Father Carey was different. He'd come out to replace old Prichard, who – retiring thankfully to Surrey – had promptly succumbed to influenza and was dead within three weeks. I hadn't liked Carey from the start. He was youngish – mid-thirties, perhaps – with a high colour, a pinched, aquiline nose, bulbous eyes which watered copiously, and a full, rather sensual mouth. He indulged in bouts of self-deprecating laughter after speaking, his shoulders jerking up and down, and he spoke with a faint Cornish burr which would stand him in ill stead once his curiosity value had dulled. I knew that, but he didn't. A month or so after he had arrived, Eleanor had invited him to a cocktail party after evensong to meet, yet again, some members of his new parish.

Otto, Eleanor's sable Great Dane, had moved reluctantly from his fireside place, made uneasy by the constant movement of the guests, and sat abjectly by the log basket. Angela and I, the only children at the gathering, were immediately pressed into service offering canapés and taking round bottles of sherry to replenish drinks.

The stone-flagged corridor from the kitchen was dark, panelled in heavy oak. The sound of the music and laughter grew fainter as I walked away. It took me a moment to recognize the couple standing close to each other by the leather settle against the wall. Thomas was saying, 'When . . . ?' and my mother, laughing in a way I had never heard before, like a girl, replied, 'Tomorrow, the usual place. Don't be silly.' She started when she saw me. 'Here, give me the bottle. I'll fill a few glasses . . .' and she laughed again.

When Father Carey arrived, my father had persuaded him to take Milly Milchrist on as his housekeeper. Milly, the spinster sister of one of the monks, had eked out a parsimonious existence for years on the capital of a small legacy which had finally run out. After which, at Father Gregorio's request, she'd been employed in my father's office for the past two years. Father had grumbled, but the monastery was one of his last big contracts, so there had been little option. 'I don't think that old bugger Gregorio's as holy as he makes out,' Father had said. Milly, genteel and fallen upon hard times, had evidently had a shrewd idea that the job was a sinecure, and had never proved very efficient. She was dozing in one of the wing chairs in the corner nearest the fire. Her unnaturally black wig was a little awry, and her top dentures were threatening to slip out of her open mouth. Her skin was dry, withered, as I touched her old hand tentatively to draw her attention to the refilled glass of sweet sherry on the occasional table at her side. 'What an attentive boy you've become. Thank you,' she said approvingly, her eyelids closing as she fell asleep again immediately.

Gobind Dass's syce had been giving her driving lessons on the New Road. Father Carey couldn't drive and it was too difficult to get taxis. Angela and I used to watch her jerking up the road. The syce would get out and roll his eyes to heaven when he looked at us.

My mother was offering people drinks. I didn't really approve of her black dress. When she leaned forward to pour Colonel Whitworth's drink, I had seen his eyes looking down the neckline. Father was talking to Julia Henne. Dora Wheeler had once said I should 'watch that woman': like so many of her recent comments, I found it difficult to grasp what she meant. Mrs Henne seemed stern, abstracted, but when she smiled her face suddenly came to life with pure joy. Father Carey was interested in ornaments ('Too damned interested in the material life,' my father had grumbled.) Colonel Whitworth was showing him the treasures in Mrs Weaver's underlit glass display case. His hands shook so much that he almost dropped a Jacobean wine goblet he was showing Father Carey. 'Sixteenth century. Just think of the rubbish they turn out these days. Ha?'

But it was the doll which had caught Father Carey's attention. He took it over to the light, turning it slowly in his hands to look at it, and Eleanor laid down the silver tray of canapés she was taking round and went to join him. Otto, unobserved by anyone else, helped himself from the tray with one guilty eye cocked in the direction of Eleanor: I willed him not to be caught. 'Don't tell me,' Father Carey was saying, 'this is a Tête Jumeau bisque doll . . . French . . . about 1890.' Angela had always coveted the doll. It had a closed, full-bowed mouth, fixed brown glass eyes, pierced ears, a real red-hair wig over a cork pate and a jointed composition body. I was shocked when Father Carey lifted the skirts with an odd expression on his face: 'There,' he said, holding the doll's buttocks to Eleanor for confirmation, 'Jumeau Médaille d'Or, Paris.'

Mrs Weaver was nodding with an expression of total incomprehension on her face. I don't suppose she'd ever have lifted the doll's skirt on her own. The smoke from her cigarette was drifting into her eyes and she took the amber holder out of her mouth. 'Ah, yes. That was from Paris. The year of our honeymoon — when Terence and I did the European Tour.' She spoke very quietly. I remembered my parents saying Eleanor had never gone further than fifteen miles from Iskanderabad.

Colonel Whitworth had joined Father and Mrs Henne, holding his glass out for me to refill. 'Personally I don't think there's a word of truth in the story. Those holy wallahs live in another world. The girl panicked and came up with a story and for some reason Septimus didn't deny it. I think he'll make an excellent job of the rebuilding.' Colonel Whitworth's tone brooked no argument. He was too senior for anyone to disagree with him to his face.

'You'd better fill some more glasses,' Father said pointedly to me. Under the table in front of him where no one else could see I noticed that his leg was resting against Mrs Henne's knee.

I sat on the stool by the fire for a while, close to Dora Wheeler. She bent towards me, holding the back of her hand to the side of her mouth. 'The human zoo,' she whispered. 'One day, God help you, you'll be part of it . . .' She turned back as Father Carey approached the sofa and sat down heavily beside her.

I could see that he was wary of her. Later I knew that she was someone who asked hard questions, expecting harder answers; that she was ever seeking some uncomfortable truth rather than accepting the polite fictions which passed for conversation. A few days before, over coffee with us, I'd heard Father Carey asking Eleanor about Dora. 'So sad,' Eleanor had said with shining eyes. 'Neither of the boys has married. At least Henry has a job, even if he only works for a box wallah. But Charles . . . And she's such a refined person.' In her mime her face turned upwards and her eyes flickered whitely, her raised hand drooped, so that it seemed as if mad Charles had hurt her into grief. But I knew it was not so.

Dora was quizzing Father Carey for his views on rebuilding the tower. 'Do you think it will seem like arrogance? You know the legend, of course?' and I could see the uncertainty in Father Carey's face as, sensing politics and unsure of his ground, he furrowed his brow as though giving way to deep thought. Otto was nuzzling his hand with an impatient snout, and the priest wiped his palm on his cassock surreptitiously. 'I think it is our duty ...' he was saying piously as, before my appalled eyes, I saw Otto put his front paws on the arm of the settee and then, from behind, around Father Carey's neck. Otto's head, open-mouthed with his long tongue lolling from its side, appeared over Father Carey's shoulder, and his long frame started to undulate. The priest's body began to rock as, still earnestly talking, he held his sherry at arm's length to prevent it from spilling. But Dora, looking at me with an expression which may have been panic or stifled laughter, was saying, 'Fetch Mrs Weaver, David. Go on.' What gave the proceedings a surreal quality was that everyone else was carrying on their conversations as though nothing were happening.

I was breathless with apprehension when I arrived in the kitchen. Eleanor Weaver rested her elbows on the draining board, her head in her hands. Jaafar, her *masalchi*, stood by her side. His eyes rolled roundly in my direction and he gestured towards her with a limp hand. I was hesitant, trying to find an inoffensive way of telling her the news. 'Mrs Weaver. Otto's got his paws on Father Carey's shoulders. He's ... playing a game. He's very rough and Father Carey may drop his glass.' I delivered the speech with careful precision.

Eleanor stood up. Her thin hair was dishevelled and tears ran down her cheeks. In a strangled voice she said, 'I can't find my husband. And Otto's far too strong for me. I'll have to wait until he finishes ... whatever he is doing.' And she began to ululate with laughter, throwing her head back like a jackal baying.

I stood uncertainly in the doorway to the sitting-room and Angela came over to join me. A strange normality presided:

the grown-ups still drank their sherry while they talked in twos and threes, though I noticed that their eyes avoided the sofa. We children watched in silence, fascinated and horrified. Father Carey quivered, holding his sherry glass away from his body while he talked to Dora. Kathleen Ferrier's voice sounded faintly in the background. Suddenly Otto gave a great heave and then disengaged his paws from Father Carey's shoulders before getting down rather ungraciously to settle before the fire with a great sigh.

It seemed the incident had never happened, though I had the strangest impression that Dora Wheeler was holding herself back from laughing out loud. When Father Carey stood up, I was shocked. 'It's all over the back of his cassock,' I said in a horrified whisper, but Angela only said, 'Shhh,' in an infuriating, grown-up way. It was half past eight, the earliest time that protocol permitted anyone to leave. Angela helped Eleanor and Mother with clearing up the plates, and I fetched coats for people from the hooks at the far end of the hall. In the gloom Dora Wheeler held my forearm for a moment. 'This country is full of dogs doing things in full view – and everyone pretends not to notice.' When she kissed me, her skin felt leathery against my cheek, and her breath smelt of sherry.

Father was helping Mrs Henne into her coat. 'Remember . . . tomorrow,' he said, so softly that I could just hear it. She looked at him quickly, but it was too dark to see her expression. Father was kissing Eleanor on her cheek. 'Wonderful canapés. Most enjoyable party,' he said, and I could see the flush come up her throat.

Later I said to Angela, 'Nobody said *anything*,' and we lay on the bed howling with helpless laughter.

Chapter Eleven

Years before Thomas's long shadow fell across our lives, I remember a day. I should realize better than most the sheer illogicality of happiness. Not only that — but the unexpectedness of its sudden appearance upon a day which was seemingly no different from any other. I knew better even then than to try to catch it or mourn its anticipated loss. It was a short time in which I soared beyond guilt, worry, fear, and whatever was immortal in me was released for those hours into the clear purity of a truer element.

It was Angela who had suggested we went to Camber Sands on the Sunday. She and Nico had been staying with me for a few days. The weather had maintained its unusual dryness and, to compensate for the hosepipe ban, we had watered the dying shrubs with the waste from the swimming-pool.

We were to leave at eight. Never at her best in the morning, Angela hummed to herself while she cooked bacon and eggs for Nico and me, and joined us for coffee on the patio. Nico's legs were burnt, covered in fine scratches after picking blackberries in the thicket. 'It's the best summer *ever*, Uncle David.' Angela smiled at me over the rim of her cup.

I stacked the dishwasher while Angela finished getting the picnic together. Nico ran down the slope of the garden to give the farmer's horse a lump of sugar over the fence. Angela said, 'He's the same age as you were when we went to the picnic at the reservoir. The one where we found the goat in the lime pit. Remember?'

I nodded, but it was only partly true then. Fragments, splinters only. Smells most of all. The heavy musk of *maquis*. Dora Wheeler watching Vivienne James.

In the car Nico chattered about school. 'I think I'll get into the Colts this season. Mr Hamilton, the coach, says that Jones Minor isn't fast enough on the wing.' His joy was palpable. We were told willy-nilly about 'Beezer' Wilkins, his English master, and 'Inky' Stevens who taught biology, the narrative threaded with unfamiliar argot. We've done all right, I thought; it has worked.

He and I went for a swim while Angela laid out the picnic. As I strolled down the pale ribbed sand towards the shallow sea, the sun burnt my shoulders. A stout woman with grey hair walked past us along the shingle towards the jetty, barefoot, with a frantic cocker spaniel at her heels. Far out a small boat bobbed slowly across the horizon. Razor shells, clams, mussel shells, the bleached exoskeletons of small crabs lay on the tide line, where the small pebbles crunched underfoot. Water oozed into our clear footprints. The gulls wheeled, mewling overhead, and the sea spread before us, a calm, unruffled turquoise.

Cold currents ran through the warm water and were gone. Floating on my back, I watched the vapour trail of a plane, too high for sight or sound. When I turned over to swim a few lazy strokes, I felt a momentary panic, unable to see Nico. 'Here,' he shouted, shaking water from his bobbing head. 'I'm trying to learn how to swim underwater.' He swam with graceless energy, splashing wildly towards a small boat moored to a white buoy. I followed using a slow crawl. He clung to the boat, breathless, and pointed. 'I think Mother's calling us.' She stood like a star in her white dress looking towards where the sea met the sky. 'Sometimes I think I will just get into a boat and sail out to the horizon.' Under the hand shielding her eyes from the sun her face was in darkness.

Later, we drove along the coast. The sun was low in the sky. Over a headland we coasted down a long incline, parking in a hollow beneath a ridge tufted with sedge beyond which the wind scoured the beach. There was a chalk path over the clifftop, wandering mazily through grass and succulents. To our right holiday cottages painted in primary colours stood like toy houses in small unkempt gardens. 'D'you think this could be a genuine Stone Age knife?' Nico asked, and I turned the shard of faceted stone over in my hands. Satisfied when I made a noncommittal grunt, he took an ammonite out of his pocket to show me, whorled delicately into the shape of a French horn. We walked quickly to catch up with Angela. The sky was grey-red with the approach of sunset. Over the hill we could see the lights of a pier with a funfair, the Ferris wheel outlined against the sky. 'Oh, can we . . . ?' Nico clung to both of us.

'I don't want him to learn about guns.'

'Just once, Mother. I've never tried.'

'How do you aim?' he asked. I tucked the battered stock into his shoulder and showed him how to line up the V of the backsight so that the blade of the foresight bisected the triangle and sat level at the top. I peered along the barrel and could see the skew where it had been bent out of true. But to his delight he shot down the row of cans, choosing a pink panther which he presented to Angela. 'There's your once. The last time,' she said with a smile, putting the toy under her arm. They both went on the dodgems while I held Nico's toffee apple. We walked through the thinning crowds, eating hamburgers, whilst the tawdry music surged around us.

Darkness. We meandered back over the cliffs, the path lit by a low moon and the yellow lights from the uncurtained windows of the holiday cottages. A gentle wind blew saltily in our faces. Over the hill again, the sounds of the fair were lost. Nico ran ahead, his shirt flickering palely. I put my arm through Angela's and she said, 'I'm sorry about not wanting him to use the gun. It reminded me of you when Father was going to kill the kid. Your face seemed so lost.'

'Look!' I pointed out to sea where the lights of a boat tracked diagonally towards the horizon. I knew if I were silent Angela would have said more, bringing some memory from the safe repository where it lay entombed.

Before Nico went to bed, he kissed me. 'I wish you lived here with us.' Angela did her best, but it was not the same. I saw her expression as she watched and wished he had not spoken. 'We'll have another day out soon,' I said, ruffling his hair.

I couldn't tell her that he wasn't complaining: that it was only a statement, a conclusion about the day and about other days we had shared before, which no one else could share with us. The fear of the shadow began then, even if the shadow itself was not yet born.

Shortly after the incident with Otto – another memory. There was a frightening randomness to them, once the chest was opened and the winged mischiefs had begun to take flight.

Father had gone out for the evening to a Masonic dinner. He used to grumble about the expense of being master, but I noticed how, when Mother mildly suggested he might resign, he took an hour to tell her of the benefits attached to belonging to the lodge, Light of the Himalayas. (Once, alone in the house, I'd seen the book in the drawer in his study, sick with apprehension that someone might catch me. There was a black and white photograph of a man dressed in a costume holding the back of his hand over his eyes. In front of him lay a body on a raised plinth. The legend read: 'A Mason averts his eyes in horror as he passes the Corpse of Hiram Abiff, Great Architect of Solomon's Temple.' Angela could not satisfy my curiosity, and I knew I couldn't ask the grown-ups.) Mother was having supper with Dora Wheeler, Dr Chatterjee and the Hennes. They would probably play two rubbers of bridge after dinner.

Poonomal had stayed in the family, though Angela and I were too old to need a nanny any more. She was married to one of the malis who worked on our estate. Her skin was blue-black, matt, and she smiled often, revealing gold teeth rimmed with betel juice. She still helped about the house in an unspecified, unregimented way. I loved her uncritically: more than my parents, more than Septimus, more than Dora Wheeler, she represented safety and the promise of affection unqualified by anything I might do. When we were younger, she used to tell us stories in a mixture of Hindi and pidgin English until we fell asleep. Her English had grown more fluent over the years until she seemed like some elderly relative who had lain out in the sun too long. Sometimes still, without our asking, she sensed a mood in us – the need for a temporary, illusory return to the safety of childhood. We sat, drinking our Ovaltine. The fire flared, slowly eating through the last pine-log, and a solitary jackal called far down the hill in the forest.

'Well, my *butchas*. One story and then it is time for your *ghussl*. There was once a beautiful young woman who lived with her fisherman husband in a house by the sea, near Karachi.' I settled further in the chair. Angela smiled at me. 'She was very happy, singing all day, and she loved her husband very, very much. One day, when she was walking alone by the water's edge, collecting shells to put on the mantelpiece in their bedroom, she came upon a great fish lying on the sand. When she looked closer, she saw that the fish was still alive. It's mouth and gills opened and shut, and the colours on its scales shimmered in the light. And the woman was sad to see something so beautiful about to die, and made a great effort to drag the fish back into the water so that it might recover, watching it anxiously as she knelt by the water's edge. And the fish was a magic fish and said to her, "For your kindness you may ask one wish of me and it shall be granted." And when she had recovered from her surprise, and realized that the fish really was enchanted, she thought for a moment and then said, "I wish that my husband might have his dearest wish. For I love him above everything." And the fish said, "Choose some other thing, for you do not know what may be in his mind." But the girl said, "That is my wish" – happy to think that their lives together would be further enriched, if that were possible.'

Poonomal struck the log in the fire with the poker and a shower of fine sparks sprayed out. The house creaked, settling for the night. Resin began to seep down the wood from a smoking fissure in the striated golden pine.

'So the young woman ran back home, full of excitement. The front door was open, and his nets had gone from their hooks. When she had run through the house calling him and there was nothing but the echo of her voice, she became afraid and ran back to the seashore to find the fish. Far out to sea she could see a black boat sailing towards the sunset. There was a splash in the water near her feet and she saw again the fish she had saved. In her anguish she said, "Please tell me where my husband has gone," and the fish rose to the surface and said, "He is in that black boat which you can see sailing towards the west. His greatest wish was to be free of you."'

Angela was crying silently, the tears shining as they ran down her face and dropped into her lap. I was angry and a little uncertain, as though Poonomal had tricked us. She hadn't told the story with the now deliberate excursions into babu English to make us laugh, or her uses of gesture and changes of voice to indicate the different characters. Stories should be safe, should offer fairness and comfort. How could a beautiful woman who was also good be treated like that? A sense of desolation at the injustice of life crept over me. Was it really like that? 'But what does it *mean*, Poonoo?' I asked.

Poonomal got up and collected our cups. There was a heaviness in her movements, and her face was uncharacteristically solemn. 'Time for *palang, butchas,*' she said. 'That was a grown-up story to tell you that there is no certainty in other people — or the future.'

Chapter Twelve

Septimus stood in his plaid dressing-gown in the hall. Through the window he could see the boys playing football in the street. An old Cortina began to nose slowly down between the cars, and the ball, kicked by the scruffiest small boy, bounced on its windscreen. Septimus couldn't see the driver through the curved glass of the windscreen, but he could see the man's fist shaking through the open window. The boys laughed, making rude signs at the car, drifting down the street to disappear down the alley opposite.

Patiently he spoke into the telephone. 'Perhaps you should tell David.'

After a little while he said, 'The police obviously haven't accused him of anything. It will probably blow over, given time. It's just part of their procedures – nothing personal. After all, they took David in for questioning, didn't they?'

When he put down the phone, he wondered if the police would pay him a visit in due course. David had told him that Thomas had telephoned, full of apparent shock and indignation that the police had so forgotten themselves as to question him, Thomas's own godson. But that had been Thomas's way – to do precisely what he wanted and then distance himself from whatever had truly gone beyond the pale. Septimus's own inclination had been to avoid becoming involved, even where great wrongs might be righted by his disclosures. I am not God, and must not interfere with the workings of his purpose, he had told himself sternly, never considering for a moment that he might himself be an instrument of that purpose. But, as events had begun to prompt David Lawrence to remember long past times, so Septimus had found himself unwillingly recollecting the past.

It seemed to him as though he were captive in a darkened cinema, forced to endure the sepia pictures of long ago, where cause and effect had become dim and faint with age, leaving only fragments of the dance itself.

He had not slept the night before Angela's call. He remembered the morning as though it were last week. He had grown used to N's mute company by his side, as they worked together, rebuilding the tower. N had arrived one day, months before, with a group of nomads, emaciated, lice covered, silent. It was Dr Chatterjee who arranged for him to be treated at Iskanderabad General, and had introduced him to Septimus when he had made a partial recovery. 'His mind is unaffected but he is in flight from something he cannot deal with. I think he may be German. He was carrying some letters in German in his pocket when we took him in. In time he may recover. I could only think of asking you to look after him.' And N had turned out to be biddable, eager to work. Only sometimes he would stop for a moment, and Septimus would see the vacant expression on his face before he turned resolutely to his task again.

Often David and Angela Lawrence would come to watch. She was beautiful already, a slim, graceful child with wide, dark eyes and long hair. David, younger than his sister, had the immoderate curiosity of the intelligent child, always questioning everything, squatting on his heels to watch as they cleaned the bricks or prepared the mortar.

Near noon Brother Ambrose had arrived on Balaam. The sun was piercing, and he was perspiring heavily, the drops dribbling down his red round cheeks to fall on to his cassock. Septimus stood back from the plumb-line he was setting and put his hands to the small of his back, bending to ease the ache. N continued without breaking his rhythm, examining each cleaned brick carefully for imperfections before placing it on the neat pile by Septimus. The cement that Gobind Dass's men had delivered was stacked on pallets, covered by tarpaulin. Recently Gobind Dass had spent less and less time on his police work as his business flourished. 'Wealth and the police go hand in hand,' the villagers used to say, tapping the sides of their noses with a forefinger.

Septimus had known immediately that something was wrong. Brother Ambrose got down clumsily and the mule had immediately started to crop at the sparse grass. He had taken two or three deep breaths, like a man surfacing from a long dive, and when he spoke there was a ripple of tears in his voice.

'Sep. Could you come back with me to see the Holy Father? He had a stroke, and Dr Chatterjee seems to think he may not survive.' His face crumpled, as though he were about to cry.

Septimus brushed the dirt from his knees and stood up. He had prepared for this moment for a long time, but felt suddenly panic-stricken to think of Father Gregorio lying near death. He had not seen Father Gregorio since he had left the monastery, but had known he was still there, still accessible when the sharpness of his own leaving had dulled to a point where he might return. He nodded silently, turning to N and saying, 'I shall be back.' The two children stood, wide-eyed, by the grass verge.

As he walked beside the mule carrying Brother Ambrose through the iron gates and up the narrow path towards the monastery, Septimus felt at first that he had never left. Brother Nicholas was watering the vegetable garden using the old hose, a handkerchief knotted at the corners protecting his tonsure from the sun. Through the bakery door Septimus could see one of the novices pushing the dough into the centre of the glowing furnace on a long paddle. The bees from Father Gregorio's hives on the hill above the monastery hummed drowsily in the still air. It was by the door that Septimus was suddenly conscious of a sense of loss, of exclusion, as though he were an exile returning to a country which no longer accepted him as its own.

The long stone-flagged corridor was cold after the fierce sunlight. Stood in front of the last door on the right, the entrance to Father Gregorio's cell, he paused for a moment, more afraid now than he had been in that last meeting where he had known what he must do.

Father Gregorio seemed very small, his skin pallid and waxy, and the sheet under which he lay seemed hardly to move with his breathing. Dr Chatterjee sat like a small monkey on the other side of the bed, carefully stowing his blood pressure stand into a capacious, battered Gladstone. With brisk detachment he said, 'Not too long, please. The patient needs to rest,' but Septimus knew that it was simply a professional habit, that it could only be hours at most before the figure on the bed slipped quietly into death.

He sat for twenty minutes in silence. The stroke had disfigured the old man's face so that the left side of his mouth hung open, oozing dribble which had dried in a white patch on the wrinkled skin of his jaw. There was nothing to be done. When Father Gregorio's lips puckered, Septimus thought at first that the old man was merely moving his tongue round his dry mouth, but Gregorio's eyes were open, and the expression in them seemed to carry some urgency. Holding Father Gregorio's hand — so frail and small that it felt like a bird's claw — Septimus put his ear to the old priest's mouth. He still had to strain to hear the words.

'The girl. Grace Chaudhury. It wasn't you. I know now. She disappeared from the hospital a week ago. Her body is in the lime pit . . .'

These are hallucinations, Septimus thought. He nodded, smiling at the old man. Still he could see the terrible demand in the olive-black eyes that held his. Again the old man spoke.

'I cannot tell you more, since it was from the confessional. If justice is not done, the innocent will suffer.' His lips, cyanosed from lack of oxygen, blew exhaustedly as though the effort of speech had drained him. His head rolled on the pillow to face the window. The sparse hair at the side of his head was damp. After five minutes Septimus gently let go of the old man's hand. He could feel no pulse at the wrist or in the neck. He stooped and kissed Father Gregorio's forehead. At the door he stopped for a last backward look, and then went down the corridor to tell Brother Nicholas the news.

Walking alone down the hill, he felt no grief. Rather he was aware of surprise: at the unfinished nature of things, at some lack of affirmation, of structure, in these last exchanges. He wondered what Father Gregorio had wanted him to do about his disclosure. He could not begin to speculate upon who might have told Father Gregorio about Grace Chaudhury. And if he approached the police, he could see himself becoming implicated in the matter which, if precedent were any guide, might drag on for years. What could be done now, anyway? Perhaps the old man's mind had been wandering. He felt shame, knowing that he was seeking an excuse to do nothing, and already a sense of self-reproach for the things he had never said. At the tower he had taken off his coat and begun to work beside N. Having so often wished for someone to talk to in the past, he welcomed the silence.

The boys were playing football in the street again. He was due at a Parish Council meeting in another hour. Dressing, he smiled wryly to himself. What was the point of bringing things to light after all these years? Was truth important enough to cause lasting pain in its service? There was no answer in his mind as he walked briskly down the road to his car.

Chapter Thirteen

Every man has his price. I know that we inhabit a society in which truth is often inconvenient. People cannot deal with revelation, the knowledge of how others really see them: almost all social arrangement is predicated upon a pattern of lies, exchanges which carry the whiff of an estate agent's euphemisms.

I did give in. I had hinted to Miriam in subsequent sessions that the love letters might be figments of her imagination, knowing that this might prompt her to bring them if what she had told me was the truth. And, as I had surmised, she produced them in triumph.

They were under my hand on the desk. Surprised, I saw there were also some letters from her.

'Did you keep copies of your own letters to him?'

'After he had told me it was over, he went to the lavatory. The letters I wrote to him were in his case. I took them.'

'You didn't need to bring them.'

'Perhaps you would keep them for a little. I don't mind if you read them . . .' I could sense the pride in her voice. Read them, she was saying, and see that I spoke the truth.

'What does he mean to you now?'

With a strange dignity she said, 'I know now that it was never what I thought. You must have heard the story so often. I believed he would leave his wife, that we would be together. It was what I wanted to believe, against all the evidence.'

'My bossy-boots.' Hard to imagine Thomas as the inspiration for such endearments. I took the letters home, still undecided as to what use I would put them to. When I began to read

91

them, I felt the weight of the ethics and tradition of my profession rising up in horror against what I might do, breaking the absolute trust with a patient. They were from Thomas: the early ones lubricious with descriptions of their recent coupling, couched in clichéd and unmemorable phrases of undying love; the later full of the deceits and excuses of passion cooling, full of regrets for missed appointments and extravagant over-compensatory offers for the future. When she next came, she smiled knowingly. 'You see,' she said, 'it was not only my imagination.'

With Neidermayer, too, the progress was of a different kind, closer, perhaps, to my ends than his own. Such things are hard to quantify. He seemed more in control of himself, more urbane. 'The silence was because I could not speak of the horror of what I had seen. I could not get past it,' he'd told me. But there had been nothing substantial in what he had said. There were inconsistencies as he played the game of avoiding what had really happened until he was ready for the truth. There was a girl he remembered in the camp; twelve years old, wearing the yellow star. Her face had looked up at him through the window as she lay under the guard who was raping her: a face like an angel, serene, detached from what was happening. It was for bread for her mother, she'd told him. The next day he had felt tears run down his cheeks as he watched her in the queue for the showers. Behind the building the bulldozers rumbled, waiting until the guards had picked through the bodies with their pliers, searching for rings, gold teeth. The first time he told me the story he was a Vopo: the second time he had said, 'I had to join the party. I was ashamed, but we had to obey orders.'

When he mentioned the lime pit, I had felt a momentary unease.

'It was not only used for animals, you know?' There was a knowing timbre in his voice, as though he were teasing me with some secret.

'For what else? What does it mean to you?'

'People bury things they do not want discovered. You were too young to know about these matters.'

For his own reasons he had shied away from disclosure. It would come in the end. Neidermayer did not like me. My professional judgement suggested negative transference, but that is a technical phrase which conceals much more than it discloses. It was not me he disliked, but rather what I represented. Unbidden, from imagination or memory, I saw a picture of a man surrounded by a circle of people who beat him with sticks. The figure gave an inarticulate, wordless bellow. His clothing was blood soaked and his hands, spread wide in supplication, had wounds in their palms.

That time he hesitated before he left, picking up his coat from the chair. He looked again for a moment as he had when I was a child, his eyes on the floor. 'It is not against you, you understand. But the anger must go somewhere. I cannot live with it heaped on my back for ever.'

Angela had asked me to go with her to the police station to collect Robert. Apparently he had a police record – something to do with turning the clocks back on cars he had sold – and the police had been both unceremonious in taking him in, and bloody-minded about letting him go. He could see no reason why there should be any connection between him and a burglary at Thomas's house, and it was quite evident that Angela had told him nothing. What she had hoped to achieve by enlisting my support, I couldn't say: I could not give her anything beyond my presence.

'I don't know what they were on about, Angie. Really.' In the mirror I could see Robert's unshaven face was flushed. He held Angela's hand, and I looked away from her eyes in the mirror and drove faster than normal.

Later she called me at home. 'He's gone,' she said, as if seeking my approval. She'd wondered if I could ring Thomas, ostensibly to inquire after Julia, to get some idea of what had been taken. If he had suggested the police question Robert, it could only be because what had been taken related to us. But she agreed it wasn't as easy as that. We would only expose ourselves further by contacting Thomas. And it wasn't until much later when everything had come out that I realized the extent of Thomas's anger — that after all those years he still wanted to hurt people. That is too simple, in itself, and what I found out subsequently provided a sharper focus, a clearer motive. Thomas had come to reflect his own publicity — the man who prized truth above all else. Like most who choose to cast stones, he had developed a convenient memory about his own past.

Chapter Fourteen

As a child I often used to visit Dora Wheeler. Her house was north of the hill on which the church Septimus was rebuilding stood. Whitewashed, four-square, with pink rooftiles, it sat in the middle of a restless, eclectic garden straddling the ridge of the hill which sheered down to Kala Pani on its eastern flank and north up towards Ooper Iskanderabad, hidden from view by the forested hills and the low cloud. She might show me Theodore's escritoire, with its neat array of pens and the tooled leather writing case. Or she would take down one of the albums from the bookshelf and turn the pages, pointing out figures dressed in the fashions of late Victoria, and tell me about them. Sometimes she read to me from one of her two favourite books: from Marcus Aurelius's *Meditations*, 'whatever may befall you was prepared for you from all eternity; and the implication of causes was from eternity spinning the thread of your being'. Or from Genesis, 'then shall ye bring down my grey hairs with sorrow to the grave'. And, looking at these quotations later, and the oblique comments she made whose meanings I could not see then, they were all part of a pattern. She saw more than the rest, even if she was ultimately wrong.

I went early that morning. Father would come by and I would join him to walk to Iskanderabad. 'I've been burgled, look!' She showed me the marks on the rosewood cabinet where it had been forced. 'Only some old plates Theodore and I bought years ago.' She didn't seem concerned at all. After I sat with her in the garden and we drank our tea together, watching the sun rise through the night-mist.

The muezzin call came reedily from the mosque at Kala Pani fifteen hundred feet below. One hundred yards across the

95

plateau Karim Baksh, the halal butcher, was slaughtering the chickens for the Nawab's wedding banquet in the village. Dora sat with her back to the scene, but I could see the headless chickens performing their grotesque reflexive *Totentanz*, their feathers floating like frail boats in the wind, while Baksh stolidly carried on with his work.

Dr Chatterjee was walking up the hill, bent forward. He always reminded me of a monkey, wizen faced, with a bald, shiny head and a shambling gait. Dora's face was alight with pleasure. She and Theodore had worked hard to gain acceptance for Chat and his plump, laughing wife, Premla. 'Wog lover,' I'd once heard Colonel Whitworth mutter to his wife, but he had been careful to keep his voice too low for Theodore to hear.

Now Dr Chatterjee was panting slightly as he sat down in the roorkee chair: the air was cooler here where the wind blew, but the coming monsoon made the air thick, almost palpable. He felt in his waistcoat pocket and brought out a bottle of pills which he placed carefully on the table. 'It would be better if you could try to sleep without these. I don't like prescribing powerful drugs, you know.' But Dora just laughed and teased him for being an old woman. 'All this trouble with Charles ... It's better that I sleep than lie awake worrying,' she said.

The sound of hammering came from the direction of the church. Dr Chatterjee said, 'Why don't you go and play, David?' but Dora wouldn't have it. 'How else is he to learn unless he listens?' and Chat looked at me for a moment with old eyes before nodding. 'You know that Father Gregorio died the other day? I haven't seen Septimus. How's he taking it?'

'I think his silent companion helps. And the work, of course.'

Dr Chat sighed and leaned forward to take a sip of his coffee. 'I was worried that people might complain, but I gather the man is a good worker. Of course there has been speculation about him, but I'm surprised at how well he has been accepted. This is not the most tolerant of societies as you know.' He smiled at her sardonically, an old friend, knowing she would not take exception.

Dora snorted her derision. 'Closed minds and small preoccupations. The requirements for colonial living.' After a moment she went on, 'He does not talk, but Septimus told me he was in the camps and is nearly mad. Sometimes, when I pass, I see him standing for a moment absolutely still, looking into nothing as though he is remembering something terrible.'

Abdul came out on bare feet with a fresh pot of coffee. When he had placed it on the table, he took a small shovel which rested against the side wall and started to clear the jackal's faeces from the lawn, putting them into a rusting bucket, and turning his head away to spit copiously from time to time. 'K-a-a-a *thoo*. Kha-kha-kha-kha *thoo!*'

'It is strange the way our minds work,' Dr Chatterjee observed gravely. 'We are often not aware of the unconscious reasons for our actions, behaving in ways which we could not justify rationally. But I am telling you with complete conviction that Abdul is washing out his mouth *because he imagines eating the dog's dirt*. Not literally, you understand, but the thought is there. For there is no other explanation for his behaviour. But to find the *true* significance of this one act would be the work of years. We are all operating our lives through repetitive metaphors, symbols, similes, whose birth is lost somewhere in our infancy. Often our senses of malaise, of disillusionment as we grow older, are merely a consequence of these hidden and inappropriate remnants of childhood.'

I felt a sudden, enormous excitement, as if I had at last found a means of looking into the adult world. Dora said, 'That's a bleak view, Chat.'

'Why bleak? I am simply recognizing a fundamental truth. That we have largely understood the physical nature of the world, but cannot comprehend ourselves and the forces that drive us. I am truly believing that after the age of ten we are merely repeating the activities of childhood. The boy who loves the power his air rifle gives him becomes – perhaps – a Lothario.'

'You don't believe the story about Septimus and the girl, do you?'

Dr Chatterjee took a pair of rimless spectacles from his top pocket and polished them on his handkerchief before replacing them. 'No. But I don't believe the rumours that it was Charles, either. You know Grace Chaudhury has vanished without trace?'

It was then that so many things fell into place. I knew that Dora Wheeler did think that her son had done something with the girl who had gone missing. It seemed to me that Dr Chatterjee might think so too, that his emphatic denial showed his concern for Dora rather than what he really might feel. There was something worrying about this knowledge, for other things that had concerned me suddenly returned, as though presenting themselves for my newly enlightened inspection: the behaviour of my parents on the evening of Eleanor's party; Dora's comment as she prepared to leave. I felt both enabled and unsafe, as though the cost of this new insight was the recognition that grown-ups were fallible.

They talked about the burglary. It was commonplace for things to disappear. Recently several people had lost glass, silver, crystal. Dora had gone to church the previous Sunday for the first time for weeks. She had a distaste for Father Carey and his High Church rituals, but the priest from Koti — an old friend — had recently been conducting services while Father Carey was temporarily laid low with a bout of amoebic dysentery, and she had attended the last two Sunday evensongs. Returning the previous Sunday, 'the day Charles went missing,' she said — and I could see the connection in her mind — she had found the cabinet forced and various items gone. 'It is not,' she said, looking into the distance, 'the loss of the goblets themselves, but who has taken them and why.'

Dr Chatterjee said, 'If you don't mind, I'll discuss this with Thomas Henne in confidence, eh? I think he is a careful man and won't jump to conclusions before having the evidence.'

I heard Father's greeting before his head suddenly appeared over the hedge. 'We're late already,' he said, consulting his watch as he declined Dora's offer of coffee. He smiled at Dora, waving his arm in the direction of the church. 'You see. They're getting on with the work. Soon it will be finished.'

My father rarely spoke to me. He walked fast, preoccupied

with his own thoughts, and I struggled to keep up. The road was cut into the flank of the hill which reared above Kala Pani. The pines looked denuded, their lower branches roughly hacked away. Even now the woodsmen's axes echoed, and there was the shattering sound of a pine falling further up the hill. Father left the road and we began to follow the steep winding path, slippery with pine needles, which threaded erratically through knotted roots exposed by the erosion of past monsoons and round great grey boulders. Usually Father would have ridden to his meeting with Gobind Dass, but sometimes he would say to Mother, 'I'll take the boy with me. A bit of exercise will do him good.'

Meandering down the slope towards us, the young Nawab of Alabargh came into sight, his guard a respectful few paces behind him, and his two cocker spaniels pricking to and fro, their stumpy tails never still. The Nawab had a gentle notoriety: two years ago (so Poonomal had told us) on his accession to the nawabship he had taken the precaution of killing his own brother − a procedure honoured by immemorial precedent. He had always seemed a little simple to me. Later I learned that he was more concerned with the poems of Iqbal and his never-ending translation of the *Mahabharata* into flowery English than with politics or social affairs. It was unthinkable to execute or even imprison a nawab, so he was assigned a full-time constable as his guard as an alternative to house arrest. Father had said, 'I'm told the Nawab and his guard are as good as man and wife,' and Mother had looked at us, and then they had both laughed. He had the permanently smiling moon face of an idiot, his eyes half hidden under deep Mongolian folds, and his skin was the colour of almonds. He spoke in his lapidary, over-accentuated English, while Father and I sat on a granite boulder and rested. In the distant valley I could just make out the notorious Imber Pass in the mist.

'My cousin from Kashmir has finally arranged my marriage. She is fourteen and we have no language in common. Such are the ways of my people.' He spread his hands for a moment, palms upward, then folded them across his round belly. 'If I am not mistaken, you are going to visit Gobind Dass, the box wallah?' For a moment, shooting a sly glance at Father, his face seemed transformed into a cunning mask.

People knew everything as soon as it was arranged. Intrigue, gossip, the passage of secrets was endemic. I could see Father was surprised. He nodded shortly, saying the automatic blessing, 'A long life and many children.'

The Nawab laughed drily, glancing towards his companion who stood deferentially a few paces away. 'Such things are hidden from us and are only for Allah. But, take care with Gobind. Like the krait, he seems small and insignificant, but do not be misled. For protection you may remind him that your family has always been in the bosom of mine. My father – Allah be merciful to his great soul – gave Gobind's ancestors shelter and sustenance. Your great-grandfather spoke for our ancestors' loyalty in the Mutiny. Though little touches Gobind, that reminder may be better than nothing.' He started to move off down the hill and then stopped. Half turning, he said over his shoulder, 'He has taken care of the matter of the girl. For that he will expect payment.'

I said, 'Are you all right, Father?' His face, turned towards the Nawab's retreating back, looked grey. I knew that some important exchange had taken place, but it made no sense to me. I also knew better than to ask my father what he meant.

Chapter Fifteen

Neidermayer moves over to the drinks cabinet. Like all the furniture in the flat, it has the heavy Teutonic functionality of the thirties. The panelling is dark, hung with works by William Etty and Alma-Tadema which he bought before their prices began to rise again. It is the home of a successful man who wishes to impress without having the taste to do so. All Septimus knows of the sources of Neidermayer's wealth is that it is connected with import and export. Neidermayer has a facility for vagueness when certain matters arise: sometimes he varies this by simply not answering. After a break of fifteen years Septimus has run into him in London. After forty years he is still not certain if he likes Neidermayer. It is the past that binds them together.

'Whisky. That's your poison. Ach, how you can drink it . . .' Always the same jokes. He pours a generous measure and a vodka and tonic for himself. *Carmina Burana* sounds faintly from the other room.

'How are you getting on with David Lawrence?'

Neidermayer's eyelids come down over his eyes and his face looks closed. Seated in the armchair, he waves the spatulate fingers of one hand vaguely to suggest uncertainty.

'At first it was helpful. I know people here are against it, but to talk to a neutral observer who makes no judgements can be . . .' – he searches for the right word, his mouth open and his eyes roving round the ceiling – 'liberating. And it helps that you pay for it, so that it is not like burdening your friends. It is like going to a prostitute for your pleasures; not that you would know . . .' He laughs wheezily at his own joke, and then coughs. 'But now I find I am being drawn into other things. Perhaps because of his infuriating superiority – I mean that he is the doctor and I am the patient – I find myself almost telling him things he was too young to know.'

'About his family?'

Neidermayer gives a sour half-smile. 'There is no need for pretences between you and me. We know what happened, how it was kept quiet because the people concerned were from the English upper classes. Not like me, eh? Just a refugee from the camps. Nothing of value, eh? Not like you, either, a priest dispossessed of his heritage. We did not fit into their . . . their scheme of things. Of course, because of the way things were, they knew you were not responsible for the girl so – why did you take that on yourself? And it affected you in other ways, too. After all that careful work the tower fell when the earthquake came. All gone for nothing.'

'That was because Gobind Dass supplied inferior cement.'

'And why did he get away with that, eh? Because he and Amyas Lawrence were like that . . .' Neidermayer holds out his hand with the first and second fingers entwined.

Septimus says, 'What is the benefit of making David Lawrence unhappy now? Nothing can be undone. All of this was years ago.'

Neidermayer stands at the window looking across at Parliament Hill. The branches of the mountain ash outside quiver in the wind. In the orange glow of the street lights Septimus can see the fine driving drizzle. When Neidermayer speaks, his voice is thoughtful, reflective. 'I am doing for David Lawrence what he has done for me. I am showing him the truth of how things really were. For I believe what he says – that to face the past and the truth frees the spirit.'

Septimus makes an effort to control his anger. It is no business of his, after all. He tries to keep his tone light. 'Like Thomas Henne and Amyas Lawrence, you're another old man seeking revenge.'

Neidermayer smiles and draws the curtain. 'That too,' he says.

Over dinner of red-cabbage soup and goulash served by Greta,

Neidermayer's monosyllabic housekeeper, they talk about politics. Look at Romania and Albania, Neidermayer says: they show how we will always choose the evils that we know instead of some other system which might be better – or worse. He talks with his mouth full, like a peasant, gesticulating with his knife to make his point.

Afterwards Septimus says, 'You won't really tell David what happened, will you?' and Neidermayer says, 'When one grows old and the end is in view, one becomes selfish. Who knows?'

*

When Miriam Cohen asked me for the return of the letters, I lied. I said I had taken them home and put them in my strongbox for safekeeping. Yes, I had read them as she requested, to see if they might provide some insight towards helping her. She was silent for so long that I was prompted to ask what was in her mind. Thomas had visited her. She had made coffee, talking desperately all the time. I thought, she said, that he might have decided to come back to me, after all. She'd asked after Julia, wishing to prompt some sudden confidence that they could not, after all, go on together. She would know more from the tone of his reply than from what he said. But his voice had been warm when he spoke of Julia's courage. She said that a hope she had never known she had nurtured suddenly died then. More than the warmth, it was the use of certain phrases: he spoke always of 'we', and he spoke of the cases he had known where cancer had gone into complete remission, until she could no longer hide from the fact of his concern. It was then that she had thrown caution aside: what about me, she had asked. Was I just someone to be used and then thrown aside? Had he ever considered what his defection had meant?

It was when she had said she was seeing a psychoanalyst that she had noticed a change in him. He had begun to question her for his name, and she could see the urgency and anger under the appearance of teasing. Why him? Why do you suppose it would be a man, she had asked, relishing even this small evidence of jealousy. She had felt a sense of gratification at arousing something in him. It was then he had quite cold-bloodedly got up and begun to hit her. Not on her face, where it might show, but in the stomach, in her ribs. And, she said, in the midst of my fear of what he would do I felt that I deserved to be punished. In the end she had told him. He said nothing, just watching her with a speculative look in his eye. I had the impression that he knows you, she said. I made no response. Thomas had asked her for his letters. When she said that she had torn them up, he had laughed. Come on. They must be here. Women didn't tear up letters from their lovers. Finally he had said that if she didn't give them to him he'd have to think of a way to persuade her. It was strange, she said, to find I still loved him despite all that he had done. She wanted to post the letters back to him. That was why she had asked for them. To be done with him, once and for all.

'Didn't you think of going to the police?'

'It crossed my mind. But I didn't think they would believe my word against his. Besides' — she gave a bitter laugh — 'as I told you, I still love him.'

'I will give them to you next session.' I could photostat them before returning them to her. How far I had come down that road in so short a time.

But there was no next session.

Five days later I received a letter from her. 'You have been the only one I could talk to these last months. Forgive me. I just couldn't find a reason to continue.' I called her flat. Her voice on the answering machine sounded eerily normal. I asked the receptionist to cancel my calls for the day.

Miriam's sister Sophie was married to a colleague of mine and we had met three or four times socially. Their house was Georgian, with a sloping garden and views over Hampstead Heath. She was brisk, her face pale and unmade up, and her paling red hair was knotted at the nape of her neck. The maid brought us coffee in the chintzy drawing-room.

'There isn't much I can tell you . . .' She made a despairing gesture with her hand. 'I was the one who found her. We'd planned an expedition to the sales and I went to pick her up. There was no answer when I rang the bell, so I let myself in with the key. She was lying across the bed . . .' Her voice faltered, and she bit her lip and looked out of the window.

'Was it pills?'

She nodded. 'There was an empty bottle on the bedside table. Sleeping pills, I think. And the remains of a bottle of vodka. I called the police. There was a note for me which I read and they took away. She asked my forgiveness . . .'

'Why do you think she did it?'

She was too polite to put her surprise into words. Undoubtedly I had known of her sister's depression. Miriam had always been – well – not quite stable. She seemed to become involved with men with whom there could be no long-term future. It seemed almost deliberate. Carefully, neutrally, I asked if she knew who her sister had been involved with at the time of her death. She looked away then, and I got the impression she was telling me less than she knew. The man was much older than Miriam. She suspected he was married. She also thought he was probably quite well known. No, Miriam hadn't actually said anything, but there had been something self-satisfied in her attitude when the affair began. 'But there was a pattern of self-destruction in everything Miriam did. It was always only a matter of time before things began to go awry.'

I had been wrong to try to evaluate Miriam Cohen's pain. What she had told me in the few months she had come to me was only the outward show. As Sophie talked and the tears ran down her face, I could see that her grief was for herself. 'If only,' she said, 'Miriam had been able to accept that life is largely a question of making do . . .' But I saw a different script: Miriam trying to compete with Sophie, who had done everything by the book and succeeded with her degree in literature from London and her respectable Jewish psychiatrist husband. Above all, I saw a family who had valued their daughters for what they did, not for what they were. By those standards Miriam would always have been found wanting.

Chapter Sixteen

In the days after Father Gregorio's death Septimus had thrown himself into rebuilding the tower. It was now over forty feet high, and he and N had erected scaffolding and planking around the summit, and a system of two buckets on pulleys — one for the bricks and the other for the mortar — which N filled on the ground and then — grimacing with the effort — hauled up to be caught by Septimus.

On the fourth day Inspector Malik had appeared with a constable. He had a curious, self-effacing manner, always giving the impression of washing his hands and seemingly unable to look anyone in the eye. Would Mr Septimus come with him and give him a little help, if he would be so kind? Despite the terms in which it was couched, Septimus recognized it as a command. He climbed slowly down the ladder. 'You might as well take the day off,' he said to N, and the other man nodded, beginning to gather the tools together to wash them in the bucket.

Septimus sat in the back of the jeep with Inspector Malik and the vehicle began to lurch down the rutted road to the Mughal Reservoirs. Malik talked with a compulsive, self-deprecating artlessness, but Septimus was aware that the other man was testing him, evaluating his responses to the apparently idle chatter. Malik was investigating a series of thefts which had recently taken place in Iskanderabad. It is only from the Christian community. And the thefts seem to take place quite often during church services. What we are finding very surprising is that none of these things are being sold on the black market. Of course, we are having our suspicions. There is a lady — you may know her — who sometimes takes small things from her friends. The English are very funny. They all laugh and say, "Don't worry about it. We know she acts strangely." But I am a policeman. I must worry about these things.' His air of theatrical confusion was so well feigned that Septimus smiled.

'There are so many possibilities for poor policemen. There is a young man who might be responsible. We know he has no money and he has an eye for the girls. Could it be him, we wonder. Eh? Eh?'

Septimus said nothing, holding on to the side of the jeep. In the distance he could see three figures standing by the Mughal Reservoirs. In the heat their shapes seemed to shimmer. The Inspector waved, and one man waved back. As the vehicle drew closer, Septimus realized with a sense of shock that one of the men was Thomas Henne.

There was something on the ground on a stretcher covered by a sheet. Two constables stood uncomfortably at ease at a respectable distance. Thomas Henne had an embarrassed smile on his face. Septimus had met him twice before. Henne had barely made an effort to conceal the fact that he found Septimus of no interest at all.

Malik said, 'We talked to Father Gregorio a few days before he died. He didn't think you had anything to do with the girl, eh?'

Septimus was silent. Malik watched him for a moment and then gave a little sigh, summoning one of the constables over and indicating that he should remove the sheet. Mr Henne's face was livid, pearled with perspiration. The body under the sheet had been a woman. Where the skin remained, it had blackened and shrivelled, but the face and neck were skinless, the texture and colour of hunter's beef. The lips were drawn back in a snarl over stained teeth, and a cheekbone showed yellow through the flesh, like old ivory. Malik made sympathetic clicking noises with his tongue as Septimus ran towards the edge of the clearing and was copiously sick.

'Grace Chaudhury. Her body was in the lime pit. It is hard to know how she was killed.' His voice was gentle, reflective. 'We wondered if you might have any ideas about who did it. After all, you allowed people to think that you and she . . .'

The constable covered the body. Malik lit a small cheroot, blowing a luxuriant cloud of smoke and examining the end of the cigar with apparent interest. 'You are very friendly with Charles Wheeler, aren't you?'

Later, when the shape of what was to happen was already cast, Septimus could see his own unwitting part in things. He had defended Charles, saying that he was not as bad as people had made out. He knew, for example, that people had whispered about Charles being the thief who had recently been robbing the old ladies, but on two occasions he could vouch for the fact that Charles was with him and could not possibly have been responsible. His shock and fear made him eloquent and, aware of the glances exchanged between the policeman and Henne, he interpreted them as an acceptance of his evidence. As for the girl (his stomach heaved as he thought of the shape under the sheet), he could not think who might have done such a thing.

'Who were you protecting?' Malik had asked, and Septimus had tried to explain. That he understood the girl's fear, that he could see why she had named him, because her own responsibility would be less. That, having decided that he would leave the order, he had chosen not to speak, knowing how the silence would be interpreted.

After that they sat for a while in silence. Malik lit another cheroot. In response his face had a melancholy, inward look. The heat was intense, and Septimus felt his clothes sticking to him, and runnels of perspiration sliding down his chest. There was nothing more he could do here, but he lacked the will to move. Malik stood up and gazed across the water of the reservoir. A few moments later he turned to Thomas Henne and said, 'Well. Perhaps you are right in both cases. Better that we do something now, rather than let things drift on in the old way, eh?'

Gobind Dass came down to the tower the following day where Septimus and N were stacking the new delivery of cement and bricks. Squatting in the shade, he chewed a neem stick, watching his servant help Septimus and N unload the gunny sacks. 'You have heard the news, I suppose?' He addressed himself to Septimus, who stopped to face him, lowering his hod to the ground. 'Inspector Malik has arrested Charles Wheeler on suspicion of murdering Grace Chaudhury. And Mr Henne has interviewed Mrs Eleanor Weaver in connection with the thefts. It is good that we have such a clever, upright man among us to find these things out.'

Behind him Septimus heard a half-strangled sound. Turning, he saw that N held both hands to his ears, his mouth open in a soundless O. He took a step towards the other man, but N, still holding his ears, began to stumble down the hill towards the edge of the trees. Dass said nothing, but, even in the midst of his shock, Septimus could see his eyes watching the running figure until it had disappeared in the fringe of trees.

Chapter Seventeen

Angela came with me to the inquest into Miriam Cohen's death. I was surprised by her insistence. It had begun to seem to me that our estrangement had become permanent since I had voiced my opposition to Robert. She possessed the rare gift of true compassion. Of course I offered my sympathy to Sophie and her mother, though I still felt that the sister's trauma was superficial, would soon pass. But Angela, elegant in black linen, sat with her and talked outside the courtroom, and held Sophie's hand while she talked and cried.

The recital of events was stark, read from a notebook by the police constable who had answered Sophie's call. The post-mortem had disclosed the presence of a substantial amount of barbiturates and alcohol in Miriam's system. She had probably been dead for seven or eight hours by the time her sister had found her. The coroner looked down through his glasses at the note Miriam had left for Sophie, stroking his chin with his hand. When he spoke, his voice was hesitant, as though he would like to reach some other conclusion. Having considered all the evidence, he said, there was no other possible verdict than that Miriam Cohen had taken her own life while the balance of her mind was disturbed.

In the weak sun outside, Angela hailed a taxi and helped Sophie and her mother into the back. We stood for a moment, like strangers, and I wished that I had cancelled the rest of my appointments so that I could take her to lunch, to talk, to try to bridge this growing division between us.

'How's Nico?'

She smiled abstractedly. Something was worrying her. 'All right. He's staying with Sally at the moment.'

'New girlfriend?'

She nodded, made a face. She caught my arm and I could see the confusion in her face. 'Sophie said that Miriam had a visitor that last night. A man. The old woman downstairs had come on to the landing and heard them talking before Miriam let him in. She asked if she should say anything to the coroner, but I told her I didn't think it would make any difference to the verdict.'

'A man . . . ?'

'It probably means nothing.'

I could not get past the coldness. There might be a time, but it was not yet. We kissed awkwardly, and I watched her figure until she was lost in the crowd. Walking back to my office, I wondered if Thomas had visited Miriam. If she had given him the letters, would she be alive now? I dismissed the thoughts from my mind. Whatever I thought of Thomas, I could not cast him as a murderer. People did not do such things to save themselves embarrassment.

Chapter Eighteen

Two days after his visit to the reservoirs with Inspector Malik Septimus worked alone, wondering where N had gone. The events of that day still worried him. Who had confided the secret of where Grace Chaudhury's body lay to Father Gregorio under the protection of the confessional? That net was too wide for fruitful speculation and, anyway, the confidant might have had no connection with her death. He straightened up, arching to ease the ache in his back. He'd slept little, worried too about N, who had not come home the night before. He had gone over the meeting with Gobind Dass again and again in his mind, but had found no answers to his questions. He knew more of N than most, but that was not much, elicited by a process of repeated questioning which N might sometimes qualify by a shake or nod of his head, but to which he more often made no response.

N had worked in one of the camps. He had joined the party under protest, sickened by the regime's brutality. In 1945 he had been taken by the Russians and had laboured for years in a camp. He had concluded that Stalin's regime was at least as bad as Hitler's. He had been befriended by another inmate of the camp, a German who seemed to have influence. When this man had obtained his own discharge, he had negotiated for N's release. N's eyes had shone with manic intensity and his head nodded up and down while Septimus elicited this. In Jellalabad his mentor and he had been attacked by tribesmen. His friend had died, and some wandering gypsies had taken pity on him. He had joined them in their ragged caravanserai. When he fell ill across the border in Iskanderabad, they had moved on, leaving him in the lobby of Iskanderabad Hospital.

Because he was plainly European, the harassed duty doctor had called in Dr Chatterjee. Dr Chatterjee had treated his dysentery with a course of M & B, persuaded Amyas to let him stay in a godown on the estate and arranged for him to work with Septimus. 'There is nothing wrong with his mind, you understand,' Chat had said to Septimus. 'It is just that he has taken flight from the things he has seen. It is easier for him to remain silent.'

Over the succeeding months Septimus had grown used to his silent companion. They had made the godown habitable: there were two charpoys, blankets from the monastery, an improvised range in the clearing in front where they cooked their simple meals. Septimus had found a sense of purpose which he had never felt in the monastery: in caring for N, in the reconstruction of the shattered building. Since Father Gregorio's death he had thought little of the monastery. He only saw the future day by day, defined by the slow progress of the tower, by the ache of his limbs, by the pleasant, companionable silence of the evenings. He sighed and began to fill the hod with bricks. The rope chafed his shoulder despite the pad of folded material under it. On the platform he set out the bricks neatly, setting them athwart each other four by four for stability. He was now high enough to see the car wind slowly up the road towards Dora Wheeler's house. It stopped by the gate and the driver got out. A moment later Dora, dressed in black, came through the gate and the driver climbed in and drove away. She would be going to Iskanderabad prison to see Charles.

Septimus climbed slowly down the ladder and filled a bucket of water from the tap. As he bent to pick up the water, he was overcome by a feeling of dislocation, as if for a moment he doubted the reality of his surroundings. The surface of the water shimmered with wrinkles, like wizened skin, and he suddenly felt unsteady, as though he might fall. A dog howled in the distance. The sensation lasted only a few moments. Looking down at the ground under his feet again, everything seemed normal. He grasped the handle and took the bucket slowly up the ladder, step by step.

When he had laid the first course of bricks, tamping them to the line of the string, he placed the level on them, kneeling to make sure the air bubble was located between the inner markers. The bubble sat motionless as he slid the level along the course to sit on the last five bricks. He felt, briefly, a small sense of satisfaction. Then, as he watched, the bubble began to distort, to break up into little bubbles. Under his hand the wall felt alive, moving, and there seemed to be a distant vibration as though some great tuning fork had begun to vibrate under the very surface of the earth. The planks beneath his feet started to buckle and, thrown back against the scaffolding, he saw the wall bulge like a monstrous balloon, and begin to spit wodges of mortar from between the bricks.

Halfway down the trembling ladder his sleeve caught the end of a scaffold pole. Panic-stricken, he tore at it, while the loosened bricks from the wall thudded down on the platform of boards level with his head. His stomach lurched as the ladder gave under him. His foot, jarring against the ground, buckled.

When he regained consciousness lying on the ground, he was aware of a silence more intense than anything he had ever experienced. There was no birdsong, the cicadas had ceased their monotonous shrilling and even the bees were mute. Above him the sun hung, white in a livid sky. His right leg was trapped under one of the scaffolding boards which was piled with fallen masonry. He felt acute surprise to see the tower reduced to some twenty courses of bricks, the foundations zigzagged with great fractures. He felt unreal, detached. Making a tremendous effort, he managed to free his leg. His trousers had been split and blood seeped into the material. He winced, holding a scaffolding crosspiece to pull himself to his feet, and stood for a moment, swaying dizzily. With no conscious plan, he began to limp down the path towards Amyas Lawrence's estate. The ground was fissured and cracked. As he reached the forest edge, he could see some of the tallest pines, uprooted by the earthquake, leaning at an angle supported by their sturdier neighbours. He was suddenly aware of a sound, as of distant shouting. The world has not come to an end, then, he thought, limping, numb with pain, slowly through the trees.

The house stood white against the dark trees. Without immediate curiosity Septimus noted a group of people on the lawn. They appeared to be playing some game, four of them standing in a ring around a figure in white who ran this way and that, with hands covering its head, trying to break through and being rebuffed. A man stood apart from them in the attitude of a spectator, watching, one arm wrapped round his waist, the other hand supporting his chin. As he neared the group, Septimus saw that it was Inspector Malik. He tried to shout, but his voice failed him. He stumbled forward, his legs barely carrying him.

The man in the centre of the group was N. Blood ran down his head and on to his soiled shirt. As he moved, his mouth was open in a soundless scream. One of the four men surrounding him was Gobind Dass, and the others were his workers. They carried lathis, and hit N in turn with a strange, impersonal fury as he staggered from side to side.

They ignored Septimus until he was upon them. Septimus pushed two of the men aside and held out his hands. N threw himself down in front of Septimus, clasping him round the legs. The pain in his injured leg was excruciating and Septimus had to summon his will to overcome his faintness. 'What are you doing? Don't you know he cannot even speak?' He addressed himself to Dass, but the other man only said, 'You do not understand.' The men stood around clutching their lathis, insolent, confident. Then Septimus called over their heads to Malik, who still stood like a contemplative, observing the proceedings. 'Inspector Malik. Please stop this. What are these men doing?' But Malik only smiled a weary smile and said, 'It is beyond my competence. You do not understand.'

Septimus took a deep breath. Carefully he loosened N's grasp on his legs. He bent down and said, 'Come with me. You'll be quite safe.' Gripping N's hand in his own, he pulled the other man to his feet and, still holding his hand as though he were a child, began to walk towards the house, conscious of the men behind watching them silently.

It took a minute for Mary Lawrence to answer the bell. She seemed breathless, a little distracted, putting her hand to her open mouth when she saw them. In the near darkness behind her a man walked swiftly across the hall and disappeared through a door at the end. It was Thomas Henne.

By the time the ambulance had picked up Dr Chatterjee and arrived at the house, Septimus was barely conscious. He was dimly aware of voices, of being helped on to a stretcher. That was the last he remembered.

Three days later he woke in Iskanderabad Hospital. His leg, encased in bandages and suspended from a pulley, throbbed. The ward was full of visitors, some of them eyeing him curiously. His mouth felt dry. It took him some time to realize where he was and to work out what must have happened. He lay still, remembering the earthquake, the tableau on the lawn. He craned his head to look down the ward, but could see no sign of N.

The visitors left. The evening light through the windows shaded to grey-gold. He slept. When he woke again, Dr Chatterjee was standing at the bottom of his bed reading his notes with a nurse in attendance. As Septimus opened his eyes, he said, 'You were lucky, my friend. You lost a great deal of blood. A few days of rest and you'll be as good as new.'

'Where is N?'

Dr Chatterjee's face betrayed no emotion. He said nothing for a moment, looking at Septimus as if to ascertain whether or not he was strong enough to hear the news. When he spoke, Septimus felt surprise, suddenly recalling the sense that both Gobind Dass and Malik had given him of being excluded from some secret. 'He stayed here for one night. He was mainly bruised and shocked. In the morning he had gone. The police have not been able to find him. That is all I know.'

*

Poonomal had gone away for a few days. Mother was very

vague. 'She's an old lady now. She's gone to live with her daughter. We may see her sometime ...' She didn't look at me, but out of the window.

Akbar came to cut my hair. He was unshaven, as always, and the slight scent of patchouli seemed a mask for ranker smells. The metallic snicker of the scissors echoed in my ears and I closed my eyes, feeling the hair slip down over my face. 'Your poor ayah,' he said, his voice full of assumed concern, and I felt that I had known what had happened, even before he responded to my query.

Poonomal's husband had recently given up working for us as a mali and had resumed his old work as a durzi in Ooper Iskanderabad and, once a week, she made the journey home to stay at the house. Some months past her husband had brought a young woman to the house and had announced he was making her his second wife. Poonomal had apparently taken this with equanimity: men were children, and they did such things to convince themselves that their powers were not fading. But he had begun to drink, to stay out late at nautch houses, to spend money they could ill afford on presents for the young woman. When Poonomal had tried to talk to him about these things, he had shouted at her, following her on to the Mall and saying that she was ugly, a barren woman, that she had never given him a moment's happiness. 'Poor woman,' Akbar said, his vulpine face alive with the pleasure of retailing gossip. 'Everybody could hear what was happening. She is at her daughter's house. She will not come out in case people see her.' His story told, Akbar was instantly his furtive, secretive self again. I must not tell anyone else. We were friends, weren't we? I would keep his secret.

That night I was frightened. It was very dark and the dim outline of my dressing-gown against the wall seemed to move, as though it had come to life. I lay still. I thought I heard breathing, as though there were something in the room with me. The house settled with small creaks and noises. Everything was changing. In the afternoon I had seen Mrs Weaver walking in the wood with her husband. She was crying, holding both hands over her face. Her hair wasn't combed, and one of her stockings had begun to roll down her thin leg. She was saying, 'How can we stay here after this? Everyone knows . . .' When I passed, Mr Weaver had his arm round her shoulder. He smiled at me, but it wasn't a real smile. His face looked serious, as if something terrible had happened.

Maybe the disaster was the earthquake. It had occurred only the day before Poonomal had left. She had shouted at me and Angela to get under the table. We knelt there, huddled, all three of us together. I could hear the house making sounds as if it were breaking. When we got up, there was a big crack across the wall. Angela asked Poonomal if the house was going to fall down, and Poonomal said, 'Don't be silly. Of course not.' But now I could tell when grown-ups weren't telling the truth. She didn't know. I heard Father telling Mother about Kala Pani. Fifty people had died and almost all the houses had fallen down. The Nawab is paying fifty thousand rupees to get workmen in from Iskanderabad to rebuild the houses. Mother is taking pills from Dr Chatterjee to help her to sleep.

I saw Mrs Wheeler. I had tea with her but it wasn't like it used to be. She was in black. I suddenly realized that she was very old. She looked at me with her cup almost at her lips and said, 'It wasn't Charles, you know. Justice will prevail in the end. These are terrible times.'

When my fear had become too much to bear alone, I swung my legs over the side of the bed. I had to tell myself not to be silly. There was nothing under the bed to catch me by the legs and drag me away to eat me. The loose floorboard on the landing creaked when I trod on it and I stood still for a moment, but the house was silent.

Angela's door was not quite shut. There was a noise as if somebody was breathing heavily, and I thought I heard her voice say quietly, 'Please don't.' I put my eye to the crack of the door but I could see nothing.

After breakfast Angela was going to the shops in Iskanderabad to buy some shoes. 'Why don't you go with your sister? It'll keep you out of mischief,' Mother said. On the forest path there were deep fissures from the earthquake. A tree had fallen across the path. Climbing over it, I could see a bird's nest below the branches. The broken eggs were light green, speck-led. Angela came to see, putting her hand on my shoulder to support herself. It was hard to keep my voice steady. 'I was frightened in the night. I came to your room, but there was something there.' Her eyes were bright with tears. She looked away, so that her brown hair hid her face. 'You mustn't come again,' she said. 'I can't tell you why. But you mustn't come again.'

Chapter Nineteen

Thomas and Julia lived in Scarsdale Villas. Julia had been born into one of the landowning families of gentlemen farmers who had entertained lavishly and ridden to hounds and left their estate managers to run the tenant farms and to decide upon the best way to provide a sufficient income from the land to upkeep the splendid Lutyens house, which, with death duties and increasing taxation, had fallen into progressively greater disrepair over thirty years until Julia, weary of the drain on her inheritance, had sold the house to be turned into a complex of flats just after the start of the property boom in the mid 1970s.

In the old days, when Thomas was still in office, they had a flat in Marsham Street and what Thomas used to call 'our little estate' in Buckinghamshire, bought with some of the proceeds from the sale of the big house. He still qualified for protection – Bartlett, a shadowy unsmiling young man with hooded eyes and dirty fingernails who answered the door. The house itself, decorated with conservative good taste, was littered with self-conscious memorabilia. Thomas with Dag Hammarskjöld on the sideboard, in shirtsleeves with General Ojukwu under an African sun, with the PM at a Mansion House dinner in pride of place in the centre of the mantelshelf under the June Mendoza portrait of him sitting in three-quarter face in his office.

I wasn't quite sure what to expect. Cocktails from six to eight-thirty had long since disappeared from my social calendar. I had only spoken to Thomas on the phone once or twice since the lunch when he had told me about the book. I had left the invitation on the hall table for two days, uncertain about whether or not to go, and finally decided I had nothing to lose but a couple of hours of my time. A hired waiter helped me off with my coat and I braced myself to go into the sitting-room, which echoed with the sounds of laughter and conversation.

In my youth it had been Thomas who had identified most clearly for me the High Tory ethic which had prevailed in our community in Iskanderabad and had effortlessly embraced us in our new home in England. It was he who had unwittingly alienated me from it, barely hiding, under his pink and white pretence of concern, his lack of interest in old acquaintances who, now past their usefulness, assumed on their part a friendship which no longer existed on his. There was a decency in him, but it was overlaid by the years of political envy, by his resentment at seeing himself passed over for preferment by less able men. For Thomas had never grasped one of the fundamentals of patronage of any kind: that the skilled conferred advantage only upon those who could never challenge them in turn. In some ways he had never rid himself of those schoolboy attitudes of thought which had been briefly fostered during the administrations of Wilson and Heath – the assumption of the deserved recognition of excellence. The decency showed itself in other ways, in his evident concern for Julia, in his open-handed generosity to causes which helped the poor, the halt, the infirm. I wondered why I had been invited.

He greeted me warmly enough, it seemed, smiling as he pumped my hand in his moist grasp. 'Good to see you again. You're looking well. Come and have a word with Julia.' Beyond the august white-haired figure of Lord Wheatcroft talking to a prominent industrialist I saw her, seated on the sofa. Despite being prepared for change, it was a shock. Her skin had a grey translucence, and her eyes looked drugged, but she rose to greet me with spirit, kissing me on the cheek. Her hand briefly on mine felt insubstantial.

With the noise of the party round us we were as private as if we were alone. Julia had never had any facility for small talk, and, listening to her, it seemed that the passage of her illness had shorn away the last vestiges of social pretence. She was frightened, she said. Not for herself. She'd come to terms with what was happening to her. After all, the process of dying was natural, and the fact that it would come to her earlier rather than later was simply a question of luck. It was Thomas who worried her. She'd felt for the past year that he was in the grip of some obsession which was unhealthy. It was difficult to put her finger on it. She nodded her head towards the corner of the room and I saw Gobind Dass talking to a group of men. 'He is seeing some strange people. He doesn't tell me anything, but every now and then I catch him smiling, as though he is hugging something to himself. It makes me uneasy. I think it is this book he is writing . . .'

I asked if she had ever spoken to Thomas of her concern, but she said, with a touch of asperity, 'I know the fashion these days is for absolute honesty and talking things through. Those things didn't apply in my generation. Men did their things together and women — well, we had our own separate preoccupations too. I have tried to talk to him, but it is impossible to break the habits of a lifetime.'

'Do you think there's anything I can do?'

She put down her glass and sat back, folding her hands in her lap. After a moment she said, 'Quite apart from the hurt he will do others, he may discover things which he has not anticipated. I don't think the possibility has occurred to him . . .'

'Are there such things?'

She looked away, as though to distance herself. 'You should know better than most the answer to that question. I suspect there are in anybody's life, if you look hard enough.'

She smiled her brittle, brilliant smile and put her face up to be kissed by a young man whose appearance seemed familiar. I half rose, taking his hand, and smiled vaguely as I missed his name completely. His duty finished, he straightened up and walked over to a faded blonde on the other side of the room.

'Who was that?'

Julia made a dismissive gesture with her hand. 'Can't remember his name. He's helping Thomas with some research.' After a moment she said heavily, 'I can't really see what anyone can do, more's the pity.'

I could see Gobind Dass trying to place me as I left the room with Thomas's arm round my shoulder. 'We mustn't let it go for so long again, eh? We'll have another lunch soon.' The waiter went to get my coat and Thomas, leaning towards me so that no one else could hear, said, 'You were Miriam's psychoanalyst, weren't you?' I glimpsed something unpleasant – anger, perhaps – behind the smile. Incongruously I felt some sense of being menaced. I said, 'I'm afraid I never discuss my patients with anyone.'

'Of course. Of course.' His hand crushed mine. 'Not too long, then.'

I ran through the rain to my car.

*

Things changed. Angela had moved away from me in some incomprehensible way. She was often quiet, spending a lot of time in her room. 'It's her age,' Mother said. 'Such a pity there aren't other boys of your own age for you to play with.' I didn't want other boys: I wanted Angela, as she used to be. She watched people now, covertly, but with such intensity that it felt as if she were trying to penetrate beyond what they were saying, beyond their everydayness, to some idea of what they were really like inside themselves. She told me that Julia Henne was pregnant after we had briefly seen the Hennes in church. It was weeks later that Mother said to Father at breakfast time, 'I think Julia's pregnant.' 'How did you know?' I asked Angela, but she only picked up her book and left the room.

She came with me to the tower where Septimus worked alone, in silence. He acknowledged our presence with a brief nod, carefully chipping away at the line of mortar below the top layer of bricks. We lay on our stomachs on the hot friable earth. The soil still radiated jagged cracks from the earthquake. Septimus was unshaven, his arms muscular and heavily veined. I could feel some adult sense of sadness behind his swift, precise work. The bricks he had saved, expertly dismembered of their old mortar with the edge of a trowel, were neatly stacked on one side. The broken bricks had been tossed into the ditch for use as hardcore later. In church on Sunday Father Carey had turned in the pulpit at the end of his sermon on the godly life to point to Septimus – 'working for the Glory of God – if God permits it'. Perhaps it was this I felt, this burden of obligation which had seized him and would not let him go. I could only see that the tower was again at waist height, as though all the work that Septimus and N had done was gone for nothing.

The committee had decided that Septimus should resume work if he so wished. Against Father's recommendations they had debated finding a new supplier of building materials, though without pressing the matter to a conclusion. Two days later Gobind Dass had appeared at the house with a face like thunder and was closeted with Father for an hour in his study. Leaving, he had said, 'I have done my part, now you must do yours.'

We were joining my parents for tea with George and Claire Gunter. Angela walked ahead of me up the rutted path past the clearing full of gentians, open, bell-like, to the sun. Last year Father had chased a man through these woods after returning unexpectedly to discover him in the house. He was a *badmash*, Father had said, striking his fist into his palm to emphasize the moral authority of the words. A *badmash*! Angela had already entered the grey-green gloom under the trees. Remembering the stories she had told me about Gagool, the witch of the wood, I ran after her as fast as I could. 'Wait for me. Please.' She stopped and looked at me with a strange expression of satisfaction. Through the trees I could see Inspector Malik's empty jeep far below on the road. Above, by the first clearing, the Inspector climbed slowly up the hill with Dr Chatterjee. Two constables walked behind them.

George Gunter's cottage sat on the brow of a hill, its sloping lawns spreading down in four quarters to the surrounding wood through which we came into the bright sunlight again. While Dora Wheeler schooled me without condescension in her insights into the adult world, George and Claire Gunter seemed like fairies come to life.

At ninety-three, George had recently taken to confiding his preoccupations with Man and Nature as aspects of the Cosmic Sea of Electricity, the endless dance of quarks around each other whose motions alone sustained the spinning world and all the multiplicity of nature. His conversation, keeping track with his mind, had long since left other adults behind, of whom only his wife, Claire, could still understand him. He was small, benign, shrunken clawed, his skin withered with age and his face wearing the permanent, distant smile of a benevolent visionary. Claire was majestic, a Cumaean sibyl towering over her little husband. Their kindnesses were legendary. Sita, their house servant, was blind and crippled with arthritis, and her ministrations about the house had become cursory rituals without evident effect. They had an old dog with three legs, and a near bald parakeet which flew in one morning through the skylight window as though knowing that it had found sanctuary. The very house itself had the air of an elderly relative being nursed through the terminal stages of decline with such love and devoted care as were within the gift of its elderly occupants.

'You mean he stayed here? The night after he discharged himself from hospital?' Creeping quietly into the room, I could see that Father's face was red with anger.

'Of course,' Claire said, matter-of-factly. 'He was in no condition to travel.'

'Where did he go?'

'Been camping,' George said vaguely, fiddling with the arm of his chair.

Angela and I were barely listening to the exchanges. James Crale, the aged, notorious, black sheep of a titled family, had come down from his summer lodge in the mountains. I had met him once, very drunk, at a christening years before, aware immediately with the sharpened instincts of childhood of the disapproval which followed in his wake. Now he lounged upon the sofa with the lady we had heard our parents discussing at length — Pearl, black as night, smiling with white teeth serried behind soft pink lips and holding, yes, holding his hand. Father Carey was here too, examining Claire's collection of Venetian glass, nodding as she pointed out some treasure here or there. James Crale was dribbling from one corner of his loose mouth, the legacy of a mild stroke two years before, and his dentures clicked as he talked.

'But where did he come from originally, this chap? From what I hear you might have been harbouring a murderer.'

'Camping,' George said again.

'For Christ's sake, Claire. Translation please?' Pearl patted Mr Crale on the arm and said in a warm, slow voice, 'Honey. You know what Dr Chatterjee says. You gotta take things ea-sy.'

Claire said, 'He was in a concentration camp. In Germany.'

Conversation moved to Charles Wheeler. He had still not been charged with anything, and Inspector Malik, with unfailing courtesy, sent a car daily to pick Dora up and take her to the prison to see him. Watching Father, I could see that he often looked at Pearl from the corner of his eyes. From where I sat I could see that the hem of her skirt had ridden up her thighs so that the tops of her stockings were clearly visible. With the stubborn persistence of age, James Crale had returned to querulously questioning N's provenances. Something wasn't right in a man of his age just arriving, dumb, seemingly without full possession of his faculties or any history, to expect the indulgences of work, food, a place to live. 'It just ain't right. Not safe.' He kept expostulating while Pearl tried to restrain him and George smiled vacantly, his mind elsewhere: as though there were nothing wrong, for God's sake, in him, James Crale, at eighty-three, sitting sassy as you please taking tea in the presence of a man of God in a decent household in the midst of a prim Puritan colonial community with his coal-black, ex-danseuse mistress culled straight from a Las Vegas bordello holding his hand.

It was Father Carey, holding a Venetian goblet (attributed to the School of Benvenuto Cellini), who leaned over behind James with a faintly superior smile upon his equine features to say, 'We are not here to sit in judgement upon the frailties and imperfections of the poor man, Mr Crale. Whatever he may have done, he is one of God's creatures, after all.'

There was a loud knock on the door and I could hear Sita shuffling down the hall. A few moments later she came in and whispered something in Claire's ear, and they both left the room. The conversation in the room flagged. When Dr Chatterjee came in, it was Father who asked what had happened. Dr Chat looked straight towards Angela and me, pausing before he spoke. It was Mrs Weaver, he said. Her husband had reported her missing the previous night. Early that morning a woodcutter had come across her lying in a ditch in the forest. It was too early to say whether she had died of exposure or some other cause. 'Perhaps she could not cope with people's suspicions,' Dr Chatterjee said, glancing around the room. Nobody looked him in the face.

'Off home, the pair of you,' Mother said briskly.

Angela ran and I followed, plunging from the amber late light in the clearing into the grey-green shadows of the wood. I was afraid. Everything was changing, as though there were no stability in life any more. In the clearing Angela threw herself down on the needled floor, covering her face with her hands. I lay beside her on my stomach, the needles warm against my legs. 'Black as the Ace of Spades,' Angela said, mimicking Father's voice. Her body heaved in little spasms as though she were laughing. Glad for some respite, I said, 'Do you think he does it with her?' only dimly aware of what the question meant, hoping to extend this unexpected return to intimacy.

Angela lay on her back, suddenly still. I could see her eyes behind her laced fingers, looking up at the warp and weft of needles and branches above our heads, behind which the lacy clouds glowed an incandescent salmon in the evening sunlight. Something in her face grew hard, the muscles working in her jaws, and her full lips tightened. She seemed older, no longer a child even in part, and the remoteness of the gaze she turned to me made me suddenly afraid of the return of the darkness.

'Men do *that* with everybody,' she said.

Chapter Twenty

I suspect that as time passes we rediscover the pleasures of summary judgements and instant solutions. There just is not enough time to indulge the best liberal instincts and argue that there may not be complete solutions, that causes and effects are often too complex for comprehension. Most of us fall prey to summary judgements when time grows short, and death paces ever closer to our family and friends and then ourselves. I judge now, where before I sought to understand, because judgements seem more appropriate in certain circumstances. They are the means by which I disengage from one situation to engage with the next.

However, matters were dealt with in those days so that the English might order things with impunity. The prevalent attitude was that Eleanor had overreacted to the possibility that she might be prosecuted for theft. 'Course it wouldn't have happened. We'd have sorted it out with Baksh.' Colonel Whitworth spoke for the community. There was an enormous unconscious synchronicity in the way people took these matters, as though they were aware that it was only by such communality that they could survive in this hostile land. There was never any question of self-censure, or guilt, nor any thought of questioning the assumption of rightness of those who were long since established as leaders of the community. Instead a moral indignation was the tenor of reaction, an exasperation at the wilful stupidity of someone who had not fully understood or accepted the rules of engagement. Why hadn't she allowed the community to take care of things? There may have been some mild, temporary opprobrium, but people would have put it down to her age, the change of life, an acceptable eccentricity. She would have become a story, to be embroidered and made myth and retailed with enthusiasm to the visitors passing through over the years.

Of course she and Terence would have had to expect an alteration to their standing in the community, but surely that was better than killing yourself? For there was no doubt on anyone's part that that was what had happened, despite the official verdict. Dr Chatterjee being unwilling, one of the junior locums at Iskanderabad General signed the death certificate giving cause of death as pneumonia brought on by exposure.

Terence's habit of breaking down in company and talking about Eleanor to anyone who would listen was tolerated for a few weeks: then he was simply ignored, as though he did not exist. It was stoutly maintained (too stoutly, perhaps, for bigots are not necessarily fools) that Thomas was not to blame: hadn't he shown an admirable even-handedness in questioning a member of the European community when the customary assumption would have been that it must be one of the servants? Julia, now visibly pregnant, no longer rode with Father, but they would go for long walks together. Sometimes she and Thomas came to dinner with the Whitworths, or Father Carey, or some temporary visitor from England in transit to Taxila or Mohenjodaro or one of the ancient sites on either side of the border.

The self-deception continued even after Father Carey's arrest had cast a fresh light upon events.

A parishioner returning from evening service one Sunday had surprised a masked intruder inside his house who had managed to get away in the ensuing struggle and run to the back of the house where a car was waiting. The servants, alerted by the noise, raced from their neighbouring quarters, and the driver, muffled in a cape with a handkerchief across the lower face, had stalled the engine and apparently fainted.

One of the servants was sent to call the police and, faced with the inevitable, the two had unmasked themselves to disclose Father Carey and his housekeeper, Milly Milchrist.

Inspector Malik had interviewed them intensively for two

days. On the second afternoon Father Carey had collapsed, complaining of chest pains, but Dr Chatterjee had been unable to discover any irregularities in his health beyond a justifiable fear of the consequences of his escapades. Eventually he had agreed to take the police to a store house he rented in Niche Iskanderabad, which was full of stolen church silver, glass, china, jewellery and other items. Milly, it seemed, had carried out some of the burglaries on her own at the direction of Father Carey. It had been Thomas's suggestion that the incident be played down: it wouldn't, for example, be a good idea if David Weaver were to hear of this. Nor should one bad priest taint the reputation of the Church.

The Bishop was requested to intercede and, at first angry at this unorthodox breach of his ordered regime, was mollified by the lavish hospitality organized by Colonel Whitworth. Finally, after separate lengthy conversations with Father Carey and Milly Milchrist in camera, she was dispatched to live in an old people's home in the south, and Father Carey, generally perceived to be the guilty party who had led poor addled Milly astray, agreed to serve in a lay capacity in an impoverished mission in the Andaman Islands. It was felt that the Bishop had exercised a rare balance between compassion and divine justice. People were quietly contacted to identify their property and retrieve it, and the waters of everyday life closed over the matter as if it had never happened.

Thomas, apparently, according to Dora Wheeler's uncompromising version, was distressed at first, but comforted himself when people agreed that he had been quite right to suspect Eleanor on the evidence: after all, who in their right minds could have suspected such a bizarre scenario? Only I, Dora had said acidly, pointing out to him that death was the one mistake you couldn't put right. But the community's memory of Theodore was fading, and there were many who, unable otherwise to deal with Dora's directness, convinced themselves that Dora had become a little eccentric, deranged by fear of what might happen to her beloved Charles, now indicted for the murder of Grace Chaudhury.

It was about this time that I came to grasp certain things. It was a process which had begun the day when I had sat in Dora's garden and listened to her and Dr Chatterjee talking. The events in question had puzzled me for a long time, but I was not mature enough to understand their import. Further, because discussing them or even hinting at them would suggest disloyalty, I felt unable to say anything, even to Angela.

I knew that my father and Julia Henne were conducting some covert liaison: I knew also that my mother was doing something similar with Thomas. I hadn't comprehended Dora Wheeler's words at the party where Otto disgraced himself, but they had remained with me and now fell into place with sudden logic. What still eluded me was the substance behind these liaisons.

The comfort I had always derived from Dora Wheeler's company intensified and I believe, in her own fashion, she took something from me which no one else could give her then. Sometimes Dr Chatterjee would join us, and I was flattered to listen to them talk of Theodore and the old times as though I were a third silent adult in their company. Once or twice we walked slowly (for Dora had grown increasingly arthritic) to watch Septimus silently engaged upon his lone task of rebuilding the tower. The Nawab, in addition to his generosity in paying for the rebuilding of his wife's village, had made a donation towards the rebuilding work. Often Dora would sit, shielded under her pink parasol which endowed her with a country glow, while I weeded the garden beds to her direction, and listened to her speculations which, rambling and all embracing, wound always ever closer to the subject of Charles, awaiting his trial in solitary confinement.

Old James Crale's eldest son, recently admitted as a lawyer, had agreed to represent him. 'There is very little chance,' he told her candidly, smoothing the black lock of hair from his forehead with an impatient gesture. 'We will do what we can.' Again, it was from Dora that I learned of something else, and recollected her words at the picnic: the day that nagged at my memory because of the death of the kid.

One day, climbing the hill, I saw Mr Latif, immaculate as ever in a grey pinstripe suit, white gloves, carrying his malacca cane, talking to Dora over the hedge. Dora was one of the few people whose friendship had never wavered: she would speak to him without embarrassment about his son. A listener sat upon her lawn, I had seen the tears spill over the bruised bilberry pouches below his eyes, but she had only looked at him and said, 'One should not forget, Anwar. One learns to live with the pain of loss only by remembering. If you try to pretend they never existed, you are lost. All that wasted energy used to persuade yourself of a lie . . .' He greeted me with his formal, unsmiling gravity.

That morning Dora was preoccupied. Once or twice, looking up from my task of weeding the flower-beds, I caught her mouth moving as she gazed over the hazy valley. She seemed to have grown suddenly old, her hands papery and veined, trembling as they adjusted her lace collar against the wind. It was as though, briefly deserted by her customary forthrightness, the animation had gone from her face, and the old adversaries of time and decrepitude had temporarily won their siege against her. In two days I would be back at school and would see her only at weekends. I wished I might help her, but her remoteness discouraged intimacy. Then, during that period, I could not even talk to Angela and learn the new insights she seemed to possess. Since Eleanor's death, she had retreated into a private world, absorbed with her own thoughts. Even Father had said irritably, 'What's the matter with Angela these days? I can't get a word out of her half the time . . .'

Finally, Dora had begun. It would break Charles's heart, she said, using the device which had become her means of communication lately, where she did not so much hold a conversation or tell a story as allow her listener to eavesdrop upon her private thoughts: so that, depending upon which insight finally prompted her to muse aloud, one might be at any point in a narrative. The correct procedure was never to ask questions. They would either cause her to turn her blue eyes upon one in sudden, apparent realization that she did not, after all, consider it suitable to continue in the confessional mode or else to begin an exchange which moved away from the subject under discussion.

132

Charles, apparently, had met Vivienne James when he was twenty and she fifteen, and had fallen instantly, passionately in love. 'She was a lily that festered. No good to him,' Dora said. She had tried to dissuade Charles, but he would not be convinced. Faced with Vivienne's complete indifference, his passion had grown fiercer, until, Dora said, he thought about nothing else. She was sure that all Charles's waywardness stemmed from this unrequited passion which, all consuming, would not allow him to settle to anything else. If Vivienne had responded or, better still, Charles had found a different object for his affection, he would have grown into a decent, hard-working man like his father.

Three days before, Neville had collapsed with a heart attack while playing tennis. Vivienne had demanded he be given a private room, and had sat by the side of the bed, snatching a few hours' sleep on a charpoy Dr Chatterjee had permitted the staff to install for her. As so often happens, Neville rallied strongly, and Vivienne, white faced and exhausted but buoyed up by hope, began to question Dr Chatterjee about the regime they must pursue when he was discharged. Then, quite suddenly, he had lapsed into unconsciousness again, and he was moved to intensive care. Vivienne waited outside in the passageway, attended by a young nurse. When Dr Chatterjee came out to tell her as gently as possible that her father had died, she had looked up at him and said, 'What will happen to me now?' She had become a child again, at a stroke. 'It is the death or defection of fathers which is hardest to bear,' Dora said, and I felt, once more, the echoes of a great uncertainty reverberate in some future which was hidden as yet.

The nuns took Vivienne James into the convent, enfolding her in the serene anonymity behind their gates. My parents spoke of it, that much I could hear by listening carefully by the open door of the bedroom at night, though I could only catch a few words here and there. They never talked about it in front of us. Some instinct prompted me against talking to Angela. In the old days, before her defection, she would have found some way of making me laugh, so that I would have exorcized the picture of Vivienne seated in a shuttered room like the Lady of Shalott, half mad and careless of her beauty. But I could not talk of it.

Chapter Twenty-one

Septimus found the Iskanderabad Club with difficulty. When Gobind Dass had issued the invitation, saying airily, 'In the Strand, you know,' Septimus had imagined a lofty Victorian building distinctive enough to be well known to local traders. The paper seller by Charing Cross station had brusquely professed complete ignorance, as had two passers-by, and he was searching for a telephone booth in the rain, which had suddenly begun in earnest, when a red neon sign on the first floor of a small, dingy terrace block huddled between two larger neighbours caught his eye, proclaiming itself to be HE I KANDER AD CL B.

An old bicycle was propped against the yellow emulsioned wall in the downstairs hall. The *tintawn* carpet laid in a strip over the black and white diamond tiles in the foyer had long since lost its nap. In a cubby-hole at the end of the hall an elderly grey-haired Indian sat reading a copy of the *Evening Standard*, looking up over his spectacles at Septimus without curiosity. He jerked his chin soundlessly towards the stairs in response to Septimus's question and lowered his eyes to his paper again.

The patterned flock wallpaper seemed to exude a smell of hot ghee and curry paste. On the walls sepia photographs of Mountbatten meeting Jinnah, Edwina Mountbatten walking through a crowd with a smiling Pandit Nehru, were fogged with damp and curled at the edges. There was a door marked REST R NT and Septimus pushed it open. It was like a café in a hill station: metal-legged chairs with bentply seats set around deal tables with chipped white melamine tops. A middle-aged man in a prayer cap sat at a table in the corner with a Hindi

135

newspaper propped in front of him, slowly eating roti and curry with his right hand. A dolorous female voice intoned sad lyrics of doomed love. Flies buzzed against the dusty windows.

'Mr Septimus, I presume?'

Turning, Septimus was surprised to see two almost identical plump, small, grey-haired, extremely black Indian gentlemen dressed in greying white *shalwar kameez* with Kashmiri slippers on their feet. The speaker, showing a liberal vista of gold fillings in his white smile, said, 'I am Sam and this is my brother Joseph. Mr Dass — *werry important man* — has told us to look after you until he arrives. He is *unavoidably* detained at a meeting . . .' He waved his hand vaguely in the direction of the City. He led the way to a table by the window, removing a cloth draped over his arm to give a theatrical flick to the surface before drawing back a chair for Septimus to sit down.

There was no menu. '*Whatever* you want, Mr Septimus. Nothing is too much trouble for a friend of Mr Dass.' Which, being translated, meant that Sam, by dint of many 'We have something similar's and 'Leave that with me — you will not be disappointed's while his brother Joseph stood with a stub of pencil poised over a scrap of paper, managed, Septimus was convinced, to persuade him to eat the one meal on offer. But it was conducted with such a good-natured charade of smiles, of nods, winks, gestures, touches on the shoulder, gazes into the distance, that Septimus was almost charmed into forgetting his irritation at what he was sure would be a considerable delay. 'We have today and tomorrow — the Indian has Eternity,' Dora Wheeler used to remark drily.

The food was excellent. Sam, standing behind his left shoulder, directed Joseph when to bring in the courses, and from time to time discreetly pushed a plate which had received less attention than the others nearer to Septimus. They were from the old school, Sam informed him, refusing a seat gravely as Septimus drank his coffee. After the Raj had gone, everything had changed. When Mr Dass had asked them if they wanted to run a restaurant in London, they had agreed immediately. It

136

had not been quite what they expected, he said, and for the first time the seemingly permanent smile had left his face for an instant, but, when all was said, they had a very good life here.

Downstairs the door opened and there was the sound of footsteps in the hall followed by a man's voice shouting and then, presumably, the sound of the clerk's quiet voice in response. It was startling to see the change in Sam and Joseph. They seemed to shrink like blow-up versions of Tweedledum and Tweedledee suddenly punctured with a sharp instrument. With an 'Excuse me', Sam almost ran to the door to open it. When Dass came through, both brothers bowed low, as though paying court to some Eastern potentate. 'I'm sorry to be late. Business, you know . . .' Dass put his briefcase by the side of his chair and clutched Septimus's hand in a cold, leathery grip. It was as though forty years had rolled back in a moment. The hair was grey, the dark eyes slightly cloudy from incipient cataracts, but the thin lizard lips over which his tongue sporadically flicked, the habit of looking with piercing intentness for a few seconds before looking away, were just the same. I'm sure he is remembering exactly this, Septimus thought, recalling the day at the tower, the heat, Gobind Dass sitting under the shade of the tree, N, his mouth a soundless O of terror, running away from them towards the wood while Gobind Dass looked after him speculatively.

Sam and Joseph, obsequious now, shuffled in with lamb *pasanda* and *puris* for Dass and more coffee for Septimus. Through the window Septimus could see the theatre-goers coming out into the fine rain. At first Dass's conversation had a tentative superficial quality, a recital of the names of mutual old acquaintances garnished with patently insincere codas. The India that he knew was not my India, Septimus thought, surprising himself with the possessiveness of his own memories. As Dass spoke, Septimus remembered the Nawab's story of Dass charging the villagers exorbitantly to divert part of a stream which welled from his property to irrigate their crops. 'His own mother, whom he has not seen for ten years, lives in the village. It is as well that I can pay,' the Nawab had said. It was Colonel Whitworth who had observed that Dass only survived because he knew where all the bodies were buried.

Dass missed nothing. When Septimus looked surreptitiously at his watch under the table, Dass said, 'I have a proposition for you,' leaning down to extract a folder from his case. He placed the folder on the table before him and said, 'I have here some photocopies of certain documents. There were many wrongs done all those years ago. Some of those wrongs were against me and, if I recall rightly, you also were not treated well. These documents are part of the history of that time.' He held up his hand, 'Please don't be mistaken. I do not want anything for these. But if Sir Amyas Lawrence knows that the originals are in my possession, who knows? . . . it might make him a better man . . .' He smiled, watching Septimus closely. 'As you will see, I am not motivated by desire for gain, but by a wish for justice.'

It was, Septimus thought later, the moment he had wished would never come. In the oblique, silence-haunted conversations he had had with N when they first met again, he had pieced together many of the things that took place all those years before. He had convinced himself that there was no point in bringing up the past. Justice was never done in a wicked world, and these wrongs were past righting. Father Gregorio had once said, 'Never intervene unless you know that you will improve matters by doing so,' and Septimus, pleased that the precept accorded so well with his own inclinations, had minded his own business well, never, even in his social work, going so far as to offer advice or instruction. 'What do *you* think you should do?' was one of the counters he had developed over the years to block a persistent request for help. For he had noticed that people blamed you if they took your advice and it had adverse consequences, but took any praise for correct decisions for themselves. Irresolution had become a way of life: he hated situations where people asked things of him, for refusal was not natural to him. Dass, mistaking his hesitation for acquiescence, pushed the envelope across the table and the transaction was completed. After all, Septimus reasoned to himself, picking up the envelope, my acceptance of these does not mean I am bound to act upon what Dass wants.

Driving home, he was surprised by satisfaction. David Lawrence had once observed that meekness and humility were not to be taken at face value – often hiding their very opposites, which could be startled into appearing by circumstances. Septimus knew that the buff envelope on the seat beside him held information which conferred power. Perhaps, he thought, pulling out to overtake a slow-moving car, it is this which I have been avoiding. The feeling of being engaged in life and the responsibility that goes with it. He put Di Stefano's Neapolitan songs on the cassette player. No need to make an immediate decision. He could think about things over the weeks ahead.

As so often before, his thoughts returned to the tower. If I had built that, nothing else would matter. It would have been there for all to see long after we are all dust. One could not do that with human beings.

*

One of our ways of dealing with disturbed children too young to possess advanced verbal and conceptual skills is through games. In the development of the child's libido – that is sexual function – superego and object relationship (corresponding to fantasies versus real situations) interact. The anxieties resulting from this interaction can never be completely cured by psychoanalysis and manifest themselves in destructiveness. The best we may do is to support the positive aspects of these interactions in a child's growth, to reallocate the tendencies in a manner more consistent with reality. So, at least, according to one school of thought in our increasingly divergent profession. The dynamic interaction between love, hate and the act of reparation (which, as the child grows, is done unconsciously and not acted out) is integral to the formation of feelings of love in adulthood. Children accept the rules: adults change them when they do not suit. Once they have learned. There are some things I remember which express such matters: when

139

the Indian grew up, learned the hard lesson, separated himself from the *ma-bap*, who were not supremely powerful and completely wise, he began to make decisions based in reality. To learn this, to grow, the child must give up the false safeties of illusion.

The yearly cricket match.

Ironically, it was the Nawab who decided that it must be done properly, to maintain the old tradition. Notwithstanding which, it was rumoured from the outset that he had invited three semi-professionals from the plains to bolster the village team.

Father was co-opted by the committee, chaired by Colonel Whitworth, to put together and train a team. Father's first decision was to ride down the Colonel's protests and enlist him in the team which, protocol demanded, must be composed in so far as possible of European colonials. I was to be twelfth man, standing by in the likely event of injury or some other excuse.

For two weeks nets were compulsory. At four-thirty we convened on the senior school sports ground, the older men wearing yellowing flannels and cricket boots which had a decidedly vintage look. It had been impossible to put together a totally European team. Dr Chatterjee had refused to play, but had agreed to umpire. Gobind Dass had, apparently, demanded to be included and had shown himself to be quite an adept bowler once he was shown that he must not throw the ball. Chairs were brought for the memsahibs, and tea was served under the pines at the edge of the field.

On the second day Father said, 'You'd better get some practice. Just in case.' Presented with reality, my heroic dreams of saving the day were replaced by an acute fear. Padded up, I found I was facing Thomas Henne, who had shown himself to be quite a reasonable pace bowler. While I was buckling on my pads, I had heard Julia, now eight months pregnant, speaking to him in a low voice. 'He's only a child, Thomas. Don't take advantage.' There had been a strange expression on Thomas's face, almost of triumph. 'He has to learn sometime. Never achieve anything if he's pandered to.'

I took up my stance with apprehension. There was something I couldn't understand – some hidden animus – implicit in Thomas's long stare towards me as he turned the ball in his hand, rubbing it on his trouser leg just below the pocket. The moment seemed frozen – Thomas lifting his arm and commencing his run, his face grimacing with effort; the careless sound of birdsong; the click of Colonel Whitworth's bat in the next net as he deadened another ball with his old-fashioned, Victorian stance. Delivering the ball, Thomas's grimace filled the horizon, his lips flattened against his teeth, eyes almost closed with the effort. It felt like some monstrous act of aggression, as though he were expressing some mysterious hatred towards me. Later I was told that I had not moved, and the ball had caught me on the side of the head.

When I woke up, I was lying under the trees. Voices floated over me. '. . . told him he shouldn't,' Julia Henne was saying, and my mother's voice in reply, frosty but polite, 'Just one of those things . . .' The sky seemed to shimmer above me. I felt a cold, dry hand on my forehead. Dr Chatterjee said, 'A day in bed and he will be as new, mark my words.'

I was surprised (and a little fearful) when Father overrode Mother's protestations about my playing. Tight-lipped, she walked into the house to give the *khansamah* instructions for supper. Father set his *burra* peg on the table by his side. 'Women don't understand these things, son. They can't appreciate that there's still a strain of the hunter in us. No amount of genteel chatter and sipping tea will get rid of that . . .'

The Nawab did things in style. At nine o'clock on the morning of the match two Rolls-Royces came to a sedate stop on the parade ground where the team and the wives and families were gathered. Following them, two old buses, pink curtained and copiously decorated in beaten tin with pictures of gods and goddesses and Dari Persian script, snorted clouds of smoke as they clattered to a halt. My parents joined the Whitworths in the first car. Dr Chatterjee had persuaded Dora Wheeler to forgo her daily visit to Charles for one day, and accompanied her in the second. The rest of us, players, wives, spectators, followed in the two coaches.

From time to time amidst the sprawling *maquis*, pines, deodars, a half-ruined building long since abandoned spilled its red clay and bricks, already covered in ubiquitous blue flowers, down the hillside. The ranges of hills receded — hazy in the morning mist — towards the massive far range of mountains striated with violet shadows. The jolting bus slowed as we drove through the deserted, monsoon-fissured streets of Nimbu Gali, where goats grazed amongst the blackened brick walls destroyed during Partition. The bus paused briefly to negotiate a steep bend above the great valley, and the Nawab's water palace came in sight, shining whitely against the rose-milky water of the tranquil lake.

The *maidan* had been roughly cleared. Boundaried with white posts joined by sisal, it was now graced with a long marquee, surrounded with fluttering pennants. The Nawab held court each morning to hear the grievances and requests of the villagers, so that the game had been scheduled to start at one-thirty after an early tiffin. Each time I imagined myself walking out to the crease under the brilliant sun my stomach lurched. When we bumped on to the uneven verge, the band was playing a barely recognizable version of 'The Minstrel Boy', and my parents and the Whitworths were already formally shaking hands with a few visiting dignitaries who stood outside the entrance to the tent.

The Nawab sat on a pink sofa in the shade of the marquee, his heavily veiled wife by his side. When I met him, he shook my hand gravely and said, 'You are the first casualty. And the game hasn't even begun.' His face was so solemn that I knew he wasn't making fun of me for the benefit of the other adults.

We ate at long trestles laid with starched white linen. Uniformed servants set the great tin and copper containers of curries, *dopeazas*, dhals, tandoors and salvers of pink, white and yellow perfumed rice decorated with beaten silver filigree down the centre of the trestles, and lit the kerosene burners. I sat at the men's table, between Father and Colonel Whitworth. While the Nawab was talking to a politician from Calcutta on his other side from Father, Colonel Whitworth leaned across me and whispered, 'Amyas . . . didn't occur to me to tell you that it wouldn't do for our side to *win* the match. Bad form, y'know . . .' I never knew whether his bland pink and white expression hid some joke at others' expense. I could see Father was bewildered.

'What . . . ?'

'Oh yes. It's a . . . well . . . a repayment of their hospitality, letting them win. D'y'see?'

'What's the point in playing?'

Colonel Whitworth held up his hand, as though to indicate he was not responsible for the state of affairs. '*I* didn't make the rules, old boy. But we don't want an Incident on our hands. You ask the political officer . . . Remember, half these buggers have never even seen a cricket bat . . .'

I could see Father didn't believe him.

The Nawab disdained a toss, merely declaring that his side would bat first. It became rapidly apparent that at least part of what Tom Whitworth had said was accurate. Amyas put Tom in to bowl against the first member of the Nawab's team, a ferociously mustachioed giant in a turban whose eyes rolled wildly — with either fear or rage — and who held the bat in one hand like a club whilst he scratched himself vigorously in the crotch with the forefinger of the other hand. The first two tactfully slow balls went uneventfully past his spasmodic lunges and safely into the wicket-keeper's gloves. On the third delivery Colonel Whitworth varied the pace — sending down a fast ball which, going wide, hit an uneven bump and promptly swung into the batsman's voluminous trousers. 'Bravo. Bravo.' Mrs Whitworth's voice carried faintly from the boundary and a light fusillade of ragged clapping broke out. The batsman sank slowly to the ground on one knee, holding his crotch with one hand and waving his bat in the other towards Tom Whitworth. 'Ban chod! Theire ma ki rundi . . .' His voice was strangled with pain. Dr Chatterjee put his finger in the air, saying in a quiet voice, 'He is not understanding rules of cricket and is calling you names for throwing ball at his . . . his thing. I think to avoid possibility of an Incident it is best to be giving him l.b.w.' Watching him limp towards the marquee, Tom Whitworth put his hand on Amyas's shoulder. 'Better put me in to bat at the tail end, eh?'

Dr Chatterjee excused himself to explain matters to the Nawab. 'It's best to nip possible misunderstanding in the bud.' Amyas explained to an earnest young lecturer who had come in from the field to inquire, '. . . technically incorrect but probably a sensible decision'. On the perimeter the smell of the goats grazing nearby hung in David Lawrence's nostrils. His father looked like a god, tall, broad shouldered, in control. He felt suddenly small and helpless.

Dr Chatterjee walked slowly back to the wicket, smiling broadly, holding his fist up with the thumb sticking in the air. 'Everything is all right. A-one. Asif has gone to test his honeymoon fittings with a girl from the village. The Nawab will bat at four.' Bewildered, Amyas walked down to mid-off. A second giant appeared at the crease and glared malevolently at Tom Whitworth. 'Guard?' Dr Chatterjee inquired politely.

By three forty-five Amyas sensed disaster. The sixty-two runs made by the Kala Pani team were largely the consequence of wides and careless fielding. Thomas, on the boundary and not party to Colonel Whitworth's asides to Amyas, had watched with amazement as the scoreboard clicked up an extra run here and there. 'The boy cannot add,' the Nawab had confided to the policeman who still accompanied him everywhere, 'but this is part of our good fortune.' He lay back against his brocaded cushions and sucked his hookah contentedly. Gobind Dass, who now had some rudimentary acquaintance with the game, and had missed two easy catches in the gully, was gratified (if confused) when Amyas slapped him on the back, saying, 'Well done,' with an abstracted air. When the seventh wicket fell – played on – for seventy, the game was held up while a liveried servant walked across to confer with Dr Chatterjee.

'What's up now?' Amyas's temper had not been improved by the heat and the suspicion that the ripples of laughter from the ladies under parasols on the perimeter were directed at him.

'The Nawab is not yet in the mood for batting. His head bearer is telling me that he will like to come in after tea.'

144

Amyas lifted his hands to the heavens. Tom Whitworth nodded imperceptibly, chewing a blade of grass under his yellowing sun-hat.

Tea was samosas, chicken tikka, roti, assorted Indian sweets and green tea. The Nawab reclined, smiling with distant expansiveness, while the uniformed band marched up and down playing Sousa marches. 'I think we'd better pad up pretty well,' Colonel Whitworth observed drily. 'Those buggers'll treat the ball like a rock to fell the enemy.' 'Don't understand why you men do these things,' Dora Wheeler, strolling by on the arm of Mary Lawrence, was saying to Dr Chatterjee. 'As if life wasn't dangerous enough without looking for trouble.' Her colour was high, and she held herself like a young woman. Angela, in a long dress, her hair tumbled on her shoulders, walked behind. David Lawrence felt a spasm of fear in his stomach.

The Nawab showed little inclination to come in straight after tea, picking at his toes with one hand as he waved the other at the agriculturist he had brought in to discuss agrarian reforms in the valley. Dr Chatterjee had tactfully proposed a brief lesson in bowling for the Nawab's team whilst they waited. Tom Whitworth was invited to stand at the wicket and the batsman he had injured was given the ball. ('Chat paying off old scores, wouldn't you say . . . ?' Dora observed to Mary, both now comfortably installed under their parasols.)

Amyas, turning his field-glasses toward Tom Whitworth's face, felt a moment's malicious amusement. The bowler checked at the wicket and then flung the ball with all his force at Tom's head: both Tom and the bemused wicket-keeper threw themselves flat upon the ground and the ball sped towards the boundary. Dr Chatterjee watched it go with his hands clasped behind his back, then turned and opened his arms to summon the members of the Nawab's team to him. A foot shorter than any of them, he gave them a brief, mimetic lesson on the difference between bowling and throwing. Three of the Nawab's team absented themselves to shepherd a straying herd of goats from the pitch on to the far shoulder of the slope bordering the ground. The nautch-girls in their brilliant costumes practised for the evening dance in the shade of the peepul. Tambour to the hand – shake – hold the movement – proceed.

Dass was trying to ingratiate himself. 'They are not knowing the rules,' he said with a complicit grin, but Tom Whitworth appeared not to have heard him. At four-fifteen the Nawab's guard ambled on to the pitch with the message that his master was ready to bat. Everyone waited while he was padded by two attendants and gloved by two more. A bearer preceded him, carrying his bat, and he walked towards the wicket with great dignity, very small, surmounted by his huge pink turban. Tom Whitworth had suggested that he should bowl, knowing the score, and Amyas, by now confused beyond decision, handed him the ball. ('Takes a little native cunning to cut that English arrogance down to size.' Mary smiled uncertainly, not sure whom Dora was criticizing.) Thomas stood in the outfield, obscurely worrying about Julia and the baby that was soon to be born. Perhaps it was time to leave India.

The Nawab lunged at the first gentle delivery, catching it on the inside edge of the bat so that it ran on to the stumps. Dr Chatterjee instantly signalled 'no ball'. After twenty minutes of Tom Whitworth's gentle half-tosses – the Nawab refusing to accept any other bowler – the Nawab announced that he was tired and Dr Chatterjee gave him out l.b.w. to the next ball, which was three feet wide of the off-stump. 'The game is over,' Dr Chatterjee announced, solemn faced. The band struck up 'When Johnny Comes Marching Home', and the Nawab's team ran on to the pitch, shouting vociferously, and followed their master on his stately procession towards his tent.

Tom Whitworth smiled at Amyas, closing his eyes against the sun. 'Should've briefed you before. Nawab could only be out l.b.w. Anything else too infra dig.' He avoided Amyas's incredulous gaze. Thomas was quizzing one of the lecturers, 'But what *exactly* happened . . . ?' His voice was querulous with uncertainty.

Amyas was suddenly aware that the group of ladies walking slowly round the perimeter towards the tent were giggling like schoolgirls. Suddenly furious, he turned towards Dr Chatterjee. 'Chat. What the hell is going on? When do we bat?' Dr Chatterjee's eyes grew wide under his round glasses and he splayed the fingers of his right hand to the sky in an expressive gesture. To David Lawrence his voice sounded almost amused – no, triumphant. 'There is absolutely no point. The Nawab is bored with the game and besides – his team cannot lose.' In the face of such finality there was silence.

Remembering, years later, David could feel again the relief he had felt upon not being called to bat. He recalled, too, his confusion, knowing that something strange had taken place, that adult rules had somehow inexplicably been set aside. As the bus lurched into the night, its lights illuminated gnarled trees which seemed to bend and threaten them as they passed. He had sat next to Dr Chatterjee, still full of incomprehension. 'I didn't understand,' he said to the Doctor, his body jolting as the bus laboured over the uneven road. 'Why didn't we play *properly*, Chat?' And Dr Chatterjee said patiently, 'We did play properly by our rules. It is just not really what you are calling cricket.'

Chapter Twenty-two

Some weeks after his party Thomas asked me round again. It was unexpected, and even more surprising that he had invited no one else, as though the time had come when he realized that the company of the rich and famous, his friends and fair-weather acquaintances, so many now departed shades, could not protect him from the truth. I think he had been visited by what comes to many of us who either are never caught in the seductive snare of upward mobility, or whose growing infirmity and detachment from quotidian life modify their vision: the reductiveness which sees the threadbare state of humanity, whose only redemption is human relationships. As I came to know later, his animus was not directed at me after all.

We sat in the garden, small, urned, paved, balustraded. The sound of the traffic was like the distant swarming of bees, and the sky was rosy with late sun. He had accepted that Julia, upstairs in the bedroom where she spent most of her days now, was dying with uncomplaining stoicism. 'I wish sometimes we had had one of these modern marriages where everything can be discussed. There are things I would like to say to her, but cannot.' He did not try to hide the tears.

It had not been a marriage born of initial passion. With brutal honesty, hugging his arms round his chest as though he were cold, he talked, smiling wryly. He had married Julia because he knew that she could best help him to what had seemed important then. 'I came to love her later. More than that I came to admire her for her courage. So many people I've heard say, "Why me?" as though they deserve special dispensation. Never Julia. It was she who helped me when she was first diagnosed – can you believe that? She comforted *me*!

You see, when you have failed to get the things you really wanted, you settle for what you've got. I was labelled as the conscience of the Tory party, a man of impeccable family life and devotion to truth in my career – even at the expense of being passed over. Even when my authorship of those books' – he gave an embarrassed laugh – 'somehow came out, it didn't make any real difference. That was just old Thomas doing what he had always done – setting himself above the Establishment. And for me it was a chance to try my hand at something else before I got down to the serious business . . .'

The time finally comes round for everything. I looked away, surprised to find that after all these years I still wished to hear his emphatic denial, even a sense of outrage. I kept my voice as neutral as possible. 'And Mother,' I said. 'I wondered about you and her, even as a child.'

I could hear the shock in his voice as he said quickly, too quickly, 'You were far too young to know of such things. Anyway, there was nothing in it. A little innocent flirtation . . .' But I knew then that I had been right, watching him as he made his denial at length, telling me that there would have been little opportunity.

'Julia,' I said. 'Did you tell her?'

His face had gone quite white, and I thought for a moment he was going to strike me. 'My God,' he said, 'you're so smug, so righteous. You think you can sit in judgement upon us, cast the first stone, just because you haven't lived enough to make mistakes. No, of course I haven't told her. She has enough to cope with without that . . .'

The housekeeper had left some salad on the sideboard. I forced myself to eat, washing down the mouthfuls with sips of an indifferent Frascati. Thomas's customary twinkling politeness had returned. 'There's one or two things I could tell you about your own family, you know. Not exactly blameless lives there, y'know.' I let the comment pass without responding.

Julia was reading with a shawl round her shoulders. I kissed her and sat on the edge of the bed, while Thomas was getting the coffee she'd requested. When his footsteps turned into the kitchen below, she smiled and said, 'You'd know about such things. I heard everything, you see. And I'm sure somewhere he knew I could hear. Perhaps it is his way of getting things into the open without having to discuss them. He's such a silly old duffer.' Her eyes were bright with unshed tears.

'Did you know? About him and Mother, I mean.'

Her hands on the sheet were wasted, sallow. She looked away, past my shoulder. 'It's hard to remember, now. I think I knew but didn't acknowledge what was happening. Acknowledging means facing up to things, working things out. And I suppose I was waiting to see what would happen with your father, and that seemed much more important then.' I was moved by her admission of something I had known for so long, but which could not be discussed.

'Why did it end?'

'I found out something about him that I couldn't live with. You know how one thing can be . . . impassible, cannot be set aside. He prevaricated, made excuses, of course, but it was like Thomas's denial to you just now. When it came up with your father, I'd hoped to hear him say it wasn't true, be angry with me for daring to think it . . .'

I hadn't the courage to ask the question in my mind. But Julia smiled and put her hand over mine. 'I knew about Thomas and the other women. Nothing much ever happened sexually between Thomas and me, you know. For me your father got in the way of all that. I knew about Miriam Cohen. I can only say I can't believe that Thomas would have had anything to do with that . . .'

Thomas's sharp footsteps in the hall. 'The revenges of the old,' Julia said. 'You'd think we would have reached safe haven by our age, wouldn't you?' Her voice carried a faint cadence of amusement.

The night had turned cold and the car windscreen was already misted over. Over to the south-east Robert had moved in with Angela. To the west my parents had bought three fields to add to the vineyard: the first pressing was to be next year. 'Noble rot,' Father had said, holding a bunch of grapes out to me. Their bloom was tarnished with a powdery white glaze. 'Ripeness is all,' said Father, a strange, faraway expression crossing his face for a moment.

Behind me now, as I drove south, Julia and Thomas made their accommodations to each other in the shadow of her approaching death. Theirs was what the obituary notice would call a happy marriage: they had stayed together, after all, and that was the criterion by which such things were measured. I wondered, then, about what I now know: what had Julia discovered which all those years ago had made her turn from my father?

*

Septimus held the letters Gobind had given him for three days, irresolute. The situation was so removed from his daily life, from the preoccupations he held in common with his colleagues, that he could think of no way of discussing them. In the end he decided that the only person who he could talk to was Johann Neidermayer.

He was shocked when Neidermayer eventually opened the door. The other man looked sallow, dishevelled, much older than the calm controlled figure with whom he had dined a few days before. 'Johann,' he said, his voice edged with concern, 'what is the matter? Are you ill?'

There were two cases visible through the half-open bedroom door on an unmade bed strewn with clothes. The pictures were crated, standing against a wall. The marks where they had hung were pale. With an effort at hospitality Neidermayer was trying to pour a drink. His hands shook, and Septimus gently took the bottle from him.

'Two men were here last week. The lady who lives downstairs told me they had been asking after me. One of the men showed her an old photograph and asked if it was me. She could not be sure. Her eyes are bad and besides, this was a young man wearing a black uniform with a peaked cap. It must have been taken many years ago.' He paused, took a sip of his vodka, looked out of the window.

'You know I cannot really remember what happened all those years ago. When one is young, one does so many

151

things – not from malice or bad intentions, but because one is told to, or because one has not thought enough . . .' In the greying light his features looked worn, withered. Septimus could think of nothing to say. There was a sound in the hall and Neidermayer's head turned, his face frozen in horror. 'It is only a visitor to the flat below,' Septimus said. 'Where will you go?'

Neidermayer resumed as though he had not heard the question. 'I did not remember some things until I saw David Lawrence. There was a child . . . and a woman crying. But, you see, I felt such sadness, such terrible sadness, that I could have done nothing to them . . .' His face contorted as if with the effort to recall something.

When he said, 'I'm sorry. You had something to tell me,' Septimus gave him the folder in silence. Neidermayer put on his tortoiseshell glasses and switched on the lamp by his side. 'Please . . . And me.' Septimus made the drinks.

Johann finished reading and rubbed his eyes. 'I have realized something over the years. Nothing can undermine the British upper class. They are immune to things which could destroy you and me. What do they know of our lives – yours or mine, eh? All they know of is privilege, wealth.'

They sat in the darkening room, two old men, sipping their drinks. It was, Septimus thought, listening to Johann, like a confessional. Like a man under the shadow of the gallows, Neidermayer was making his peace: speaking of the thirties and his membership of the Brownshirts, of *Kristallnacht*, of his own feelings of revulsion towards the party, of his work in the camps, there was a hesitancy, as of a man seeking the best path through a perilous field; later, when he spoke of India, of what he had been permitted to see and hear because he was dumb and was therefore an idiot, of no account, he gave a clear account. He had, he said, entered upon a period of his life, the period of dumbness, when he had lost any sense of direction, of right and wrong, so that all that he saw and heard had no effect. 'It was a moral blindness – as though *nothing* was forbidden any more . . .'

Father Gregorio was right; a time comes when one cannot

avoid responsibility, involvement in the world. The sudden realization of the power he held filled Septimus with a sense of dismay. I wish I had not been given these letters; I wish I had not heard what Johann has been telling me. He saw now the pity of things – too late to intervene or help. As a young man he had believed the truth was important, whatever the cost, but now he was less sure. We are all old men. What will be gained from exposing these things? Once it had been the tower which had shielded him from involvement. To rebuild that would have achieved something in the real world with the materials he could understand: bricks, mortar, wood, things which did not change their shape or possess hidden secrets. Things which might be relied upon.

'I do not know what I would do in your position,' he said.

'I do not know what you should do,' Neidermayer said.

Chapter Twenty-three

I read about Neidermayer's death in the paper. He had fallen in front of a tube train at Hatton Cross station. I felt a strange sense of loss. I had not known him well (as I had discovered when he became a patient), but he was part of the furniture of my childhood. There was some justice in what had happened, if one thought in those judgemental ways. He had known what was happening in the camps, despite his denials. And, thinking in that vein, I could see no possible expiation for such things.

The letter arrived three days later. I have it still. It is a sort of *memento mori* for my profession. 'You people with your degrees are so clever, do you not realize that the only way many people can live is by pretending? You make me go back, you force me to see what I was doing, the thing I am. You never look to see if I can bear these things.' He went on to say that one day I might find things I could not bear in my turn. 'Ask Septimus, if you have the courage . . .' I could almost see him, standing defiantly in my consulting rooms.

Angela cried when we talked about him. On the rattan loungers on the patio behind her house it seemed, for an evening, as though things were the same again. A bright moon, the distant sound of a car. Robert was away. 'In the north somewhere' — the dismissiveness of her tone lifted my heart for a moment. She had changed in our absence from each other, her eyes shadowed, her face thinner. 'Oh God, to be a child again. For the most part, anyway . . . It was so much simpler then.' Her hand lay on my arm, as familiar as my own.

Later, when she had moved to stand at the balustrade

looking over the dark garden, she said, 'I feel guilty that I denied you to Lydia Folkcroft. She'd have made you a good wife.' I knew that the regret itself indicated some future betrayal. The darkness hid my face from her when she turned to look. Briefly I thought, if I could free her I must. It was the last thing I could do for her.

'It didn't work with Lydia because she wanted what she has now. She'd have been miserable as a psychoanalyst's wife in London. People don't choose each other in isolation. It is a way of life they choose. You'd be surprised how much that consideration can overcome even passion.'

I thought she was crying. She covered her face with her hands as though smoothing away sleep. 'Lydia knew. That's why she left. No other reason. And she knew because I let her . . .'

'You told her?'

'There was no need. Women know when they're beaten — and why. At the last moment I couldn't let it happen.'

I knew then that she planned to tell me that she was going to marry Robert. This was the plea for forgiveness, for magnanimity in defeat, for generosity of spirit. I like to console myself with the words Septimus said later: 'You did it for her — for the best for her.' Truth is too complicated for us humans, after all. What I did know beyond doubt then was that our knowledge meant that we could never be free of each other, so whatever I did would make little difference.

'And yet you want my permission now. Is that fair?'

'You bastard,' she said. She didn't look at me, stumbling past with her head held high. The door into the kitchen slammed. It was strange that where I might have expected to experience victory I felt only emptiness and defeat.

*

It was colder than usual, that year. The snow fell, day after day, loading the branches of the Douglas firs so that they drooped towards the ground. The air froze in our nostrils, and smoked from our mouths.

It was the year of strange stories.

Gobind Dass had sent a man from Ooper Iskanderabad to repair a power line damaged in the wind. Somehow the man had become entangled in the line and had hung himself, twisting in the wind like a murderer on a gibbet. 'Face all black ... eyes popping right out ...' I heard the Colonel say to Mother, who stood in an attitude of shock, both hands clasped over her mouth.

Thomas and Julia's son had been born. Years later Mother told Angela of the rumours. That Julia had refused to suckle the child, had cried out and ignored Thomas, who came to visit her in the hospital. Had for days sat in a darkened room, refusing food, turning her face away if the ayah brought the child into the room.

Worse than all these, Charles had escaped. We had heard the tolling of the prison's bell late one night, faintly through the driving storm. Malik's men, finding his cell empty, had set out upon their grim pursuit with two bloodhounds. The snow had fallen too fast; even before the river, black and fast running between the high white banks of snow, the footsteps were lost.

In the club I sat with Dora and Dr Chatterjee whilst the others played bridge. 'I would know if something had happened to him. He is safe ...' Dora spoke with a vehement assurance, her blue eyes looking beyond us at some privileged scene. I could see the concern in Dr Chatterjee's face, though he said nothing. Loving Dora, I felt afraid: she had gone somewhere I could not follow. 'Never love anyone,' she once said to me. 'When they leave, it is almost more than the spirit can bear.'

That night Mrs Whitworth was directing the servants as they put up the paper chains. Eleanor's Plasticine crib figures stood before Mary and the stall against a backdrop of black cardboard graced with cut-out stars. Angela had arranged them this year — cotton wool for the snow, and a torch bulb throwing the figures into relief from behind.

Someone — perhaps Septimus — had suggested that Vivienne James should be brought down to join the party. It was Christmas, after all, a time for good fellowship. Perhaps being

156

among her father's old friends might return her from the place she had hidden in her mind since his death. She sat with Sister Agnes and James Crale and his wife at one end of the room, empty eyed, smiling, her beauty withered and vacant. 'She is enjoying herself,' Sister Agnes, apple cheeked and round, assured Mrs Whitworth, patting Vivienne's arm. But, until they were able to forget her presence, she cast a blight upon the party's spirits.

Thomas and Julia and their son were planning to leave for England as soon as possible. My mother had said, 'Poor thing. She's suffering from depression. It often happens after a baby.' Thomas played bridge and she sat in the corner. People avoided Julia, as they did Dora. I knew even then they felt resentful because Dora and Julia were not playing by the rules: they might make a scene, or cry, and then where would one be? When she thought she was unobserved, I could see that Julia watched Father covertly. Her face betrayed little, no animation, except puzzlement, as though she were trying to find the answer to some insoluble question.

Years later David could still remember the moment. Outside the windows snow was falling. The assembled company in the club had listened to the BBC World Service news, sipping their *burra* pegs. The mood had changed to a sentimental nostalgia. Thomas sat by Julia, holding her hand. The Whitworths were discussing Home with Amyas. Septimus, who had arrived late, had joined Dora, Dr Chat and David, who sat on the floor at their feet. Angela, at her mother's request, had changed the needle, wound the gramophone and put on 'Silent Night'.

There was the sound of muffled footfalls on the veranda outside and the door opened, gusting an icy wind into the room, to disclose Inspector Malik, half whitened with snow, with a constable behind him. For a moment everyone was still, like a tableau vivant. He looked at Dora and said, 'I am so sorry, ma'am. We have found your son's body in the Mughal Reservoirs.'

Dora sat immobile for a moment. Dr Chatterjee put his

hand on her arm, but she ignored it. She stood up slowly, clenching her fists by her side. The sinews in her neck stood out like ropes, and her face was livid. When she opened her mouth, no sound came. Suddenly she screamed without sound and turned, pointing her finger at Amyas Lawrence, who sat as though turned to stone. The record came to an end and there was only the tck-tck-tck of the needle over a crack to punctuate the appalled silence.

Chapter Twenty-four

The police came to see me again. A very polite detective inspector and his sergeant. Both young, casually dressed, with the studious, formal politeness which concealed authority. The wide-ranging artlessness of their inquiries, sipping coffee in my sun-flooded consulting room, slowly focused upon Miriam Cohen. They had the habit of ignoring my questions, the senior, lean, blue eyed, inspecting the pictures on my walls with every appearance of interest, whilst the sergeant, stolid, squarely built, fixed me intently with a level gaze and made notations on his pad.

Of course they realized that I could not ethically divulge any specific details about a patient, but it would help them greatly if I would give them some very general information which might assist them. Could I, for example, give them some idea of whether or not she might have been a drug user? Would I categorize her as someone promiscuous, as someone careless in her habits? All the while Reynolds, the detective inspector, ranged round the room giving an impression of profound boredom. Outside I could hear the aggrieved tones of Lady Romark berating my long-suffering receptionist as she made a fresh appointment, saying it was too bad, and what was the world coming to, and there are other psychoanalysts, you know.

I took refuge in vague generalizations, using the most patrician rendering of my Cambridge accent to intimidate the two, without signal success. I was certain that Miriam had never taken drugs. It was not consistent with her personality. She would have been afraid of their effect upon her looks. Besides, I was as sure as one may be about another human being that she had, as was her wont, told me everything she might consider to be important or interesting. Like many patients, she had quickly assumed a teacher–pupil, parent–child relationship to me – part of which was her seeking to tell me things that might interest me. It had been vain to tell her that this was not the point of analysis.

What I did not say was that in her case, as it happened, it was merely a symptom of her neurosis, her inability to accept that Thomas and I did not have some godlike power to protect her from life, to guide her into the paths of happiness and peace. In truth, I had felt from time to time that it was her sudden realization of all this, and the consequent feeling of being abandoned, which might have led to her suicide.

Again, without much hope of a response, I asked, 'Can you tell me what this is all about?'

Reynolds stopped his pacing and fixed me with a level gaze, seeming to come to some decision. He put his coffee-cup down with deliberation on one of the coasters on my glass-topped desk and wiped his mouth with a brilliant white hand-kerchief which he stowed carefully in the pocket of his well-cut grey trousers. He had the habit of never looking me directly in the eye, as though to do so would bring in its wake some unendurable intimacy. Sunk to a confidential whisper, his voice held a sudden, unmistakable tang of the East End. 'Her sister told us that she'd had a visitor the night she died. A man . . . You didn't visit her by any chance . . . ?'

I was shocked, as much by the smoothness of the insertion as by the implications of the question. Before I had time to respond, the blue eyes had looked me over once, very hard. 'Didn't think so,' he said. 'Leaves us with a couple of little mysteries, then. A needle mark in her arm and some missing letters. One of the neighbours gave a description of a distinctive car in the under-ground park that day.' He shot his bright, inquiring glance in my direction. Warned now, I kept my features deliberately blank.

Leaving, Reynolds shook my hand in his cold, firm grasp. 'Can't tell what's useful these days. We put everything into the computer to see if any trends emerge. But thank you. We may be in touch again.'

I sat in my chair, angry to realize that my legs were shaking. During the afternoon sessions I took refuge in the analyst's silence, only half listening to the recitals of my patients. It was just possible that Miriam had entertained another man, but unlikely. I remembered her telling me of Thomas's violence. One had to be careful in evaluating such information, particularly coming from patients prone to self-dramatize. Whilst I could perfectly well imagine Thomas conducting secret affairs, it was hard to think of him — the pillar of outward respectability — being involved in her death.

When I heard the phone ring and Janet's bright voice say, 'Just a moment, Ms Lawrence. Your brother's in,' I had a premonition that it was bad news. In one sense at least, even if, aware it concerned Robert, I had to dismiss a mean instance of pleasure from my consoling voice. Robert had been taken in for questioning. This time it was serious. 'It's all our fault, isn't it . . . ?' she said bitterly after I'd been silent for some time. And, in a curious, roundabout way, I suppose it was. Serves you right, I thought, knowing that he had, however unwittingly, driven the wedge deeper between us.

*

Two figures appeared on the hill, one supporting the other.

There was a misty sun, and the snow hurt my eyes, so that I had to shade them with my hands. The smaller figure fell, and the other patiently stooped, taking an arm round his neck to steady the other man before they commenced to walk slowly down the hill. It was Mr Latif, half carrying Henry Wheeler. I felt a strange foreboding of disaster.

Even downstairs with two closed doors and an empty room between us I could hear Henry's keening cries and my mother's and Mr Latif's attempts to soothe him. Dr Chatterjee, swathed and muffled against the cold, arrived half an hour later. Briskly, rubbing his hands now free of their gloves, he said, 'Where's the patient? Upstairs?' After a while there was quiet.

Angela and I were sent to the sun-room. We sat silently,

pretending to read, while their voices sounded clearly through the wall.

'He'll sleep now. I'll arrange for him to be taken to hospital when the weather permits. I hope that is all right, Mrs Lawrence?'

'Of course. What shall we do if he wakes up?'

Suddenly Mr Latif made a sound between a laugh and a moan. I looked at Angela and she put her finger to her pursed lips. 'I am passing the house and Henry is running out. He seems to be dancing in the snow with his hands holding his head. Then I can hear he is saying, "Oh God, oh God, oh God" – over and over again. When he sees me, he asks me to come with him. He is like a baby, you know. He takes me by the hand. The house is decorated for Christmas. Lovely streamers. A tree with lights. I am following him upstairs. On the landing he is like a baby. He is sitting in the corner and smiling and curling his finger at me. I look through the door. Mrs Wheeler, my friend . . .' – the voice stopped for a moment, choked with emotion – 'is lying on the bed in a white dress. Her wrists are cut and there is blood all over her, over the sheets . . .'

Dr Chatterjee said, 'I'm afraid the shock of Charles's death was too much for her to stand. I must go and get these arrangements sorted out.'

Through the frosted glass we watched his figure grow smaller and disappear amid the whirling snowflakes. I wished that Angela would console me as she used to, with a touch or a hug – a few words of comfort. I knew that she shared my pain and bewilderment, but I knew, too, that even this was secondary to some great thing which held her, pale and withdrawn, from us. And all the things the grown-ups said about growing pains, the sulkiness of adolescence, were the perpetuation of the lies with which they consoled themselves. Once they had reached those conclusions, they could relax, signalling to each other with raised eyebrows and covert smiles a smug agreement with their common assumption. But it was not like that at all. Even then I knew that.

The snow stopped the next day. A dandy arrived on the

shoulders of two coolies to bear Henry away to Iskanderabad Hospital. I walked with my sledge up to Dora's house on the hill. It was shuttered. No smoke came from the chimney. I lay on the sledge on my stomach, going faster, faster down the hill away from her house, as though the flight itself could leave my thoughts behind. The cold prickled at my skin. When I took my shoes off on the veranda of our house, my feet glowed with pain as I massaged them to restore the circulation.

At breakfast the next day, Father read the paper. He sipped his coffee, then took the paper-knife and started to open the pile of letters by his side. In the far distance a snowplough ground slowly up the road, growling and checking. Chik-chik — our name for the new *chokra* — was setting the fire, coiling old newspapers tightly and surrounding them with a careful wigwam of pine kindling. Father jerked in his chair, the paper dropping from his hand, and held his chest. His eyes seemed to bulge and sweat suddenly beaded his forehead. My mother called for the bearer and went round to his chair. Father didn't say anything, allowing them to lead him slowly up the stairs. I could hear the barely controlled note of panic in my mother's voice as she spoke quietly to him.

Angela turned over the letter by his plate. There was no address, no signature. Just the one word, 'MURDERER'. She didn't look at me as she went out of the room.

Dr Chatterjee only said it was 'a warning'. There was nothing physically wrong with Father, but he was evidently under stress. He should spend a few days in bed. Try to relax. The letter disappeared. Soon I could barely remember it, the scene as insubstantial as a dream disappearing from sight as morning light floods through a window.

Wrack remains, like pebbles left at the tide line. The froth of foam hisses over them, sinking into the rapidly lightening sand, shifting them fractionally this way then that, smoothing them imperceptibly. Like the strange shapes in a darkened bedroom in childhood, their significance changes, their potency begins to fail with familiarity. The dressing-gown hung behind the chair in the dark bedroom is no longer Grendel coming to avenge the death of his mother, but the prosaic, familiar garment without associations. With age we forgive ourselves, too. If we survive, that is. If we can survive.

When I first began, it was as a flight from certain things. Because of my own, barely acknowledged fugue, I caught insights which others outside my profession might have missed. Even in our infrequent social meetings I could see that Septimus ran from what he could not comprehend: the cloying obligation of personal involvements. Father, for once looking with open eyes and with rare self-awareness, saying, 'Ripeness is all,' obliquely acknowledging for once some accommodation with a less than perfect past. There are matters which we dare not reproach each other with, may not bring to the light. Such situations which, once breached, bring in their wake a fundamental change. It is a sort of collusion, the relationship we must have to each other merely for continuance.

('You should know above all: it *happened*, David!' Thus Angela, brown skinned from the summer against her white lace blouse, in the window seat. She could not enter the collusion which sustains us all. We had walked in the country arm in arm between the hedgerows, down the long lane. She had been reading Alvarez – *The Savage God*. And it was then that everything changed. Or is that my weakness, my self-absolution?)

*

Septimus thinks.

I have never married. Over the years I have got used to that inquiring glance, that wordless exchange, particularly between men when we first meet: one of *those*. It has never worried me, or even been a factor in my life, possibly because I am secure in my preferences, however muted and unassertive they are. Possibly because of Father Gregorio, and the Order's inveighing against the sins of the flesh, cycles of passion and indulgence have alternated with periods of austere self-recrimination and abstinence.

164

Lately – the last fifteen years or so – I have realized that self-denial makes sense only if one is buying favours in some post-death world in which one might have an individual and continuing existence: having lived so long, I cannot countenance that, even if I ever did. The appalling awfulness of an eternity of good works!

Miriam was a surprise, coming long after I had thought that side of my life was over. I was interviewing prospective Samaritans in a small, shabby office in a run-down Victorian building in Southwark. An airless summer day, dull and close, with the smell of dust and poverty in my nostrils. There had only been one possible, a fifty-year-old banker who wished to give back some of life's generosity towards him – a Christian construction, given his story. (The first thing I ask is what is in it for them.) For some it has a social cachet ('Thursdays I answer the phone for the Samaritans, my dear . . . One must do *something* worthwhile'). For others the fascination stems from their own neuroses: in my experience social workers have a higher incidence of nervous and mental problems than the world at large. But he had been gentle, non-judgemental, open. The children had grown up and his wife had gone off with a younger man. 'Of course I hoped it would blow over if I didn't insist upon a confrontation. She's a well-preserved fifty-eight with a strong sex drive, he's an immature thirty-one-year-old who's looking for his mother. Already she misses the kind of social life we had, and he calls her from the office to say he's working late. We still talk, you see. Except I cannot tell her what she really knows. That in four or five years it will be over, and she'll be alone in her sixties. Maybe, for both of them, four years of that is enough. Better for her than another twenty-five being bored with me. I gave her the house and as much as I could afford. There's no point in useless anger, or dismissing the good years, the children . . .' His smile was resigned, accepting.

The next appointment was late. I drank a cup of sweet tea. The voices from the operations room next door were indistinguishable through the partition wall. She was almost seated before I was aware she had come into the room. 'I'm so sorry

— the traffic . . .' she said, smoothing her hair from her high forehead with a slender white hand. Her face was eager, wide-eyed, her mouth parted as though in excitement. I felt an instant shock, the subliminal recognition of her openness to me. I was very formal at first. This was no place for such feelings.

Her mannerisms hinted at her nervousness. Quick, like a bird. Her hand over her mouth while she spoke, her eyes resting on my face for an instant before she looked away. She was not conventionally beautiful, her mouth too wide, her nose a shade too retroussé, but there was something of the appeal of a wild animal, poised for flight.

Of course the interview continued under false pretences: I knew that her presence here was nothing to do with a desire to work with us. She had come for a confessional, for comfort. I smiled noncommittally and looked away when she said wryly, 'I'm not really right for this, am I?' 'Tell me about your life. I am interested,' I said.

That's where it all began, I suppose. David Lawrence wouldn't approve. His view is that cruelty is a prime tool in the search for truth — that the comforts of listening, of appearing to understand, are superficial, visceral and transitory. That it is fundamental change which succeeds, and that may only be attained through self-knowledge, which is usually lonely, painful and permanent.

It was closeness she wanted, not understanding. I think she was wise enough to realize that was beyond most people. When the time came, on our fourth meeting, drinking brandy in her flat after dinner, and I could see the familiar signs in her eyes, in the heat of her thigh against mine, the confidence of her hand on my arm, I said (*pace* Father Gregorio), 'I am too old for you, and too poor.' Almost as if it were the awaited signal, she was covering my face in kisses. Her hair in my nostrils smelled sweet, fresh; the skin of her cheek against mine felt soft. 'None of that matters. I want you for what you are.' It sounded like a line from an old movie, and I a poor substitute for the father who had never given her his love as unstintingly as she had wanted.

166

I felt devoured by her. She had both the charm and the petulance of a child. Often I would return to my flat to find three or four messages from her on my answering machine. Once, letting myself in late after attending a conference in Rochdale on child abuse, I was startled by a sound in the dark flat. Arming myself with a walking-stick, I inched quietly through the rooms, straining my eyes. In the bedroom I lifted the stick above my head and switched on the light. She lay naked under the sheets. I could not resist her laughter for long. In my arms she said, 'You wouldn't really have struck me. Even if I had been a burglar.'

It was only later that I came to see the depths of her despair.

I take things as they are. Her clear laughter, the suddenness of her impulses – so many of them sexual, the apparent transparent artlessness of her expressions dazzled and carried me along. Her mother didn't approve: not in words – she was glacially polite and correct – but more in what was left unsaid. We spoke amiably enough about her garden, we seemed to find a certain rapport in the disenchantment of age in the current political situation. What did it matter, anyway?

It was Neidermayer, after we had dined with him two or three times, who had frightened me. 'If she does not find help, she will die ...' Delivered with absolute certainty, in his guttural accent. I could not think how I had been so blind. It was plain that she was in distress even if she could not articulate it. I was horrified at my own selfishness and determined to make amends. For the first time in my life I intended to *do* something. Responding to my anxiety, my covert questions, she became reckless: what right did I have over her life? How dare I assume responsibility? Despite which, she did eventually take up my suggestion that she should get her GP to arrange for her to see David without disclosing it as my idea. My ambivalence towards him does not extend to doubting that he understands such things better than I.

After that she began to slip away from me. At first it was almost imperceptible. A day to return my calls, an expression of mock frustration that she could not make dinner – 'perhaps next week . . .' It took a month to dawn upon me that there was someone else. Piqued, I decided to resort to silence. If there was anything left, that should bring it out.

I managed three months. I was annoyed at the extent of my dependence. I missed the warmth she brought into my life – the sudden, unexpected gestures of affection. I realized that – without acknowledging the fact – I had, for the first time, begun to assume that we would remain together. I had accepted her capriciousness, that my role was as much father as lover: and I had come to appreciate that the gains she brought – her presence in the flat when I returned from work, the smell of cooking, the flowers standing brightly on the polished table in the hall – more than compensated for my loss of privacy. I had, in short, fallen in love with her.

I will not punish myself by thinking I might have saved her. There is a pattern, but it is beyond our feeble abilities to comprehend either its shape or its meaning. Perhaps the pattern is that there is no pattern. One evening I knew that there was only one thing to be done, even if I could hold out little prospect of its success. If I could see her, talk to her, perhaps there would be some way of returning things to the way they were before.

It was raining. I held my breath as the starter motor whined and almost died before the engine fired. The traffic in the West End moved slowly. I felt a little light-headed, realizing I had eaten nothing beyond a slice of toast in the morning. In the last weeks I had deliberately taken on a heavier workload than usual, and was used to a snatched sandwich halfway through the afternoon.

I parked across the road from her flat. The light faded and the street lamps began to blink on one by one. My hands were wet and I could feel my heart palpitating uncomfortably fast against my shirt. There was no light in her flat. I would sit quietly and wait for her return.

It was an hour before I saw her figure moving up the street. At first I did not realize that the tall figure swathed in a greatcoat by her side was accompanying her. There was something oddly familiar about the man's walk, but he was wrapped up against the rain, and the umbrella he held over both of them cast a shadow over their faces. As they drew nearer, I could see that she held his arm and was talking, turning her face up towards him in a gesture I knew well.

I'm ashamed to recollect that I cried, hidden in the darkness behind the rain-spattered windscreen. If there's one thing more foolish than a man suffering the torments of unrequited love, it is an old man suffering the torments of unrequited love. It made me feel valueless, of no account.

It was her mother who rang and told me. Tempering the genuine sorrow in her voice there seemed a note of near triumph, as though she were saying, you see, I told you so. 'She was seeing an older man, I think. She only chose people with whom there couldn't be any future . . .' There was the faintest note of censure in her voice. It was only later I knew that Miriam was probably dying as I sat outside in the car, weeping.

Chapter Twenty-five

All week I had the feeling of being out of focus, prone to accidents, so *distrait* that even my receptionist asked anxiously if I was all right. I felt a sense of paralysis about the wedding. Angela had, of course, sent me an invitation, stiff and formal and without any personal message. There was nothing I could do to change the course of things. My mother rang to tell me how delighted they were. Playing the game, I tried to sound approving, embarrassed at the hollowness of my responses. But Mother hadn't noticed. 'Pity it's going to be in a registry office. Still, it's how they do things these days. It's too far for your father, I'm afraid. But you'll be there, so she won't be alone.'

I made a last effort at reconciliation on the Wednesday before. I hadn't seen Angela for almost a month. When she answered the door, I was shocked into silence for a moment. She had lost weight, and the light tan barely disguised the sallowness of her skin. Her eyes were puffy, as though she had been crying. She bit her lip and smiled wryly, going before me into the cool interior. 'I'll only be a minute. Help yourself to a drink.' She looked unfamiliar with make-up. Harder, somehow older, more remote. And with the make-up and our long absence from each other came an awkwardness I had never felt with her before.

I'd booked at a restaurant in Cobham. We had a drink while waiting for our table, and she forestalled me by saying, 'It isn't going to work, you know. You can't change my mind. Of course it alters nothing, but it seems the only thing I can do in the circumstances.'

The police had barely left Robert alone. He had to report

each day. They had taken his passport away. He'd said that he was with Angela the evening of Miriam Cohen's death. I didn't ask if that were true, though it seemed not from the way she presented the information. 'I know he isn't ideal, but I am getting older. It will be companionship — and it is what Mother and Father want . . .' She talked with bright determination of other things, but I could feel the hard edge of her old anger with me beneath the surface.

Outside the registry office it was raining. Angela, in cream, looked severe and unsmiling. Robert wore a grey suit and a cravat. His smile for my benefit seemed to hold a hint of triumph. 'We're going to Fethiye. Had a marvellous holiday there once, didn't we, Ange?'

Her grey eyes held mine, without expression. Surprised, I said, 'I thought the police held your passport . . .'

'Let me have it back. I think that's all over . . .'

I was busy. My paper was well overdue and I had recently had a spate of referrals. My sense of loss — not because of this inappropriate marriage, but for the deepening rift — was modified and ameliorated by work. For a time, at least.

Chapter Twenty-six

I couldn't rid myself of the image of Dora Wheeler lying in her bed with her wrists cut. At night I would wake, sweating with terror. I would imagine her lying like Miss Havisham, her eyes pebbled like fish eyes that have been exposed to the heat, cobwebs swathed across her face and over the outstretched finger that she pointed at me, her mouth open showing a black cavern behind those bleached lips.

In these fantasies she was always upon the verge of speech, trying to overcome the barrier of death to tell me something of great importance. The image had the same nightmarish half-reality as Pinocchio or the Brothers Grimm had held for me when I was six or seven. If I didn't move, I would be safe. At times I cried out in the night, and my mother, half drugged by sleeping pills, would sometimes come and hold my hand until I fell asleep.

I was feverish one morning and Dr Chatterjee came to see me. He spoke in front of me, as though I were an adult. 'The nightmares are not surprising. A lot has happened in his young life, and he and Mrs Wheeler were great friends. The nightmares will do their work of dealing with things and then they will pass . . .' He seemed immensely old and wise, packing his instruments into his Gladstone with phthisic, bloodless fingers. '. . . All that psychological rubbish . . .' I heard my father say later to my mother.

James Crale's buxom black wife, Pearl, had left him. 'Couldn't wait for him to die and leave it all to her. Bet she's run off with some fancy man . . .' Colonel Whitworth downed his *burra* peg and looked expectantly round. The bearer padded away to refill his glass. Mrs Whitworth made sounds of mock disapproval. 'Oh, Tom! That's an awful thing to say!' but the comment was for form's sake only. Mother had gone up to Crale's house the past three evenings accompanied by the bearer to cook his supper and keep him company. 'Preserve me from the legion of the socially concerned,' Septimus once said.

A sound woke me. It seemed like some animal trying to come in through the window. I lay in bed, straining my eyes to try to see what might be there. An old witch, that's what Vivienne James had once called Dora. People's fear had been based upon their belief that she knew more than most people − wouldn't play by the rules. In life she had been my friend. But − out there in the stormy darkness − what had she become? What did she want of me?

(This was part of what I denied for so long. Strange that now, forty years later, the memories return with a scarcely bearable, crystalline precision. I am doing what my patients do. Forced to remember, I still, in a sense, deny the reality of the experience. It has become part of the rich myths and textures of childhood, along with the mosaic of Greek and Roman legends, of manticores, and hydras, and chimeras, winged horses, Titans, anthropophagi.)

I had to get away from the bedroom. The terror was so great that I was ready to face Angela's coldness and derision. But in the dark corridor I could hear the sound of a voice, very low, which said, 'I had to do it. Don't you see? − if she had said anything, it would have been the end of our lives − don't you see? You must never say anything about it, you must never say anything about this. Do you understand?' The voice was insistent, sounding almost in pain. It was my father's voice.

I moved along the wall very quietly. My father was pleading now. 'It was an accident. The girl tempted me. I was stupid. I tried to tell her what was best, but she wouldn't listen. Don't you see?'

The door was ajar. My father, still talking, lay on top of Angela, moving as he talked. They were both naked. Her legs were apart and he lay between them, his bottom moving with a rhythm which jarred with the words he still spoke. Her eyes stared up unseeing at the ceiling as though she were in shock. I knew that something terrible was taking place. Suddenly, I felt very old. I would never again fear Dora Wheeler's return. The world contained far worse things than that.

Much later, in our ruin, she told me she had seen me. 'What could I do?' she said. 'He was grown-up and my father, and he said it was all right, was what he wanted. And part of me thought that it must be all right because he was doing it, that I must want it, too.' It was so sad. I could not comfort her, absolve her from that stain which would never leave her.

'What about Charles?'

She sat up with her chin on her knees, clasping her feet. 'He would never have allowed the trial to come to that . . .' she said, but speculatively, without conviction.

*

Septimus wrestles with his conscience.

I gave David the letters. Dass had called me a couple of times. He'd changed his tune a little, realizing perhaps my distaste. He stressed again that it wasn't money he wanted, nor revenge. But didn't the English have a tradition of seeking truth and justice, whatever the cost? I cannot find it in my heart to like the man, but I know in that careless sunset of the Raj things were done which cried out for settlement.

I'd always wanted to be an innocent. That was the side of me that Gregorio fostered: like the rest of the brotherhood, his vocation was not chosen for any positive virtue in self-abnegation, but from a fear of his own impulses. As the saying goes these days, that later realization of what he had missed went with the territory. I suspect if the rule had permitted some sexual licence I would have stayed; the conscious avoidance of responsibility has chimed with something in me which has never changed with age, despite the work I do. Even now, with tragedy a part of my daily life, I am essentially unmoved. 'One should take things like Septimus does,' Dr Fabricius said.

174

'He has reconciled the apparent paradox of sharing his compassion, yet saving it for others when it fails, as it sometimes
must.' So blind for such a clever man! He does not see the
coldness at my core. The only person who does, I suspect, is
David Lawrence. Perhaps that is why I love him, but wish to
hurt him also − or, at least, to get beyond that professional
detachment he assumes at all times.

When the tower finally crumbled, I could not comprehend
what had happened for a few days. The north corner had split
and spilled down like a sandcastle caught by the tide. On the
first day, half crazy, I became wildly enthused and then as
suddenly disillusioned with several schemes. I would construct
an armature to brace the missing section, and build from
within: I would weld steel girders together set deep into the
foundations, and rivet the stonework to them. I scoured the
library in Iskanderabad, reading catholically in the work printed
on the buildings of Wren and Vanbrugh and even Brunel's under-
takings − hoping that somewhere I might chance upon a solution
which would permit me to salvage part of what was standing. In
some measure I knew I did not have the strength on my own to
undertake the complete dismantling of so much work before
beginning again: also, I had not been paid for over a month, and
was afraid to ask for money, in case the funds had dried up. In
retrospect it seems as if I must have been a little mad, like
somebody who has unexpectedly arrived to find his wife or
child killed in some appalling tragedy. I spoke to no one.
Once or twice I was aware that people had moved from my
path to avoid me, but my mind was too full of calculations −
of stresses and strains, of materials required and where I might
be able to hire the specialist equipment I needed − to notice.

On the fifth or sixth morning after the storm I was setting
up a wooden system of scaffolding so that I could test the
structure remaining and loosen and remove those sections
badly damaged. I felt a strange lack of concern, as though the
damage were limited, and I would be able to put it right very
quickly. As I stood on the scaffolding, I could see the children
coming out on to the playing-field of the school, small, black,
busy as ants. Looking ahead of me, past Dora Wheeler's

175

boarded-up cottage, I saw the Nawab slowly walking down the path with his silent guard in attendance.

He called out a greeting and I responded, and he settled himself under the peepul, like a bland buddha. Despite his history, which I knew, I always had a sense of being at ease with him. His eyes, under the Mongolian folds, had a distant, other-worldly register, and he exuded an impression of peace. His guard, grizzled now, stood at a respectful distance. Village gossip held that the Nawab's wife had tried to have him dismissed immediately after the marriage, without success.

He watched me for a while in silence. Far to the north the boom of dynamite sounded where the Public Works Department were blasting the road into the mountainside. 'Sit with me for a while,' he said. 'I have some cold *nimbu-pani*. It will be good to talk to someone other than the women of my family for once.'

He had the reputation among the English of being either simple or a little mad. It was hard for them to see that his killing of his brother was entirely justifiable in terms of the history of his family. Far from being either mad or simple, he had no interest in what he considered to be inessentials. He knew, he said, that building this tower was important to me. Some could not bear the burden of the direct relationship with God of working in his temple. It might be that their path to salvation would be an indirect one, accomplished by their hands. Provided that what they did did not become an end in itself, something to be proud of for its own sake, their service was of the same value as that of a priest. But if it was for their own glory, or to avoid the involvement with others which was one of our obligations upon this earth, then such work was of no importance.

As he spoke, I saw the truth in what he said. That my building of the tower was as much of an escape from the real world as my life in the monastery had been. It was only much later that I could appreciate the artifice with which he had dealt with the situation, so that when he came to tell me of the events of the past few weeks, of which I knew nothing, I felt, even in such a short space of time, the relief of a prisoner unexpectedly released.

176

It was not my ability or care that had failed, but the materials that were at fault. And in this matter one could not solely blame Gobind Dass, the supplier. Sitting cross-legged, he invited me into his confidence with a crooked finger, dropping his voice. It was, he said, one of the English diseases to be preoccupied with possessions, with temporal power and recognition. These things were totally unimportant, and, more than that, were evil in their effect, because they kept people from understanding the true nature of temporal life. He shocked me then, telling me that James Crale's runaway black wife was now working as a courtesan in Garianwallah, forty miles to the south. 'She has nothing, but she is happy. For she is connected again to life, not to the sterile possessions of which she had become just one more.' He beckoned and his servant set down a basket covered with a linen napkin. We three sat under the peepul and ate roti and pakoras with our fingers and drank water from the spring which splashed down the mountainside and irrigated the Nawab's village.

I should have felt a sense of loss, but did not. He understood the English, he told me, because of the oral history passed down from the days when a distant ancestor allied himself with Henry Lawrence and became rich – 'the same money, increased many times, that I am using for the benefit of my people. From evil beginnings good may come ...' They had fallen out finally when Lawrence – a man of insatiable sexual appetites – had killed a girl who would not succumb to his advances. 'I think my ancestor might even have forgiven that – for, after all, we do not value life upon this earth greatly – but Lawrence had then tried to cheat him in a business arrangement. Here, such things are sacrosanct ...' When he came round, phrase by phrase, to draw a parallel between Gobind Dass and his ancestor and Henry Lawrence and his descendant, I was ahead of him. 'Though Dass is dishonoured and in prison, he will never forget.'

In part I had already decided what I would do. He tested me then, telling me that James Crale was dying, and the lawyer who had drawn up his will, being a friend of the Nawab, had told him there would be ample money for the church to be restored in time. I was not seduced. Something had died in me, and could not be replaced.

When Dass gave me the letters, maybe it was some obscure urge to revenge which prompted me to take them. Later I was tempted, of course, particularly since I would merely have acted as a go-between, but persuaded myself that I was interested in justice, not mischief. After a little I realized I was interested in neither. I did not want to carry any burdens: not the weight of Gobind Dass's expectations, however legitimately based they were, nor the responsibility of opening up the wounds of forty years ago. This is David's territory, the uncharted shoals of human emotions. In the end all I had intended to say to him about the letters, all the phrases with which I would disburden myself of any blame for such consequences as might flow, came down to little. At dinner, after an indifferent modern-dress production of *Lear* at the National, I placed the buff envelope on his napkin. 'You may find these interesting.' When we left, he put the envelope in his pocket. That was all.

Chapter Twenty-seven

I was sent to school in England.

Six weeks aboard the SS *Caledonia*. The long wake of the ship spreading behind in a widening V to the horizon. The purser told me that eleven times round the deck made a mile. Father had placed me in his care. Before breakfast I would try to match my steps to his long stride, walking round and round, past the ladies swathed in blankets sitting on their deck-chairs on the top deck. 'You'll find it all very strange, old son,' he confided, his freckled red face turned to mine. But England was still half a world away: Simon Artz, the Gully Gully men, the Captain's party were still bulwarks against the day of my arrival.

Liverpool. Six in the morning. The air grey with smoke. Rigs, derricks, the superstructure of other ships, the oily grey-brown water. The cobbles on the slipway were slick, glistening with the persistent rain. The beginning of a feeling of exile which has never quite faded, though my return to Iskandera-bad, years later, showed only too clearly that I no longer belonged there. The exile was from something else.

Without passion I did well enough at school. Under the surface, other things worked on in me, more potent in their influence than the rigid regime, the competitive environment, the emphasis on qualifications. Dr Chatterjee, my talks with Dora, above all, Angela, whose loss I mourned daily. I wrote dutifully to my parents. I wrote to Angela, describing my life, my friends, without hope that she would ever reply.

I had been there for two years when my housemaster summoned me. To my surprise he told me that a Mr Henne and his wife would be taking me out at the weekend. He was a very important man, a Member of Parliament, and I must be on my best behaviour. Despite myself, my deliberately nurtured coolness was tested when the chauffeur-driven Daimler came up the drive. 'You've certainly grown,' Julia said, standing on the windy parade ground in her tailored suit. Thomas gravely shook my hand and stopped to speak to the headmaster, who stood behind me, waiting to meet the important visitor.

Over lunch at a hotel in Taunton Thomas told me that my father had been very ill. 'Our generation cannot help doing our duty, whatever the cost. He's worn himself out serving that community. And the church . . .' He lapsed into abstracted silence. It was strange: the figure here, the frequent portrayals of him as 'the coming man' for the Tory party — all bore little resemblance to the Thomas I remembered, running down the crease to deliver a ball to me. There was something faintly risible in this new, mock-heroic mould. Julia's face was as noncommittally glacial as ever, as she looked at Thomas. 'It's all right. Your father's much better now,' she said. I knew she would not lie to me.

I didn't see them again during my schooldays. To my delight I got a letter from Angela the week after the Hennes had taken me out. The acute sense of loss I had felt at her withdrawal had long since dulled to an ache: not knowing what I had done to offend her, I had accepted I would not hear from her again. I felt involuntary tears spill down my cheeks.

'Dear Dibs,' it began (her old term of endearment). Wandering the perimeter of the Great Field, I was lost in Iskanderabad again. The old intimacy had returned in part, but, where there had been simplicity, I felt a sense of distance, of things left unspoken. The money for the Church Fund, swelled by a considerable cash donation by James Crale on his deathbed, had disappeared. At first, Gobind Dass had been arrested and everyone thought that was the end of the matter. Mother had said, 'To think you were in business with him, Amyas. What a lucky escape . . .' Then Inspector Malik had come down 'and questioned Father about the girl who died: you will

180

remember all about that, I'm sure . . .' While all that was going on — over several days — there was a terrible storm, and part of the tower fell down again. Father had brought in a surveyor who had tested the mortar supplied by Gobind Dass, and said it was corrupted. In the end Gobind had gone to prison. Mother had said it was the strain of all this that had made Father ill.

Septimus had gone to England. 'It's hard to see why men get so worked up over a pile of stones and mortar. There are so many more important things than any of that . . .' James Crale had left Angela his piano. She played every night now — the 'Moonlight' Sonata, the 'Pathétique'. At Christmas she had played while the guests sang carols — 'all those cracked old voices. And lots of umm-umming because they didn't know the words.' She would — she promised — write again soon.

In the vacations I stayed in London with Father's cousin and her sister — both spinsters. The house was chintz and patterned carpets. They were both small, upright, weathered by gardening, kindly, uncertain about boys. They had retired — one from teaching, the other from the Civil Service — some years before, and devoted much of their time to Good Works. I wrote to Angela: 'I can understand what drives people to murder. They cannot accept that there is anything but good in people. It is so cloying — like being forced to eat too much chocolate.'

Angela's letters continued while I made school captain, got my scholarship to Cambridge and went up to read medicine. They held so many of the references of our common childhood, even in those things which we avoided saying to each other. Through them I kept a picture in my mind's eye of what was happening at home — for I never learned the trick of abandoning Iskanderabad. Tom Whitworth had a stroke: 'it has produced in him a rather endearing artlessness — like a child who has no conception of what one may or may not say. The sad thing is that Mrs W is embarrassed by it, and scolds him, and he looks quite crestfallen . . .' Mr Latif had become more and more melancholy, obsessed with the memory of his dead son: one day one of the woodcutters had found his body floating

181

in the Mughal Reservoirs. Gobind Dass had come out of prison and would soon be a rich man again. The Nawab had four children and was a contented family man – but his faithful constable, now honourably retired, was still his personal body servant. Vivenne James was well enough to be the occasional companion of one of the nuns when they went to shop in Ooper Iskanderabad bazaar. She had gone prematurely grey, but, Angela said, remained beautiful, with a sad, sweet smile and absent eyes. Dr Chatterjee was unchanged – small, spare, caustic. 'I think,' Angela wrote, 'that he knows about everything that has ever happened here.' A year after she had first written she said that Poonomal's daughter had asked them to visit her mother in hospital. 'I held her hand and cried as I haven't for years. She remembered us so well: you and I had remained children to her, of course. Last week she died – but peacefully, in no pain.'

It was curious. While Angela said nothing about our long estrangement from each other, the letters were, in some way, about virtually nothing else. There was never any hint that she was seeking my forgiveness, or even acknowledging the years of separation, but from time to time I detected a faint note of desperation in her tone as she reminded me of some long forgotten, shared moment. It was as though my exile to a strange country had conjured some fear in her mind of a permanent parting between us from which, at the last moment, she had drawn back. I could sense, too, her loneliness: on the few occasions I permitted myself to think about that, I knew the reason. I would wonder then if what I had witnessed that night had continued. When I thought of these things, I felt an incoherent, fierce anger confused by guilt that I could ever think thus about my own father.

When I had not seen my parents or Angela for almost ten years, and my memories of Iskanderabad had begun to assume the fuzziness, the loss of resonance, of the old sepia photographs in my album, I received a letter from Angela.

'I didn't want to tell you before in case something went wrong,' she wrote. 'I'm coming to England in a couple of months to finish training as a librarian, and M and P are negotiating to buy a place in Devon and will follow on. I can't say how much I look forward to seeing you again. There's so much to tell you, so much to explain. And letters are no substitute for the real thing. Can you find me somewhere — just a room with a kitchen and bathroom — somewhere in Bayswater or Notting Hill? All these strange names which mean nothing to me at all . . . I feel as if I am awakening after a long sleep . . .'

Chapter Twenty-eight

Nico had asked me to join him for a holiday in Turkey, touring the sites. I was touched to find that it was a genuine request. I had always tried to avoid invasive inquiries, but, in passing, had gathered that he was quite heavily involved with Sally's successor. He had the bloom and charm of youth, the artless arrogance which life had not yet begun to chip away. 'I'd much rather go with you,' he said with an engaging grin, his brown hair trailing over his eyes so he had to flick his head. 'She was getting a bit too serious for me. I want to have a look round before all that . . .'

I hadn't spoken to Angela since the wedding. She was distant but polite. Nico was old enough to know his own mind. Better that he should be absorbing some culture than moping around at home. I knew from a few asides Nico had dropped that he and Robert didn't see eye to eye. There was a pause when I suggested to Angela we should meet after I got back. Is it hindsight, or was there a tremor in her voice when she agreed?

On the fourth day we toured Ephesus in the baking heat. The sun struck from the cobbles as we walked up the main thoroughfare with the Library of Celsius behind us. 'Look,' Nico said, his voice awed, as though in the presence of a great mystery, 'these ruts were made by chariot wheels when St Paul was giving his address to the Ephesians.' I stood patiently in the sun while he tried to photograph me against the curving, waist-high wall, with the reconstructed library beyond framed against the brilliant white-blue sky. 'It is all here for us to find.' As though he had just realized the emotional truth of that banal insight. I was amused, remembering my own excitement on my first visit, twenty years before.

Two days later, standing in the cool of the glade above Pamukkale, with the great necropolis sprawled in ruins about us, he was silent. Ahead there was a small group of tourists — a fat man in checked shirt and red shorts and wearing socks taking photographs, an elderly couple with white cotton hats, hands on hips — to whom the guide spoke in guttural and barely understandable English. To our left the limestone cascade glittered like glaciers. Oddly enough, I had been thinking, for the first time, of the letters Septimus had given me, which lay, unread as yet, in my safe.

By now I had convinced myself that Thomas would do nothing. His had been a careful life, characterized by his attachment to possessions, influential friends, power. Yet, even judged from the harshest viewpoint, and one that did not condone his mistakes, he had never been a petty man. In the terms in which I saw these matters, he had been caught and held by things which held no intrinsic merit and failed to achieve the maturity which eschews most of this as unimportant; but, in that, he was merely one of a goodly company of politicians and industrialists with dynastic ambitions who would always see matters so. In short, it seemed unlikely that he would jeopardize all this with the possibility of a squalid court case, even if the memory of his passion over lunch that day about writing something lasting for posterity occasionally came back to me with uncomfortable force. On the other hand — as Beckenbauer once told me — sometimes age brings a return to the irresponsibility of youth: values change, one is less concerned with the judgements of others.

At first I didn't hear Nico's question. We were walking down the winding road between the tombs towards the hot springs. In front of us a Turkish woman, swathed in black, carried a basket on her head which she held with one hand, while with the other she switched the withers of a laden donkey. An ancient Anadol crawled by us in a swirl of red dust.

'Did you know my father?'

I was spared this for so long. But finally, there is a time for everything.

185

'Yes.'

'What was he like? Mother's always been evasive when I've questioned her, and I didn't want to press too hard. Was he like Robert?'

Before us, to the right of the road, there was a raised rock which seemed to bleed in streams of red and green and yellow. Two Turkish women, lifting their dull skirts to just above their ankles, danced on the rock, laughing and talking to one another. Their bare brown feet moved in the sunlight. The water running over the rock steamed. A big man in a white cotton shirt bumped into me, moving to get an angle for his photograph. 'Entschuldigung . . .' he said, smiling.

'All I can say is that your father loves you,' I said. 'The rest is not my place.'

'So he is not dead, then?'

I was silent.

Only once, as we came ashore after swimming over the underwater columns in the harbour at Phaselis, we two alone on the curving shingle behind which the *maquis* crawled over ruined stonework, he said, 'I wish someone would tell me about him.' It is such moments that one must guard against: taken unawares they can prompt disclosures which might change everything. And what profit would there be in such changes, and where might the ripples end?

Curiosity got the better of me. I'm sure Septimus had never asked how Gobind Dass had got hold of the letters. I was surprised Father had kept them, though, on reflection, I could see that they were too flattering to throw away. It did occur to me that their disappearance, and his consequent panic over their whereabouts, might have played a part in the breakdown Angela had written to me about when I was at boarding school in England.

I read them one evening in the conservatory, a whisky soda by my side. They were bad photocopies, of course, stapled together and creased with dirt. There were no dates beyond reference to the day of the week, but I could roughly ascribe them to a certain period. I was astonished by the recklessness of Julia's passion. 'I don't care about honour or reputation or vows. The worst sin would be to abandon this for a lifetime of regret. Don't tell me that you do not feel it also — this mad, irrational passion to be with you — whatever the cost. I know we didn't intend this when we started. We were going to be so adult and so careful about Mary and Thomas discovering anything . . .'

Dora Wheeler had evidently suspected. After the party (the party I still remembered, where Otto had climbed on Father Carey's back and I had watched the adults playing games) Julia had written about Dora: 'I almost hope she does say something, so that we can dispense with this awful hole-in-the-corner business once and for all. But seriously, my love, whatever dark hints she might choose to give, I don't see her as either an avenging angel or a common gossip. There would be no profit for her.' At the end she suggests they go riding the next day. 'At least, thank God, neither Thomas nor Mary even likes horses . . .'

Beyond the line of trees at the end of the garden the horizon was white-yellow under leaden clouds. I poured myself another whisky soda. In the hall I heard the telephone ring four times followed by my voice on the answering machine. I closed the door into the hall and put the lights on in the conservatory and settled down to read.

Later (judging by the context) the tone of the letters changed. They were shorter, often apologizing for her inability to get away, less preoccupied with the obsessive physical passion of the early letters. The tone of these chimed more readily with the Julia that I remembered. 'I was sorry to hear that Mary hasn't been well . . .' These either were the tones of cooling passion, or were intended to convey that impression for some reason. There were evidently no letters for a month. Then: '. . . thank God you know I'm telling the truth. It doesn't mean we have to *do* anything, but I couldn't bear the coldness that had begun to grow up between us. I know you won't feel about this as a woman does, my darling, but to me this is another affirmation of what we mean to each other. Don't worry, we'll work things out somehow, and I promise it won't be as messy as your forebodings suggest . . .'

The last letter. Something irrevocable had happened. Try as I might, I could not improve upon the perspectives of childhood nor hazard a guess as to what lay behind the words. 'I didn't think anything could come between us. Oh, I don't mean in the physical sense: of course I could imagine circumstances in which we might be separated, but nothing essential would have changed. This has altered everything and I'm afraid, my dear, it is something I cannot accommodate or overlook. If we continued to see each other, it would always be there. Perhaps it is some flaw in me: I raised you too high at first and now I cast you down too low. But the fact is that I just can't help it — I can't will myself to feel as I did before. I believe you when you say it could never happen again, and we can still be friends . . .'

I surprised in myself a small quickening of sympathy for my father. My profession does not acknowledge right or wrong: life is difficult enough to negotiate without imposing an artificial set of moral imperatives regarding relationships. It was the finality of that ending which seeped from the page, from the bare, flat text. It conjured a world of love lost, of joyless accommodations to be made. Looking back, I was forced to admit that Father had hidden it well.

I would see Julia. I suppose that put off the moment of confrontation with Thomas. I hadn't spoken to either of them for months. Perhaps, now that Julia was in hospital and the end was near, he no longer had the time or the heart to carry on.

I went into the hall and played the message on the answering machine. It was Angela. 'I must see you soon. Please call.' A picture of her and Robert together in the house came into my mind. I would call her later, after I had seen Julia.

Chapter Twenty-nine

I arrived at Heathrow an hour before Angela's plane from Iskanderabad was due. I had found her a small, one-bedroomed flat in Notting Hill Gate, opposite the police station. The night before I'd barely slept, besieged by memories of our childhood, half sick with anticipation, half fearful.

I saw her first, wheeling a trolley piled with luggage, her eyes scanning the crowd by the barrier. There was a sense of shock, as though something within me had burst, to see her as a stranger, but one with whom I had shared so much. She wore a blouse open at the neck with a gold chain round her throat, a full skirt cinched at the waist, neat court shoes. I was suddenly, painfully aware that she had grown startlingly beautiful. She showed small, even white teeth in a wide smile, her eyes crinkling with pleasure. In my arms her hair felt soft against my cheek, and I caught the scent of a faint elusive perfume. She held me fiercely for a moment. 'God, how I've missed you.' Her voice was breaking, and her eyes were bright with tears.

Later, we spoke of the awkwardness we both felt, our separate recognitions of what was happening. There was business to be done: getting the luggage to the car park, loading the car, driving through the traffic to Notting Hill, and incoherent half-questions and answers which passed the first moments. There was, too, her curiosity about everything, so that, for the first few hours, I thought I might have been mistaken – about her, at least. 'All mine,' she said, clasping her hands together, her elbows tucked tightly to her body as she looked round the sitting-room of the small flat. She couldn't possibly sleep yet.

We had lunch in a workmen's café round the corner. Father

had bought the house in Devon. They were visiting a few people on the way back – 'A sort of Grand Tour,' she said, laughing. She had been moved when all the servants had joined their friends to put garlands round the family's necks, and say goodbye. 'They kept asking what would happen to them now we were leaving. They wanted to come with us. Mota – he was after your time – the *khansamah*, said that he would work for no pay and sleep outside the parents' bedroom. "No need even for charpoy"' – she mimicked his delivery gently. 'I felt almost a traitor to be so happy.'

I said I'd return in the evening. I had to get back to the hospital and she could unpack, perhaps sleep for a while. She came towards me, then stopped. 'I'll see you at seven, then?' Her voice carried the faintest trace of apprehension. She waved from the window as I drove away. I was beset by hope and fear, unwilling to admit the reason for either.

It was inevitable. Now, with the wisdom of hindsight, with the benefit of studies dealing precisely with the feelings aroused by these circumstances, I can see that. In the lecture room, barely concentrating, I did think of taking Peter, a houseman friend a year older, or even Caroline. We would go out for a curry in Bayswater and return to the flat for coffee, and convention would take over and still the wild desire for ever, and that would be the end of matters. I took no one.

After supper we went back to the flat. I had brought my record player and some old records that I had found in Portobello Road market. We drank some Chablis, chilled from the refrigerator. She lay back on the sofa so that the light from the lamp shone along the planes of her face and reached for my hand. 'You cannot know how long I have waited for this moment,' she said, and I could feel the denseness of our shared life between us, could sense the desire in her voice. Then she was in my arms.

I don't know if anything was said behind our backs. I said I was too preoccupied in getting a foothold in my career to have the time to take girls out. It made sense, too. Angela would never make very much as a librarian, and we could afford a better house on two salaries than one. I could not believe that passion could continue like this, that each day it would seem again like that first evening. It was as though we lived in each other's minds, knew without discussion what the other wanted, both in the small things and in that leaping, violent joy which time upon time brought us together so closely that it seemed we did not know where each ended and the other began. It was she who absolved me from my guilt. 'There are no rights or wrongs. Only love and the absence of love . . .' There were things I could now understand: that this struck some balance with what our father had done to her, released her. For when she spoke of that with shame, I told her that it was quite commonplace, and she had done what almost every child placed in such a situation by an adult would do: and in time I freed her of that, so that she could throw it aside carelessly enough. In public we were at pains not to touch, to act with the slightly tolerant weariness of siblings towards each other. On our infrequent visits to our parents – for Christmas or a birthday celebration – we endured their matchmaking, laughed off the coy hints about grand-children. Once, in some complex exorcism, Angela had come to me there in the night, and I had understood her need without words, so that we had made love until the birds began to sing away the night and she had stolen to her own room on bare feet, her hair loose about her shoulders.

When she became pregnant, it grew more complex. I was shocked into a recognition of what we were doing, but she saw it as a seal upon what we had made between us, and could not understand why matters might not continue as before. We could invent a brief affair for her, an absentee lover who had disappeared upon being told the news. A sailor, perhaps? A married politician? She giggled, a little drunk, determined not to take it seriously. She was sure that all would be well if we behaved as if this were entirely normal. We concocted such a story of sorts, and I persuaded her that it was best if I lived elsewhere for a decent interval. Later – well, we could live together again.

Then a curious thing happened. Our son Nico was born. Decorously, I waited at the hospital until given the news. I drove her home later, almost jealous of her preoccupation with the child. But as I embarked, without conscious deliberation, on the process of persuading myself of what I wanted — that people's malicious gossip didn't matter and that we should live together again, Angela became fearful, as though my arguments had infected her. Now it was my pleading which met with stony resistance: not directly, for she would use the child's supposed needs to avoid any confrontation. He was upset, or he needed feeding, or he must not be exposed to an atmosphere. Our affair continued and, nurtured again by the condition of secrecy and the sense of flouting convention, resumed the obsessive, passionate intensity of old.

Years later, when we had both tried, and knew that we could never be rid of each other, we were, for a few short weeks, on the verge of living together again. It seemed as though we had exhausted every other possibility. It was then, when I told her of my lunch with Thomas, that her fear returned in greater measure. Not for herself, but because she never wanted Nico to know. I could not persuade her that marrying Robert would provide no disguise for our relationship — that, in any event, Thomas was concerned with things that happened long ago and to another generation. 'I think I'm a bourgeois provincial at heart,' she said. 'I just want to have some experience of a normal life.'

After religion, the desire to conform has most to answer for. There was some lack, some stability, I could not give her, and I was excluded by definition from this new expectation. Quite separate from my own despair, I found it sad that she, with so much to offer, took Robert, who had nothing. Perhaps her marriage to Robert was the hidden spring which began Nico's curiosity. If I had satisfied that, things might have been different. But the moment came when she was confronted in turn, and must have thought, in that instant, to have an end with lies.

Chapter Thirty

I saw Julia before the end. She was in the Royal Marsden. The ward was suffused with some indefinable, sweet smell which I fancifully thought of as the smell of death. I was surprised to find her in a public ward, but that was what she had wanted. Two old ladies sat propped against their pillows. A third, in a long cotton nightdress with a pink bedjacket about her shoulders, sat wearing headphones, watching one of the serials I never saw on the television set bracketed high on the wall. The nurse who conducted me to Julia moved with spare elegance, prim in her uniform.

Julia's flesh had shrunk so that her nose stood like a sharp prow over her thin mouth and sunken cheeks. Julian, just taking his leave, had shaken my hand rather stiffly, as though he disapproved of my visit. 'Such a prig,' Julia said, with faintly contemptuous affection, watching his retreating back. The bedside table was covered in flowers and fruit.

'Has Thomas been in today?' The awful, forced cheerfulness of my voice.

Her eyes were still bright with sardonic humour. 'He comes in like a reluctant pachyderm being forced to consort with mice. Sits at the edge of his chair, stuck for anything to say, looking desperately around. These places really aren't him, you know. I send him off after twenty minutes, and he's at the door in a trice saying, "Are you sure?"'

'How do you feel?'

She laughed with genuine humour. 'OK. Drugged up to the eyeballs, of course. But I can't take any of it too seriously any more. Even what's happening to me.'

We talked generally for a while. When I told her of Angela's

193

wedding, she didn't say anything immediately, but I was aware of her sudden scrutiny. Later she said carelessly, 'If nothing else, that will please your parents, I suppose. Do you think she's happy?'

I saw no point in polite dissembling. She was too clever for that, anyway. 'I doubt whether Angela has been really happy since she was a child.'

Julia put her hand on mine. The efficient nurse was wheeling the drinks trolley to a halt beside her bed. 'Yes. The usual, please, Nurse Peters.' Julia's smile was genuine, not the guarded rictus of old. After the nurse had moved away, she said, 'When there is very little time, one wants to put things straight, make a neat end. I think both you and Angela know. I mean, about your father.'

In that moment, I knew. 'Grace Chaudhury . . . ?' The name had come from some unconscious spring. I had never acknowledged the thought, even to myself, until that instant.

Julia nodded. I realized her eyes were bright with tears. 'Strange how things happen. I went for a walk in the woods one day, up by the convent . . .' She paused, and her face twisted in pain at some memory. 'I was thinking about leaving Thomas, if I remember rightly. It was very hot and still. There was an open slope below the estate and then a copse of trees. Walking towards it I realized that there was a man there, bending down and peering through the thicket. He didn't hear me approaching. As I came closer, I realized it was the strange dumb man who had been helping Septimus rebuild the tower . . .'

'Johann Neidermayer . . .' I said.

She looked at me and nodded. 'He was so preoccupied that he wasn't aware of me until I was right behind him. I heard voices coming from further up, by the boundary fence. I recognized the man's voice and must have called out, for . . . Neidermayer . . . jumped up and began to run diagonally across the open slope. There was a noise further up, and I heard a woman scream, 'Please, no.' Something like that. Amyas stood above her with his fist raised to strike her again, and I could see the terror in her face as she held up her hands to ward him off. When I called his name, he turned towards me, and the girl scrambled to her feet and began to run. He stood quite still while I walked towards him, his arms hanging by his sides. I reached him and saw that he was crying. I was so confused and afraid. His face looked empty and I wanted to comfort him, wanted some explanation that would make everything safe and normal again. He pointed towards the copse and said, 'That was N, wasn't it?' and I nodded, and he knelt on the ground and buried his face in my skirt. I think I knew then, even before he had told me everything like a child, that it was over.'

She paused and wiped her eyes with a tissue. An elderly couple came in, the woman blue rinsed, walking in front of her husband with a deliberately cheerful face. 'Soon have you out of here, dear. Not that it isn't a marvellous place, but it isn't home, is it?' The woman whose pillows she was plumping with such missionary fervour was probably her daughter. The man smiled painfully, shifting from foot to foot.

She resumed and her voice was lower, deliberately conversational in tone. 'It is a strange moment when you are faced by something so terrible, so cataclysmic, that you *know* your life will never be the same again. A few minutes before I had been thinking of our future together, wondering how to tell Thomas. I was expecting Amyas's child, you see . . .' My shock must have registered in my face, for she smiled gently, shaking her head. 'In the end all these secrets are of no importance. I don't think Thomas knows. Julian doesn't, of course. I think your father couldn't understand my reaction. Sitting there with my arms about him, I had felt cold with shock, despite the heat. He told me that he'd met her in the woods by the stone the villagers make jokes about. He and I had seemed to be at odds – it was the first time I would see him alone after writing to tell him about the baby – and Grace Chaudhury had turned up and been provocative. He said she must have followed him, and that may be true. He'd given in, just once, he kept telling me. He kept justifying himself: though she was very young, she was experienced. After that he hadn't thought about her for months until she got a message to him that she must see him. She was pregnant. "Why should it be me?" he said, and I was appalled by his unconcern for her and the child. It could have been Charles Wheeler's child, or one of the other men with whom she had slept. She insisted that it was his. He tried to persuade her to have an abortion. He could arrange it through Gobind Dass. But she was frightened and, besides, she wanted the child. He couldn't believe that. He suggested she said Septimus had taken advantage of her. I remember, he laughed then, trying to get me to see how funny it was. All the while he was talking I couldn't get it out of my mind that she was only a child herself — that he had used her and was now going to abandon her. Then he had become angry and hit her. "I don't think she'll be any trouble. I've frightened her ..." he said, as though that would put my mind at rest. And it had evidently never occurred to him that this would be the end of us. He just couldn't understand ...'

'So Neidermayer was attacked because of what he had seen. Was driven away?'

'At first I thought that. Nobody believed Septimus was guilty and people started to talk. I suppose Neidermayer was a potential danger. Dass must have arranged that. He had some sort of arrangement with Amyas. After the girl disappeared, I wondered if ... your father ... Until Inspector Malik confirmed that they were looking for Charles Wheeler.'

Her courage had not been quite enough to face everything. 'So Malik was in it, too,' I said. I had balanced the truth against convenient falsehoods in my own mind and decided that Julia would know if I lied. The approach of death had stripped away most inessentials, had left no time for fabrications and compromises. It was strange, whispering to a dying woman in an overheated ward which smelled of decay, almost the last secrets of forty years. She turned her face away sharply as though I had hit her when I told her. Not only Grace Chaudhury, whose death he had probably arranged, but his own daughter. She cried quietly, turning her back to the other beds. Stricken with remorse, I suggested that I should go, but she held my arm with surprising strength. 'It is the best thing you can do for me. Give me the truth at the last. It

196

is what I have always needed, if only I had realized it.' Talking, I was aware that she had dismissed the suggestion that Father had killed Grace, the defence of denial which we all use. I lied only when she turned to me and asked if Father would have remained silent if Charles had been indicted. On balance, I said, I thought not. I said that such men were ill, and much more common than one might suspect. Inadequates who, unable to attain true intimacy with another adult, sought to dominate a child. One could not judge them, for they were snared by a neurosis over which they had no control, which marred and stilted their own lives, too.

She said passionately, 'If only Dass had left us alone, instead of coming to Thomas to get his revenge on Amyas. Thomas knew some of this, you see. Not about Angela, but most of the other things. And Thomas sat there and listened, and it became an obsession to write the book, to set the record straight. He still has connections, you know. He had a couple of men investigating Neidermayer. He said he wouldn't write a history, but something must be done before it faded into oblivion. I decided to let him do whatever he wishes, though I think it is wrong. I have no right to do otherwise.'

That was too easy. 'Remember, Eleanor Weaver committed suicide because Thomas frightened her. He couldn't wait to get the evidence, could he . . . ?'

Something closed in her face. I think her strength was failing. She said, 'I know you have no cause to love Thomas, but he is not an evil man. I can tell you that he has never recovered from that.'

'Regret never brought anyone back. I was too young, I know, but I think he did what everyone else did – blamed Eleanor for overreacting rather than looking for the real culprit.'

Her eyes were clouded with pain and tiredness. I felt a sudden sadness: that I had not known her well; that when I should be bringing her peace, I was presenting my anger, my need to know. She had courage, and I could only speculate at the price she had paid in keeping these secrets for so long. If she would not walk the whole way, see the precise mechanisms of what had happened, I could not blame her. When she said, 'You can take my word that he has suffered, whatever you might think,' I was silent. We had not spoken of Miriam Cohen, or her death, but I could not ask that of her.

I had intended to ask her to intercede, to stop Thomas. I would not do that. Whatever waited for us — my parents, Angela, myself — in the future was insubstantial, a shadow, a passing scandal, to be borne somehow. But Julia's end was close, a few weeks, maybe a month. She had served her time with strength. I could see how Thomas had come to love her.

She said that she would not wish me happiness, because she knew it was unattainable for me. Divorced from the pettiness and business of everyday life in that ward, I had the sense that she knew everything. Not in the literal, factual sense — the precise details and narratives of events — but in some far more profound region to which we might have no access until we, too, sat in the creaking boat separated already from the silent watchers on the shore, saw the slipway recede and turned our faces towards the dark, impenetrable sea and the baleful light of an unknown horizon under leaden clouds. I kissed her, knowing I would not see her again. 'There are only two great things,' she said. 'Pain and love.'

Angela's voice was brittle at the end of the telephone. I was too tired to care much, one way or the other. We had been apart for too long to have any other expectations. I felt that I had been fighting shadows only, that the real battle was somewhere else and had already been lost. I knew, for a host of reasons, that I would never confront Father. I said, 'We seem almost strangers these days . . .'

She said nothing for a while and I was about to speak when I realized she was crying. Her voice was low. 'I was going to phone you. I've made some terrible mistakes — got everything out of proportion. I can't wait to see you again. I don't care what people think any more. We're away for the weekend in Cornwall. Can we meet next week? Please say yes.'

It was Angela as I'd never heard her — except in those last letters she had written from Iskanderabad before we met again.

I felt oddly reluctant, as though I had become so used to this new life that I was wary of the prospect of change. A fancy took me then that, in accepting the honour, I had also acquiesced in society's valuations of people and things. I could not imagine again committing the act to which we attach such importance. In my mind that possibility had been set aside by some process whose mechanism was foreign to me. We might, after all these years, be able to live together again as brother and sister. And I could see a shape, a sense of symmetry, in that.

She caught my hesitation. 'Do you not want that?' she asked, and I knew that she was referring to things beyond the meeting, that she was really asking me to accept it all: the flouting of convention, the censure, the embarrassment of friends, the loss of acquaintances. I said I was at a low ebb, tired, that work had been very exacting. All the ways in which one avoids a simple truth. Of course we must meet. I could hear the note of hope and optimism in her voice as she said, 'Until next week, then.' I mixed myself a whisky and water and took it out on to the patio. I was aware of a complex of feelings, but mostly anger because I knew that the old balance could never be restored.

'Ich sage ihr: Wenn du noch Schmerzen hast, so ist es wirklich nur deine Schuld. Sie antwortet: Wenn du wüsstest, was ich für Schmerzen jetzt habe in Hals, Magen und Leib.' (Will I ever deliver the paper?) I translate. 'I say to her: "If you still have pains, it is really only your fault." She answers: "If you knew what pains I have now in my throat, stomach and abdomen . . ."' The repetitions and assonances in my own life at the moment make it difficult to treat the study with the intellectual rigour it requires. I watch television mindlessly and wake at two, chilled and stiff.

Chapter Thirty-one

I woke from a troubled dream about Father Gregorio to hear someone hammering at my door. The clock on my bedside table showed three as I struggled into my dressing-gown. It was rare but not unusual to be disturbed in the middle of the night, and I expected to find one of my clients, fresh from some marital upheaval, coming round for sympathy and the use of my divan.

I was shocked to find David Lawrence on the doorstep, exhausted and soaked to the skin. He was clearly in great distress. I took him by the arm, led him into the sitting-room, made him change out of his wet clothes and sit in front of the electric fire wrapped in one of my sweaters and an old pair of trousers. I brought him a coffee laced with whisky, and sat opposite him with a brandy while he sipped it, his teeth chattering against the rim of the cup and his eyes absolutely vacant. Even in his distress he apologized. 'I couldn't think where else to go. I'm so sorry.'

His usual fluency had deserted him. As the light outside slowly brightened, and the sound of traffic increased from an occasional car passing to the steady roar of vehicles on the through road at the end of the street, he walked round the room, occasionally picking up an object and putting it down, without interest, telling me a story so disjointedly, in such flat tones, that it had no sense of chronology or coherence. Once he paused and looked at me. 'She had great courage, but no instinct for survival. If only I'd been there ...' Even when he had finished, and I knew why he was in despair, there was something missing: it was like a book in which the author creates a spectacular effect which catches the imagination, and it is only later that one sees that some internal logic has been mislaid.

Robert kept a boat in Cornwall. Taking Nico with them, he and Angela had motored down to spend a long weekend. They had stayed just outside Portscatho in a farmhouse Robert had known over the years. The weather – till then uncertain enough to keep the tourists away – had suddenly changed to brilliant sunshine. On the first day they had driven to Tintagel and walked across the causeway to the castle, and eaten Cornish crabs for a late tea, looking out over the darkening sea. The following day – the Sunday – Robert and Angela had had a disagreement. She had wanted to go to church and Robert wanted to go to Castle Drogo, over the border in Devon. Robert, apparently, had suggested they could drop in on her parents for tea: it rankled that they had never really accepted him. Angela had refused and went to church and Robert sulked and Nico went down to browse round the bookshop in the village until she came back. When she returned, Robert once again tried to persuade her, but she said, 'Can't you see they don't want anything to do with you?' Robert was furious, and had got into the car and driven away.

When Nico had come back from the village, they went down to the pub. There had been an atmosphere – Nico said: not in what was said, but in the silence. Angela had been *distraite*, barely talking. At first he had put it down to her exchange with Robert. Later in the afternoon a wind blew up as they walked slowly down to the shore together. He had felt an odd sense of apprehension. He'd wondered if her marriage to Robert had been a mistake. She had become more reclusive, her moods darker – shot through with sudden, unexplained bursts of anger. Something she told Nico had brought about a violent argument. David said something strange here: 'After all this time she'd decided to tell him.' Listening, while David paced the room, I wondered if Nico had told him what the disagreement was about and whether he would come to it in time in his episodic, disjointed narrative. I could not ask: if he knew what it was and wanted to tell me, he would do so in time.

Angela had gone ahead, down to the beach. On the telephone, in tears, Nico had said, 'I knew the one thing she wanted then was to be rid of me . . .' Suddenly panic-stricken, he had run down the shingle, but the boat was moving fast now, black against the livid light of the evening sky. Standing with his feet in the foam, he called as loudly as he could, but the roar of the breakers drowned his voice. On the cliff there was a figure in a red anorak against the dark-green field; two children ran diagonally over towards a white house in the near corner, from whose chimney a wisp of grey-blue smoke curled into the air. Something brushed against Nico's leg. It was a dead fish. The next wave threw it up on to the dark sand.

By the time Robert arrived, running down the cliff path, white-faced with fear, Nico had called the police. The sea was high now, hurling wrack and weed far up the beach, the spray wetting them where they stood well above the high tide line. At ten o'clock the police sergeant had told them with gruff kindness that there was nothing more to be done until morning, and had sent them back to the farm in a police car. When Nico fell asleep at four o'clock, Robert was talking; an hour later, when he slowly woke to a feeling of dread, to the hollow realization of what had happened, Robert was still talking. 'If only I had not gone . . .' he said again and again, like a litany of despair.

The helicopter found some wreckage in the morning, but it was still too rough to send out a boat. 'We can't say, sir,' the police sergeant said with his slow, kindly burr, 'but it is best to prepare yourself for the worst. There were warnings out yesterday. Nobody should have gone out.' By late afternoon they had identified the wreckage of the boat, but there was no sign of Angela.

It was then that Nico had called David. Once David said, almost to himself, 'If only we had told him years ago . . .' but I did not ask what he meant. I heard the morning paper drop on to the mat, and the sound of the radio from the flat below. There is nothing one can say to people in despair. One can only listen. David sounded like a child when he said, 'I just don't know what to do, Sep. I don't know if I can bear it . . .' and I said something pompous like, 'There is nothing to be

202

done. You can only endure. She came early to what awaits us all . . .'

I pressed his clothes while he showered and shaved. He was pale but composed. I asked him if he would be all right as he drank his coffee, deliberately draining my voice of inflection, and he said, 'Oh, yes. I've got a very busy day today.' His voice was infused with an artificial lightness, as though he were holding himself together by a great effort of will. I watched him drive away, concerned that there was nothing more I could do.

I was left with that sense of distance which always accompanies tragedy. People go away into some remote part of themselves, and I am reminded, time and again, of the fleeting and illusory nature of friendships and of love. There is always something in the mechanisms of these things which eludes me, some cosmic insight into the cause and effect which creates these patterns. I cannot do what Father Gregorio did: acknowledge that it is impossible to know the mind of God and that it is we who cannot comprehend the pattern which is there. Standing with my face to the darkness, my answer is no better, though I think my questions have more courage. For they are addressed to us – the people who put together these things in the subtle recesses of our minds.

*

Robert telephoned me two weeks later. At first I couldn't recognize the voice, seemingly old and trembling on the verge of tears. Guilty, I began to apologize for not calling, but he cut through my stilted phrases. 'A body has been washed ashore, David. They need someone to make an identification. I thought as you're a doctor it might be . . . easier . . . for you.' The relief in his voice as he thanked me was almost palpable. 'We must have dinner . . . talk . . . when all this is over,' he said, but it sprang from his relief and we both knew we would not meet.

There are a few scenes from my life which remain indelibly

printed on memory. I arrived at the hospital in the late after-noon. Stone-grey clouds delivered a flat, monotonous drizzle. After the tactful sympathy of the duty nurse I sensed a prurient curiosity in the sideways glances of the old attendant as we took the lift and then walked the long corridor to the morgue. Despite the livid bloating of the seawater, there could be no mistake. Perhaps I felt nothing because there was so little connection between the Angela I had known and what she had become, covered in a white sheet, laid in a grey metal refrigerated drawer. I could not conjure one single recollection of her alive, standing there under the harsh fluorescent light with the two men watching frozen into silence. I nodded, wondering what they must make of my coldness, and the old man pushed the drawer shut. After I had signed the forms, I asked if I could use the telephone.

Then it was hard to bear Nico's silence. 'Are you still there?' I asked, and distant voices sounded in the wires. It was worse than his anger. He was going to America, he said. Perhaps one day we would meet again, but he needed time. I know those flights: you take your baggage with you wherever you go, slung round your neck like Coleridge's albatross. There is no other way than through the middle, confronting all that rears up in your path. But you cannot tell people of these things, for they are the parts of life which only make sense at first hand.

I had thrown almost everything away. Now I must continue to the end.

My parents did not attend the funeral. On the telephone my mother said apologetically that it would be too taxing for my father. They coped by ignoring bad news, in a world of determined brightness. There were so few of us. Robert, in dark glasses, Nico, two girls I vaguely recognized from the library. The vicar's voice had an orotund cadence, as though he were delivering his brief sermon directly to the Almighty.

'When are you going?'

Nico rubbed his finger over a mark on the car door, avoiding my eyes. 'Two weeks' time. I've got a place at UCLA. Robert's going to help with the fees.' There was the slightest edge to his voice. I had intended to ask if I could pay, but it was the wrong moment. I put my hand on his arm and said, 'I hope you'll write,' and walked away before he had time to answer.

At the beginning I coped because there were things to be done. Also, because we had been estranged since before Angela's marriage, I had grown used to memories, to thinking of the times we had been together in the past. The thought of Angela with Robert had never worried me beyond superficial sexual jealousy: I had known the crux and causality of that arrangement and my only feelings had been sadness for her, and a rather unworthy sense of irritation at Robert. What had never occurred to me until very late was that Angela and I would change places: that her Bohemian youth would mutate into a desire for a conventional life, just as my caution had begun to disperse. Wrong timing is at the heart of most tragedy.

Thomas had heard the news before I called him. He spoke quickly, betraying nervousness. He would have come, of course, except that he was spending most of his time at the hospital. Julia was very weak, and it was only a matter of days now. It was not hard to stifle any hint of charitable concern in my voice. I told him that I needed to see him very soon on matters which concerned us both. Preferably somewhere where we could not be overheard. Even as we arranged to meet on Saturday afternoon in Hyde Park I felt a mild sense of discomfort at how melodramatic it all sounded.

I put the letters in my pocket. That impulse seemed like a betrayal of the ethic by which I had lived. I hadn't the faintest idea of how one went about such things as blackmail. What could I threaten which would carry any weight? Thomas would know me too well to be worried by any suggestion I would show the letters to Julia. He'd remarked the mutual affection between us in the past. There was the threat to expose him in the papers, but I didn't know how I would go about it, and Thomas would undoubtedly be aware of that. Eventually, sleeplessly tossing in bed, I concluded that making no threat, thus permitting his fears full rein, might be the best approach of all.

Walking across the grass from the car park by the Serpentine, I saw him at once in the distance. Incongruously enough, he was holding an extending dog lead, at the end of which a diminutive Yorkshire terrier strained and pulled. Slightly shamefaced, he confessed he'd bought it for Julia on an impulse, when he'd had to spend a week away attending a conference in Cambridge. Thomas had never given way to an uncalculated impulse in his life: one of his staff — his surly detective — could as easily have walked the dog. It was for effect. Sat on the bench by his side, I was aware of some uncertainty in him, a reflective quality which I had not seen before.

His professions of sadness about Angela were curiously anodyne, as if he wasn't prepared to make the effort to dissimulate. Yet that was honest, in its own way: he had barely seen her since we were children, and anything more would have been too much. 'I had the impression the marriage was a mistake . . .' he said, wrinkling his eyes against the sun as though dredging whatever he could from his memory.

But he began defiantly enough, testing my mettle to see how far he could go. A wind riffled the water of the lake and the leaves tinkled above us. The dog, tired of questing, returned and curled up on the grass at Thomas's feet.

'I've nearly finished the book, you know. It's the best thing I have ever done.'

'What do your publishers think of it?'

'I've got a bit more work to do on it before I send it off to them . . .' He laughed suddenly, as though a thought had just struck him. 'Trouble is that Christopher — Lord Silbert, that is — has ancestral connections with India. I suspect he believes that the English were responsible for civilizing a benighted nation and bringing them into a modern democracy. He's published several of those post-imperial histories. You know the sort — patronizing about the Indians, about the violence that accompanies each essay into democracy, about the graft and corruption and bribery. Written by reactionary paternalists pretending to be liberal intellectuals whose true beliefs are that we should never have left . . .'

'And you have put together a rather different story . . . ?'

He had become more confident, as though my neutral questions had allayed some sense of unease. A couple passed with a dog along the slope beneath us and Thomas checked the little terrier with a sharp pull of the lead.

'I told you I wanted to write an authentic story. What better than my own experience? A superior, sheltered colonial enclave, contemptuous of the rules of civilized behaviour, subject to no checks and balances but their own. You were just a child, but I had come out as a young man, full of idealism. What I found was as savage in its own way as the destruction of the Aztec civilization by the Spanish. With the exception of Dr Chatterjee — who was a special case — our community there used the Indians. Just look at the history of your own family, for instance.' I could see why the press had sneered at Thomas's moral crusades. His wattles were flushed, and he had the demeanour of a man confronted with a gross inequity which he had a duty to correct.

I said, 'That is what I want to talk to you about, Thomas — your use of real characters and events in your book. I hope that you have decided against that.'

I hesitate to say that one can find the mind's construction in the face. Mostly we Anglo-Saxons hide from each other, so that one must learn to infer reactions from the merest hint. But I saw naked triumph on Thomas's face in that instant, the unguarded delight of the hunter closing upon its prey. It was here, I knew, where the spring that had begun to turn the wheel was first wound. It was an old man, nearing the end of his life, seeking to find a focus for his rage at the world's treatment of him. I could feel his heat, his anger, the banked, rancorous hatred which must have simmered for years. As he spoke, all that I had known of Thomas disappeared. The courteous, smiling politician, trimming his purpose to the prevailing wind, was gone — to be overtaken by this loose-mouthed, venomous old man. Even in the midst of my shock I felt a moment's compassion. When it was over, he would regret what he had said and punish himself for his loss of control before me.

'Your father was given a knighthood for his services to the English and Asian communities in Iskanderabad. What service! Your father basks in the sunshine of a reputation which is founded upon nothing but lies.' His face was a foot from mine, and I could feel the spray of his saliva on my cheek. 'Do you know where the money came from? He stole it – from the community, from the Restoration Fund. Worse than that, he got that girl from the convent pregnant and, so I'm told, either killed her himself or arranged for someone else to do it. When I first came out, I admired him. I was taken in, like everybody else. Who knows? – if he had stood up and accepted everything like a man, I might still have thought well of him. And those sheep let him get away with it. It was never even discussed. The fact that he was English conferred a total immunity upon him even to the extent that he was able to have poor Dass sent to prison.'

I realized what a fool I'd been. As I knew from Julia, Dass had talked to Thomas and gained a sympathetic audience. Of course Dass had nursed a grievance against my father. And it was not money he wanted, but revenge. He could not face confronting my father on his own, so he had chosen the only person he knew who might act as an intermediary. But Dass, too, was eager for revenge as soon as possible. He had obviously intended the letters in my pocket for my father and had chosen Septimus to perform the deed, not knowing how ill he chose. Septimus had done what Septimus always did. Had passed responsibility to someone else as soon as it was decently possible.

I had hoped that Thomas would have changed. That Julia's illness, the less than onerous demands of the mastership, might have relegated the book to some less important place in his life. After all, I had reasoned in the days just after that lunch (so long ago), anything might happen in the year or so it took to write the book. Quite apart from the normal hazards of life at his age, I had thought of the amelioration time so often brings to petty anger. I had not seen then what I saw now. That the book had become Thomas's *raison d'être* – the compan-

ion, the fixed star which would see him through Julia's deser-
tion, the indifference of his old colleagues, the departure of his
friends. With Angela gone a brief thought came to me, sat
there on the bench listening to Thomas pouring out his splen-
etic narrative. That I should walk away, and let him do it. But
there was my mother and, above all, there was Nico. I could
not do what Septimus had done, and avoid the issue.

I had, I told him, done some of my own research, and the
conclusions might surprise him. Did he recall, for example,
that it was his assumption of Eleanor Weaver's guilt and his
blundering interview with her which had led to her tragic
death, only for the real thieves to be revealed later? And (here
I was on dangerous ground indeed, but I swept on, holding
the advantage) hadn't Charles Wheeler's death and Dora's
suicide again been partly attributable to him? But over the
years Thomas had found a means of accommodation to these
events. No one could accuse him of stupidity and, even as he
justified himself, I could see that these things had caused him
pain. I was too young to have understood what happened
then, he told me. How could I possibly know the circumstances:
he, fresh from college, faced with the prospect of advising
experienced officers much older than himself in an alien culture.
I saw the politician's trick of using only what was convenient
and discarding the rest. He pulled the dog back viciously so
that it whimpered. I had not touched him at all, I saw.

'You know Miriam Cohen was my patient? She gave me
some letters for safekeeping. They were from you.'

I could see incredulity in his eyes as he battled to keep his
face under control. Watching him, I wondered again if he had
been her last visitor, if he had arranged for the police to
interview Robert, if he had known of Angela's fears about the
book, even if he had, somehow, driven poor Neidermayer to
his death. And in those moments, even before he spoke, I saw
beneath the mask of avuncular gentility to the venality beneath. I knew that Thomas was guilty of much more even
than I suspected, and also that, being who he was, he had
always escaped any culpability for his crimes. Sitting there in
the sunlight while the tourists walked along the path by the

lake, I was suddenly aware of his rage, his contempt for others. His smile now was defiant: it said, there is nothing you can do to me; I am beyond your power to hurt.

'Miriam killed herself. So, I sent her a few letters. What of that?'

'Miriam told me that you attacked her physically. I gather that she had a visitor on her last evening and that there was the mark of a needle in her arm – things that didn't come out at the inquest. Was that visitor you by any chance?'

He sneered. 'Quite the little detective, aren't we? I suppose you thought that these few snippets would give you the power to do a deal – to stop me telling the truth about your precious family.' He licked his lips. I could see his head shake – though whether with anger or fear I could not say. 'I even know about Amyas and your sister. Now that's all the rage these days, isn't it? Gobind Dass got that information from your ayah's husband. I suppose Amyas didn't even bother to hide what he was doing from the servants. You can imagine how well all this is going to go down, eh?'

There was nothing else to be done. I took the buff envelope from my pocket and laid it on the seat between us. 'If you go ahead, I shall arrange for these letters to be published – with a full history of their provenance. As I'm sure you will be aware, there is a fashion in the media for exposing politicians – particularly those who have set themselves up as being morally superior.'

He tied the dog lead to the arm of the bench and took the letters. It seemed he had suddenly grown old: the colour had gone from his face and his fingers trembled. I willed myself to remain neutral, to keep before me the insights which had just come to me. If there had been another way, I would have taken it, for, faced with the knowledge of what the letters would reveal to him, I was reminded of childhood, of Thomas and Julia coming to the house, or walking down the rutted red path to the picnic area near the Mughal Reservoirs. I had never loved Thomas and Julia as a child, as I had loved Dora Wheeler and Dr Chatterjee, but they had been part of the safety of childhood, and I, more than most, knew the power of

210

the illusions of that time and their persistence even in the face of adult knowledge. What I was doing now, engaged in a contest which was not of my making, and one that I had no stomach for, seemed to strike at the very core of our lives – as though this would despoil some place once sacred, would disinter it from memory and soil it so that I would never again remember those years with pleasure.

He stood up abruptly. At first I thought he was having a heart attack. He clutched his chest and his mouth opened, but no sound emerged except for his laboured breathing. 'Oh, God,' he said, and a couple walking by stopped to watch, the young woman laying her hand on the arm of her grey-haired companion. 'It isn't true. It can't be true.' He began to run down the slope towards the lake, ungainly, lumbering. The woman who had stopped was laughing, looking up at her escort. The little dog sprang up to follow and was checked by the lead. It danced frantically on its back paws, whining. I ran after him and caught him by the arm. 'Come and sit down for a moment. You've had a shock.' He allowed me to lead him back like a child. He sat with his head slumped on his chest while I gathered the photocopies which lay on the grass and put them into the envelope. The couple walked on.

Thomas gazed upon some unimaginable horror. We sat in silence for perhaps twenty minutes. I felt a curious detachment, as though free from myself, an observer only, watching the swans and Canada geese swim forward to be fed, a small boy dressed in a red track suit zigzag his skateboard expertly through the crowds, an Alsatian run for a stick. When Thomas spoke, I had to strain my ears to hear his voice. 'All these years,' he said, 'I never knew.' He gave a small laugh, as though at his own stupidity. Now was no time for weakness. 'Julian is not your son,' I said. It was not spite or revenge, but I had seen his capacity for self-restoration, the processes by which he might in time learn to justify his intention. The threat must be real. He put his head in his hands and tears spilt through his fingers on to his trousers. The terrier stood with his front paws on Thomas's leg, its ears pricked, whining, and Thomas put out his hand and ruffled its ear.

211

Finally, not looking at me, he asked me what I would do.

'Nothing. You will never know the pain and tragedy which has come from this. If you give up the book, then that will be the end of it.'

I asked him if he would say anything to Julia. 'What could I say?' he replied. 'Besides, she is all I have left. It was long ago and I haven't been blameless.' Perhaps there was hope for him, after all. I might even visit him, much later. I understood his motives and that was at least halfway to forgiveness.

I sat for a moment in the car, watching him. In the distance he was small and insignificant. An old man sat on a park bench with a little dog playing at his feet. It was an ending of sorts. Not the one I had hoped for, perhaps, but peace of a kind.

I had an unexpected visitor a few weeks ago.

One afternoon I was writing up some notes. I heard the door open and a man's voice and then my receptionist said, 'I'll see if Dr Lawrence can spare a moment. Can you wait?' She closed the door carefully behind her and dropped her voice to a discreet whisper, mouthing like a mummer on the stage. 'A Mr Wheeler. Says he knew you years ago in Iskanderabad. Can you allow him a few minutes?' I realized immediately that it must be Henry. I couldn't refuse to see him without being churlish.

'I was having my annual BUPA check across the hall. Just thought I'd drop in for a moment.' The voice, cultured and slightly smug, matched his appearance. Bald, with a tonsure of greying hair, a bucolic face, an immaculate pinstripe suit. He had left Iskanderabad after selling up Dora's estate. He had the gift for self-deprecation. He'd been lucky, he said, in stumbling on a growing market for Indian artefacts, and had been well positioned to take advantage of the consuming interest in India which had started in the mid 1960s and had never died away. 'I know my parents loved Iskanderabad and I sometimes feel guilty – as though I am selling my family possessions to people who merely want something for their mantelshelf or hall ...' His little bursts of self-mocking laughter were unconvincing. I looked at his cold eye appraising the contents of my office and felt the comment was for form's sake only.

Anything we may have once held in common had long since disappeared. I professed interest in his family, his two sons, one at Oxford reading law, his news of the changes in Iskanderabad, which he visited from time to time to see what else they were producing which might be saleable, but I knew that any observations he might have would be alien to me, would hold no interest. He shook my hand on leaving and there was a note of curiosity in his voice when he said, 'You've done well for yourself . . .' as though I had violated some universal law. He gave his self-mocking laugh, excusing himself for his ineptitude. It was just something he remembered his mother saying: that I had all the capacity for a tragic life unless I learned to feel for people. 'Whatever *that* meant, it's stuck in my head all these years. She had something,' he said, shaking his large head; 'she wasn't always right, but sometimes it seems she saw further than most people.'

For the first time I went to an Iskanderabad reunion. In my experience these functions are frequented by those who have failed, who try to keep their fear of the present and the future at bay by reinventing the past. I would know nobody except Septimus, if he decided to attend. Against all reason I accepted the invitation when it arrived.

It was in a church hall in Southall. Brown paint, metal-framed chairs clad in orange canvas, chipped deal tables. All the traditional furnishings of the Church decadent. A notice proclaimed that a million pounds was needed to save the church spire. An accompanying graph showed that £30,000 had been raised to date. Yet, ordering a drink at the bar amidst the conversation of strangers, I was aware of a conviviality expressed by the tones of people's voices, the frequent laughter. There was a video showing on a television screen in a corner of the room, surrounded by people. When the church came into sight, I realized, with a sense of shock, that it was Iskanderabad. But the tower was complete.

A voice behind me said with dry amusement, 'In the end the Indians rebuilt it with the aid of a government grant. It has been deconsecrated, and is used as a museum. It is full of artefacts from the Raj, including some letters from an ancestor of yours, Henry Lawrence, to his wife, Matilda.' The speaker was a small, totally bald elderly Indian, whose features seemed vaguely familiar. We sat at a table in the corner and he regarded me with quiet amusement for a moment. 'Dr Chatterjee. You would hardly remember me. You were just a *butcha*. But I understand you've done very well over here. Dora always said you had perceptions beyond your years.'

'Many of them came from her.'

He laughed. 'Discretion wasn't one of her virtues. She believed that truth was more important than filling young heads with lies.' I had falsified his speech in my memory. His voice was precise, uninflected.

I told him that Henry had visited. Dr Chatterjee said that it had taken a long time for Henry to recover from the trauma of finding his mother's body. Then, one day, he had announced that he had come to terms with the fact that his mother was mad. Having dealt with the tragedy thus, he was able to move on. Chatterjee's wry amusement seemed permanent. Only, when he spoke of Angela, I was thankful for his hesitance. He said something curious then, after the silence with which we confront things for which there are no words. 'I knew what was going on, but it wasn't possible to do anything about it because of the collusion of others. One has to balance the attempt to right matters against the possible benefit.'

There was no need for silence any more. I said, 'With my father, you mean? Who colluded in that?'

There was a grey-haired, handsome woman in the corner. Though her hair straggled to her shoulders and she had made no effort with her clothes or make-up, her face still carried the evidence of beauty. Only her eyes seemed dead and lifeless.

'You remember Vivienne? I seem to recall you had a crush on her when you were a child. She lives on the charity of an uncle. Her father's death unhinged her. You asked me a question a moment ago. In the context of the England of today I would have made a report of the matter and it would have been dealt with by your social services. But you must remember that forty years ago in Iskanderabad the English still ruled in everything but name. Such absolute power corrupts both men and communities. In the absence of a judicial system, and men who would implement its controls against them, they become arrogant. If I had said anything, do you think your mother would have believed me? Do you think Colonel Whitworth and his wife would accept that a man who had dinner with them would do such a thing? I would have been reviled and excommunicated.'

'So you kept quiet and saved your position?'

He laughed gently, reprovingly. 'For an eminent psychoanalyst you reach snap decisions. No. In the end I concluded that permitting that to continue within the family was preferable to the guilt and confusion your sister would feel in the failed attempt to expose what was happening. And, whatever happened at the end, you healed her for a while, I believe.'

The certainties of youth eventually return in the certainties of age. Only in the middle – chaos. Becoming a psychoanalyst was – I suppose – an attempt to impose order upon the messiness of human feelings, my own and those of others. But entropy and the narrowness of our vision confound the plans: the tower fell, my order has turned out to be an illusion. The substance, the reality, seep from the cracks and we are powerless. As though reading my thoughts, Dr Chatterjee said gently, 'When you reach my age, you realize one fundamental. That you cannot control events or alter people.'

'You think it better to do nothing? To be uninvolved?'

'I didn't say that. Involvement is an indispensable part of all our lives. But these things are not controllable. In the end you must either accept us for the poor sorry things we are – or reject us.'

He was going back. His daughter was working as a doctor in Southall. His wife had died two years before. I see England, he said, and it is not what I imagined at all. He had not thought to find dirt and poverty, cupidity, hypocrisy. He was laughing at himself when he said he was eager to return. It had been his last naïvety that he had believed he would find a just and honourable society, buttressed by fair laws and a civilized democracy. The only way in which it differed from Iskanderabad was that the Indians never pretended corruption didn't exist.

Chapter Thirty-two

It is some time since Angela's death. She is in my mind every day: the last thing at night, in the slow realization each morning as I wake that something is wrong. She will remain thus, an icon, until I die. I cannot speak of what we were to each other to anyone. Nico, even if he had not gone to America, least of all, for he will not grow into understanding in my lifetime. If Dr Chatterjee had remained, he might have comprehended, though at his age, I suspect, few of life's passions impinge any more, so that his understanding would have the austerity of the confessional.

There is no fault, as such. It has taken all this to demonstrate one simple fact. My own inextricable connection with others and our common heritage. I met Thomas at Julia's funeral, and he wept openly. I see him from time to time at his house and we eat a meal prepared by his housekeeper. He has remembered only the things he wants to. 'How happy we were,' he said without a trace of irony last time I visited, his hand upon a faded snapshot of him and Julia with my parents by the Mughal Reservoirs. Perhaps that is the way of it, for we can bear very little reality. And he is dying, so that compassion distorts the picture. My impulse to blame him came from that instance in each of us which must ascribe responsibility for misfortune to someone.

Such fault as there is was my own. Despising the instinct in others, I, too, wanted to change people, to make them bear the burden of my expectations. If you have no expectations, they cannot be disappointed. If you have no wishes, they cannot be thwarted. If you have no ambitions, they cannot be blighted. Only then are you freed to hear the truth in all its

217

irrational complexity, without the desire to control or change it. That is more than most people have, and there is peace in it. And perhaps that is what I have, now, in my role of confessor at work, and here in my russet garden where the last remnants of autumn past – black, gold, red – hang briefly in the foliage before the bareness of winter.

Septimus quoted Yeats to me. 'The years like great black oxen tread the World/And God the Herdsman goads them on behind/And I am broken by their passing feet.' That is our function once the growing season is past. Like the Fisher King, we corrupt and pass and die for the future. And shall those who follow escape?